CRISIS: BLUE

CRISIS: BLUE

J. A. DAVIS

VIREO / RARE BIRD • LOS ANGELES, CALIF.

THIS IS A GENUINE VIREO BOOK

A Vireo Book | Rare Bird Books
453 South Spring Street, Suite 302
Los Angeles, CA 90013
rarebirdbooks.com

FIRST TRADE PAPERBACK ORIGINAL EDITION

Set in Minion
Printed in the United States

10 9 8 7 6 5 4 3 2 1

Publisher's Cataloging-in-Publication data
Names: Davis, John Alvin, author.
Title: Crisis : blue / J.A. Davis.
Description: First Trade Paperback Original Edition | A Vireo Book | New
York, NY; Los Angeles, CA: Rare Bird Books, 2016.
Identifiers: ISBN 978-1-942600-84-8
Subjects: LCSH Terrorism—Fiction. | United States. Department of Homeland
Security—Fiction. | Doctors—Fiction. Spy stories. | BISAC FICTION /
Literary | FICTION / Espionage. | FICTION / Thrillers.
Classification: LCC PS3604.A9585 C85 2016 | DDC 813.6—dc23

John Alvin Davis Jr.—*Los Angeles, California.*

Commanding Officer of the USS Greenfish (SS-351) and the most highly decorated submarine skipper of the Cold War. Gathering intelligence on the Russian Pacific Fleet in Vladivostok Harbor with half of your submarine below crush depth and Soviet torpedoes racing by the hull was rather gutsy. However, with the United States lagging so far behind the Soviets in the space race in 1959, capturing the first Soviet telemetry package north of the Hawaiian Islands by snagging the cords of the parachute with your periscope was truly courageous.

What wonderful memories; I can still envision Diamond Head through the crosshairs of the periscope. What a thrill!

May the sands in front of the Royal Hawaiian always keep shifting—a virtual certainty after a few rounds at the Mai Tai Bar!

INTRO

Iran continues to threaten Israel, while North Korea taunts the United States by detonating nuclear weapons and launching long-range missiles across the Pacific. However, these threats are suddenly overshadowed by the destruction of the John C. Stennis *Carrier Strike Group as it traverses the Strait of Hormuz and enters the Persian Gulf.*

As this crisis of unimaginable magnitude escalates, little attention is paid to several blue, bloated, and grossly disfigured Asian sailors who wash ashore in Galveston, Texas. Likewise, the North Korean cargo ship Il-sung *is able to slip into Whiskey Bay, Louisiana, unnoticed, where she off-loads her weapon of mass destruction.*

As more Asian sailors become deathly ill from the many weeks spent at sea in close proximity to their lethal cargo, they are transferred to a small hospital in Carencrow, Louisiana, for treatment. Dr. Rex Bent, an emergency room physician, immediately becomes suspicious and notifies the proper authorities.

With their coup de gras in jeopardy, the Islamic extremists realize that not only Dr. Bent, but also his wife and confidant Trissy, must be eliminated without raising suspicion. Pursued and hounded like traitors who have betrayed their country, the Bents are in a race against time, determined to discover the significance of Prussian Blue.

CHAPTER 1

THE DIESEL ENGINES ROARED to life, disrupting the peace and tranquility of a glorious evening. The skies were clear and the moon nearly full as all hands hastily made preparations for sea. Moments later, the order was given to cast off all lines, and the Soviet-built Kilo class submarines, *Tareq* (901) and *Yunes* (903), were underway.

The propellers dug into the warm, dark waters, leaving an eerie, phosphorescent glow in their wake. Tricolored flags with bright bands of green, white, and red snapped in the breeze, and the gray exhaust from the diesel engines quickly whisked away as these ships of war entered the Gulf of Oman. The naval base in Jask soon faded into the distance.

A-uga, a-uga, a-uga, the alarms wailed as the order, "Dive—dive—dive," rang throughout each boat. Instantaneously there was a loud collective hissing sound, and large clouds of white mist clung to each hull as air was released from the ballast tanks. Soon, the decks were awash. Silently, both diesel-electric boats slipped beneath the surface. They immediately changed course and increased speed. Their direction: north/northwest. Their mission: to honor the great and glorious Islamic Republic of Iran.

Eighteen hours later, the *Tareq* and *Yunes* slipped through the Strait of Hormuz and entered the Persian Gulf. The sun had just begun to set, casting a magnificent orange glow, which would soon retreat beyond the horizon. The crew had just been informed of the mission, and their spirits soared.

"Sonar, do you have any contacts?" Captain Rahirimi, commanding officer of the *Tareq*, inquired.

"No, Captain," Seaman Jannati responded without hesitation.

"Very well. Raise the snorkel and recharge the batteries," the captain ordered. "Nasrin, find me the American fleet."

"Yes sir, with pleasure," the executive officer replied enthusiastically as the satellite antenna pierced the surface. Nasrin had the utmost confidence that soon the captain would gain all the valuable intelligence necessary for their rendezvous with destiny.

"Up, periscope," the captain ordered.

"Lieutenant Sadeq, what's our position?"

"Two miles south/southeast of the island of Tunb al Kubra, Captain," the navigator responded as the captain looked through the periscope, adjusted the focus, and shuffled his feet in a clockwise manner. Slowly, he completed a 360-degree turn. The sun had set, and the moon's reflection sparkled off the gently rolling waves, making the scene surreal. There were no vessels in sight. "Down, scope."

"Captain, the American fleet is twenty-four miles south/southwest of the Strait of Hormuz," Nasrin proclaimed as the captain walked over to the computer screen for a better tactical picture. "Isn't Google Earth fantastic?" Nasrin chuckled. A red pin marked the position of the fleet. After a few keystrokes, the *Tareq*'s position appeared, as well as the fleet's projected course, speed, and time to intercept. "The American fleet will be here at o-three-hundred."

"Excellent. Is our sister boat *Yunes* in position?"

"Yes, sir, and awaiting your orders," Nasrin confirmed.

"And what of the Islamic Revolutionary Guard's operations coordinator on Tunb al Sughra?"

"Major Sayyari reports six Zolfaghar (Seraj-one) fast attack patrol boats have just pulled into the cove on the westerly side of the island. The Karrar 'Ambassador of Death' drones are ready for launch, and our frigate *Jamaran* is in position five miles north/northwest of the island."

"Very well. Inform the major that the anticipated time of the attack is o-three-hundred. Also, request he order the *Jamaran* to stop all outbound traffic in the shipping lane, effective immediately," Captain Rahirimi ordered.

"Yes, sir, it will be done."

"Jannati, any sonar contacts?"

"No, Captain," the sonarman responded as the captain looked at his watch. It was 2100, and all was proceeding as planned.

"Nasrin, instruct Captain Taqipour and *Yunes* to begin mine-laying operations as instructed."

"Yes, sir," the executive officer replied before whispering, "Allah be praised."

"Helm, left standard rudder. Come to course two-seven-zero. All ahead slow."

"Aye, aye, Captain."

"Hasan, commence mine-laying operations. Deploy all sixteen mines at three-hundred-yard intervals," the captain ordered.

"Yes, Captain," Hasan replied as the first of the Russian MDM-UDM 1100-kilogram mines rolled off the specialized mine rack secured to the hull. Slowly and silently, it drifted toward the sandy seabed. Captain Rahirimi felt a surge of pride. The Soviet mines would detonate in response to acoustic, magnetic, or pressure influences within a fifty-yard radius.

Yunes was on a parallel course one mile to the north. Iranian intelligence had reported that the USS *Olympia* (SSN-717) had deployed with the carrier strike group. Undoubtedly, she would operate two miles ahead of the *John C. Stennis* Carrier Strike Group, and on a track that would take her and the fleet directly to the United States Naval base in Juffair, Bahrain.

The trap was soon to be set. The *Los Angeles* class attack submarine would slip through unharmed, not knowing the gruesome fate that awaited the surface ships and their shipmates. The fleet would be vulnerable to attack by sea and air. As with all battles, confusion and panic would ensue, and victory would be theirs.

Captain Rahirimi had developed a passion for naval warfare. *Sea Power: A Naval History* by E. B. Potter and Chester W. Nimitz had proven invaluable in his intellectual pursuit. He alone had devised the battle plan and considered every contingency. Yet over and over again he rehearsed the execution of his plan.

Initially, all vessels in the Carrier Strike Group would bring up flank speed and take evasive action. However, the wind was blowing from the north. Should the carrier somehow survive the torpedo attack, she would have to turn to the north in order to launch her aircraft.

The escort ships would have three, and only three, options: they could continue to screen the carrier, attack *Yunes* and *Tareq*, or turn broadside in order to bring all weapons to bear on the frontal assault launched by the Seraj-1 high-speed patrol boats and the Karrar drones. All scenarios would most certainly result in an abrupt change of course to the north or the south and a rendezvous with the Russian mines. Captain Rahirimi knew with the greatest confidence that the American fleet would soon be decimated. The power of Islam was far too great. Death and a watery grave awaited the nonbelievers.

"Allahu Akbar," he whispered, as another mine rolled off the *Tareq*.

CHAPTER 2

A THICK, GRAY HAZE had suddenly descended upon the tranquil waters of the Persian Gulf. Hours before, the skies had been clear and the stars unusually bright. Now the light from the moon struggled to pierce this ominous veil.

Their batteries fully charged, the Iranian submarines *Tareq* and *Yunes* were submerged and rigged for silent running. Six supercavitation Hoot torpedoes had been loaded into the bow tubes earlier, but the outer torpedo doors remained closed.

Yunes was positioned a thousand yards north, and *Tareq* a thousand yards south, of the respective minefields each submarine had lain. The trap had been set. It was now a waiting game. The captain appeared calm and collected, but tensions amongst the crew ran high. All were convinced that a historic sea battle was about to commence.

"Captain, I am picking up a low frequency vibration!" Sonarman Jannati shouted as he strained to identify the unusual sound he had just picked up.

"Bearing?" Captain Rahirimi requested.

"Zero-zero-five, sir."

"Our *Los Angeles* class submarine, no doubt. The Americans are so predictable," Nasrin whispered to the captain.

"Yes, and this gross error in judgment will be their downfall. Allah is great! This shall be a glorious day," Captain Rahirimi assured Nasrin as the American submarine continued on its course, its underwater signature quickly fading.

Hours before, the *John C. Stennis* Carrier Strike Group had passed through the Strait of Hormuz and entered the Persian Gulf. The aircraft carrier USS *John C. Stennis* (CVN-74) was accompanied by the guided-missile cruiser USS *Antietam* (CG-54) and the ships of *Destroyer Squadron* 21: USS *Wayne E. Meyer* (DDG-108), USS *Dewey* (DDG-105), USS *Kidd* (DDG-100), USS *Milius* (DDG-69), and USS *Jarrett* (FFG-33). All were steaming in formation, yet nowhere to be seen by the naked eye. Visibility had been reduced to less than one hundred yards.

It was 3:00 a.m. Admiral Ted Frederick, commanding officer of the Carrier Strike Group, had an uneasy feeling and had been unable to sleep. He stood on the bridge of the Nimitz class nuclear-powered aircraft carrier with Captain David Crisalli, the carrier's commanding officer. Both were long-time personal friends and Naval Academy classmates. Given the low visibility, flight operations had been temporarily suspended. The deck, which was usually bustling with activity, was eerily quiet.

Both officers were gazing out to sea when the admiral broke the silence. "David, I've never liked operating in the Persian Gulf. We must remain extremely vigilant."

"I share your concern, admiral. Frankly, I'm not comfortable operating in this Persian puddle either," Captain Crisalli complained.

"It's not just operating in restricted waters that I find troublesome—it's operating in restricted waters so close to hostile, irrational countries," the admiral emphasized.

"Surely you can't be referring to Iran?" Captain Crisalli quipped.

"Well, Mahmoud Ahmadinejad and his band of Islamic fanatics are certainly at the top the list, but in reality, danger could come from any point on the compass."

"I concur. We're effectively surrounded, and there's no telling from where the threat will originate," Captain Crisalli replied.

"You know, David, my dad was stationed at the US consulate in Tehran in the early sixties. I found the people, their culture, and the history of the Persian Empire fascinating. And the country— the country is one of startling contrast and great beauty," Admiral Frederick confessed.

"That's interesting. Well, I can't imagine what the Iranian people have had to endure since the fall of the Shah. What worries me are the recent crippling economic sanctions imposed by the United Nations. I can't help but believe that Iran is going to behave like a wounded animal," Captain Crisalli rationalized as Petty Officer First Class Wolfgang approached the officers.

"Agreed. However, I am more concerned with Iran's accelerated development of nuclear weapons, their sponsorship of worldwide terrorism, and the threat that country poses to the State of Israel," the admiral replied, although he did not want to get into a political discussion. Yet he found himself briefly reflecting on how dangerous the world had become and the recent discovery of a Russian Akula-class nuclear submarine armed with long-range ballistic missiles patrolling in the Gulf of Mexico. Yes, indeed, the world had become a more dangerous place, and, with a five-hundred-billion-dollar cut in defense spending looming, he felt certain that the greatest nation on Earth would soon be ill-equipped to defend either herself or her allies. Additionally, he carried a heavy burden. Before deploying, the admiral had been briefed by Naval Intelligence that a strike by Israel was imminent. Indeed, Iran's uranium enrichment facilities would have to be destroyed. *Would this attack launch World War III?* he wondered.

"Admiral, Captain, there is nothing better than a steaming cup of java on a hot and muggy night," Wolfgang said as he handed each man a cup of coffee. "Of course, that's coming from a snipe who was lucky enough to escape the confines of the boiler room for the wide-open space on the bridge," the petty officer added appreciatively.

"It was my pleasure to have approved that transfer, Wolfie. Thanks for the supercharged caffeine," Captain Crisalli replied.

"You're welcome, Captain. By the way, this special brew contains my magic beans. Just one cup will bring you incredible luck—assuming it doesn't eat through your stomach lining," Wolfgang added reassuringly, but with a broad grin.

"That's comforting. Thanks, Wolfie," Admiral Frederick responded before cautiously taking the liquid stimulant from the petty officer.

"Yes, sir, Admiral," Wolfgang replied with pride before returning to his duties.

"Admiral, why don't we move outside to the bridge wing for some pristine Persian humidity?" Captain Crisalli joked.

"Good idea, David. I could use some fresh, damp air."

"Officer on the deck," Captain Crisalli barked.

"Yes, sir," Lieutenant Kuo Wei responded promptly.

"The admiral and I will be on the bridge wing," Captain Crisalli announced.

"Aye, aye, Captain," the lieutenant acknowledged as both men stepped out onto the open bridge.

"This soup is so thick, Admiral, that I can't even see the running lights of the vessels in formation," Captain Crisalli complained as he set down his coffee cup.

"I should say," the admiral replied while gazing off into the darkness.

"Hell, the *Antietam* is only a thousand yards off our starboard beam, and she's not visible. Even the light emitted from the carrier seems to be absorbed by this dark haze. It's as if we're in a black hole," Captain Crisalli concluded with a sense of real concern.

"In my thirty years at sea I've never seen anything like it," Admiral Frederick agreed.

"Well, Admiral, although we're visible on unfriendly radar, it is comforting to know that the Stennis Strike Group's silhouette can't be seen from shore. And, thankfully, the safety and security of our naval base in Bahrain is only four hours away," Captain Crisalli said reassuringly as Lieutenant Kuo stepped onto the open bridge.

"Captain, Combat Information Center reports the sudden appearance of a large surface contact," Lieutenant Kuo said.

"Very well, Lieutenant," Captain Crisalli replied after receiving the disturbing news.

"Admiral, if you would excuse me, I need to evaluate this situation."

"I understand, David. Keep me informed."

"Yes, sir," Captain Crisalli replied before quickly making his way to the Combat Information Center (CIC), where the executive officer (XO), Commander Mike Mauri, was closely monitoring this new development.

"What do you have, Mike?"

"Captain, radar had a large surface contact heading directly toward us at fifteen knots and ten miles out. We originally thought it was probably a large tanker in the outbound shipping lane.

However, this one large contact now appears to be six smaller contacts, all abreast."

"It would certainly be an unusual time of the evening to set sail looking for tuna, so I don't think they're dhows," Captain Crisalli quipped as he analyzed the tactical picture and evaluated the potential threat.

"Is there any chatter coming from these vessels?" Captain Crisalli asked with increasing concern.

"No, sir. No communication at all. Additionally, we have been trying to raise them for the last ten minutes, without success," the XO replied.

"Mike, I smell a rat. Get two choppers in the air immediately to investigate. With night vision goggles maybe the pilots can see through this muck."

"Captain, there are two other troubling facts. These contacts appeared suddenly, and the only explanation, which makes sense, is that they were on the western side of Lesser Tunb island, thus shielded from our radar."

"Interesting. And your second concern?" the captain queried.

"We have no other contacts on radar. This is a busy waterway, and there is always a constant flow of commercial traffic through this area at all hours, day and night," Commander Mauri injected as Captain Crisalli turned to face the XO. There was no doubt that this subtle observation proved equally disturbing—Mike Mauri could read it on the captain's face.

"Keep me informed and make sure that the other ships in formation are tracking these contacts," Captain Crisalli ordered, as he was about to leave the CIC.

"Yes, sir," the XO responded.

"Bogies, two-seven-zero, twelve miles out!" a petty officer manning the anti-aircraft radar screamed. Captain Crisalli stopped dead in his tracks.

"Mike, get the admiral down here," the captain ordered.

Moments later, Admiral Frederick was in the CIC.

"Speed, course, and altitude?" Commander Mauri requested with a sense of urgency.

"Speed is forty knots, course is one-seven-zero, altitude is five hundred feet," came the reply.

"Admiral, there are six small surface contacts ten miles out heading toward us at fifteen knots. I've ordered two Sea Hawk helicopters to investigate. Additionally, we just picked up these bogies."

"Captain, the bogies are traveling in a southerly direction. There may be ten to fifteen aircraft. The bogies, as well as the surface contacts, appear to have originated from Lesser Tunb," Commander Mauri explained.

"I don't like it, David—get two F-Eighteen Super Hornets in the air," the admiral responded curtly as the crew worked quickly to plot and evaluate these new threats. They had trained countless hours for scenarios such as this one, but those were only drills. This was the real deal!

"The bogies have changed course and increased speed to one hundred knots. They are now heading toward the fleet," the radar operator announced.

"Sound General Quarters," Admiral Frederick growled.

"Mike, inform the other ships in the Carrier Strike Group to go to General Quarters and to *lock and load. Weapons release—authorized!*" the admiral ordered as Captain Chrisalli continued to reassess the tactical picture.

"Admiral, it appears that these seagoing desert rats are coming to pay us a visit," the captain observed.

"General Quarters, General Quarters, this is not a drill," the bowswain's mate announced over 1MC as the *John C. Stennis* roared to life. Thousands of sailors were rudely awakened from a dead sleep at the sound of the alarm, yet all scrambled to their duty stations. Hatches were slammed shut and dogged as to make compartments throughout the ship watertight within minutes.

"Commander, I recommend coming to course zero-one-zero and increasing speed to thirty-five knots," the flight officer, Lieutenant Helfrich, announced after completing his calculations.

"Very well, Lieutenant, make it so," Commander Mauri ordered as Lieutenant Helfrich notified the bridge of the new course and speed.

"Let's get the Hornets and the Sea Hawks off the deck," Captain Crisalli insisted, knowing that time was now critical.

"Admiral, I assure you that we'll have the remains of these audacious bastards buried deep beneath this sandy seabed momentarily," Captain Crisalli said with unwavering confidence.

CAPTAIN RAHIRIMI AND THE crew of the *Tareq* were at battle stations, and anticipation ran high. Yet all remained silent. Sonarman Jannati had detected the fleet some twenty minutes prior. The captain ordered that the sounds from the multitude of thrashing propellers be piped in throughout the boat.

Whoosh—whoosh—WHOOSH; the sounds grew louder. Now there was no doubt that the fleet was rapidly approaching.

Captain Rahirimi was aware that the six Seraj-1 fast attack boats were in position, ready to strike, and the fifteen Karrar drones were in the air. Each sleek Seraj-1 fiberglass boat carried an anti-ship missile and was capable of quickly reaching speeds in excess of eighty knots.

The Karrar unmanned drones carried four cruise missiles each. They were controlled by pilots in a makeshift tent on Lesser Tunb. Each had a joystick and sat patiently in front a computer screen. In the nose cone of each drone was a camera, so the battle could be monitored in real time. In all, the destructive power from both sea and air was overwhelming.

"Captain, the bearing to the fleet is zero-three-zero," Jannati reported.

"Excellent. Up, periscope." Captain Rahirimi trained the scope to 030 and adjusted the power and the focus. The carrier and her escorts were now entering the east side of the trap.

"Nasrin, send the following message to *Yunes:* 'Allahu Akbar. Commence your attack on the cruiser. Good hunting!'" Captain Rahirimi ordered. "Helm, come right to course zero-one-zero, all ahead one-third. Make your depth four-zero feet. Flood all tubes and open all outer torpedo doors," the captain ordered. "Nasrin, notify Major Sayyari that we are commencing our attack. Unleash the Seraj-1s and the Karrars."

"Yes, Captain."

"Captain, the fleet has increased speed but their course appears to remain unchanged," Jannati reported, although the captain had instantaneously detected a change in pitch. He had little doubt the higher frequency indicated that the propellers were turning faster.

"They have gone to General Quarters, but it's too late," Captain Rahirimi observed as he watched the carrier through the periscope. "Bearing—mark."

"Zero-two-zero, Captain," came the reply.

"Range—mark."

"Twenty-five-hundred yards."

"Angle on the bow—thirty degrees," the captain relayed.

"Captain, I have a firing control solution," Mustavi, the weapons control officer, announced.

"Very well. Set torpedo running depth for thirty feet," the captain ordered as he remained focused on the carrier. "It's time to release the Hoots—fire one." Seconds later, "fire two" rang out...and again, and again, until all six fish had been set loose.

The spread was precise. There was no way the carrier could escape *Tareq*'s self-propelled messengers of death.

"All torpedoes are running hot, straight, and normal. Time to impact: ninety seconds," Mustavi announced with exhilaration as the high-pitched whining from the supercavitation torpedoes trailed off.

"Very well. Mustavi, reload all tubes."

"Yes, sir."

"Captain, the Seraj-ones and Karrars have increased speed and are commencing their attack," Nasrin reported as Captain Rahirimi watched continuous flashes of light suddenly erupt from all of the vessels in the Carrier Strike Group.

The thick gray haze that had engulfed the fleet earlier had started to lift. As weapons were discharged, great, irregularly-shaped plumes of fire and smoke roared over the waves. Suddenly there was a loud explosion, and a wall of water engulfed the guided-missile cruiser *Antietam*.

"Captain..."

"Not to worry, Mustavi. The torpedoes from the *Yunes* have found their mark," the captain reported, knowing Mustavi was concerned that his torpedoes had detonated prematurely. "How long until impact?" he asked as he watched the naval battle unfold.

"Twenty seconds until the first torpedo hits."

"Captain, several of the vessels appear to be changing course," Jannati concluded.

"Very well," the captain replied, knowing full well that there was no way the carrier could turn in time to escape his grasp.

"Nasrin, it would appear that the infidels might have to adopt a new naval doctrine."

"Ha, the infidels are not that smart. Besides, how do you have a naval doctrine when the American fleet is no more?" Nasrin chuckled.

Boom—Boom—Boom—BOOM! Four torpedoes, each with a five-hundred-pound high-explosive payload, had slammed into the aircraft carrier. Captain Rahirimi watched as sheets of the once tranquil waters shot hundreds of feet into the air. The crew cheered. Their success was now undeniable.

Suddenly, a multitude of rockets streaked over the water and across the sky toward the fleet. For a brief moment the weapons discharge from the American fleet intensified, and the wall of fire and shrapnel appeared impenetrable. Yet most of the missiles found their mark.

Fires raged and black clouds of smoke billowed skyward within a one-mile radius. Captain Rahirimi turned his attention back toward the carrier. The *Stennis* was engulfed in flames and listing to port.

Jannati continued to listen intently. Amid all the explosions he detected a well-known sound. "Captain, I'm picking up high-pitched screws. Bearing zero-one-zero. One of the frigates is heading toward us."

"Got it. It's a DDG. Open torpedo doors for tubes one and two. Bearing—mark. Range—mark."

"Zero-one-zero, fifteen hundred yards, Captain."

"Angle on the bow is zero degrees. Set torpedo depth for thirty feet."

"Aye, aye, Captain. I have a firing solution."

"Very well. Down, scope. Fire one—fire two," Captain Rahirimi ordered calmly. "Right full rudder, come to heading zero-eight-zero. Ten degrees down bubble; make your depth one-five-zero feet."

"Captain, a down-the-throat shot?"

"Yes, indeed, Nasrin, but it's difficult to say if the mines or our torpedoes will send her to the bottom first."

Seconds later, three loud explosions could be heard, followed by several intermittent explosions in the distance.

Captain Rahirimi looked around at his crew. All were smiling and laughing. They had performed admirably. The naval battle had been decisive.

As the submarine *Tareq* slipped away silently, Captain Rahirimi was convinced that this was a new dawn for the Persian Empire. Only daylight would reveal the extent of the death and devastation. However, this was but one battle. Undoubtedly, greater battles were yet to come.

Jihad bil Saif had been decreed. The Islamic Republic of Iran would once more rule the world. Believe in Allah or be wiped from the face of the earth. Infidels beware, our crusade will soon return to American shores.

"Allah be praised," Captain Rahirimi whispered as Jannati reported the sounds of ships breaking up and drifting down— down into the depths and the obscurity of time.

CHAPTER 3

I T WAS A COLD day; the air was unusually still, and black, low-lying clouds drifted slowly overhead. The only sound that could be heard was the excessive chirping of thousands of confused birds. They flew in one giant, turbulent circle over the little town of Carencrow, located on the banks of the Cajun River in southern Louisiana. Oddly enough, this funnel cloud of wings appeared to touch down over Carencrow Regional Hospital, an affiliate of Lambed HCA. However, instead of creating a vortex powerful enough to suck up this monstrous for-profit hospital, nothing but droppings rained down.

It was October 31, and a massive storm was approaching the little town. Suddenly, in the distance, multiple lightning bolts shot toward the earth. The light was blinding, and the energy reflecting off the ominous clouds gave the town an eerie glow. Soon thereafter, the sound of the rolling thunder could be heard far off in the distance. All that was missing was the deadly warlock and his ravenous pack of goons and goblins. However, they were soon to arrive, as the workday was about to begin.

GeeHad Bin-Sad, founder, president and chief executive officer of Lambed HCA, had just arrived at the hospital. It was

5:00 a.m. He parked his Bentley on the sacred ground reserved for his eminence. As he stepped from his car, he looked toward the sky, thinking how much he loved stormy days such as this one. But it was neither the awe-inspiring force of nature nor the sweet smell of the approaching rain that captivated him; it was the thought of cash flow. He knew so very well that inclement weather generated more traffic accidents, resulted in more heart attacks and strokes, and exacerbated the inherent paranoia of the simple people living in this rural community. He was confident that the emergency room would soon be overwhelmed and the cash registers singing. Yes, it was going to be a great day.

But GeeHad's euphoric thoughts were soon shattered. As he approached the entrance, his feet slipped out from under him. He lost his balance and fell backwards, landing on his backside. The force of the fall was partially broken by his outstretched hands, which slipped in the muck beneath him. He was momentarily dazed, but, after regaining his senses, managed to crawl to his feet. It was then that he became overwhelmed by the pungent smell engulfing him.

"*Yil'an shaklek!*" GeeHad screamed, so loudly that he awakened the sleeping security guard. Realizing this was not a call to prayer, Jimbo, a seventy-five-year-old semi-retiree, staggered toward the front door to find GeeHad covered in bird crap. "Son of a bitch!" GeeHad blurted out as he tried in vain to brush nature's alterations from his fine, tailor-made suit.

"Are you alright, Mr. Bin-Sad?" Jimbo inquired, without any genuine concern.

"Hell, no!" GeeHad shot back, locking his fiery eyes on Jimbo. Jimbo couldn't help but notice the bulging veins on GeeHad's forehead begin to pulsate. He was certain that it wouldn't be long before steam would billow from GeeHad's ears. Sensing danger, Jimbo instinctively stepped back.

"Jimbo, you sorry, decrepit bastard! What in the hell do I pay you ten dollars an hour for? Certainly not to sit on your ass and read RV magazines! Every goddamn day there's bird shit at this entrance. I have told you countless times to hose down this area every morning. Since I can't seem to get rid of these fucking birds, then I need to get rid of you. You're fired!"

"Yes, sir," Jimbo replied instinctively, although he was not yet fully awake. However, when GeeHad's tongue-lashing finally registered, Jimbo was ecstatic! "It's time to go RVing!" Jimbo shouted with joy, and started to do a jig. "Thank you, Jesus, this was just the excuse I needed to leave this dreadful little town," Jimbo said out loud while the thought of traveling the country became more and more appealing. "Yes, indeed, it's time for old Jimbo to kick up his heels, enjoy several ice cold beers, and chase a few new dreams," Jimbo concluded with a great sense of pride as he watched GeeHad storm off in a huff, trailing a toxic cloud of Carencrow's claim to fame—buzzard excrement.

CHAPTER 4

GeeHad had just left the doctor's lounge, where he had showered and changed into red surgical scrubs. It was 6:00 a.m., and his monthly administrative meeting was about to get underway. The members of his team slowly shuffled into the conference room, each sipping on coffee in a vain attempt to vacate last night's alcohol-induced blues. The group included his corporate chief operating officer, Ms. Martha Mulch, the chief operating officers representing representing each of the twelve hospitals controlled by Lambed HCA, the corporate chief financial Officer, Mr. Johnny Cinch, the hospital's medical director, Dr. Cornelius Lyon, and Abdul Salah, Mr. Bin-Sad's personal assistant. GeeHad stood with his back toward them, staring out the window. The rain had begun to fall. His bloodshot, bleary-eyed executives did not focus on this strange man in scrubs until he turned to face them.

GeeHad Bin-Sad was a portly man in his late fifties. He was completely bald but sported a grey scraggly beard. His eyes were a cold jet black and only seemed to glisten when he received reports of revenue increases. No one had ever seen him smile. This morning GeeHad appeared to be in an unusually foul mood.

Without warning, his fist came crashing down onto the conference table, startling all those present. The meeting had been called to order.

"Martha," GeeHad growled as Martha Mulch snapped to attention and listened intently.

"Yes, sir?"

"This hospital is filthy, and the grounds look deplorable. Furthermore, I am tired of walking through a hundred yards of bird shit just to get onto my own property. I don't know why in the hell thousands of birds have collectively decided to roost and poop on Carencrow Regional Hospital, but enough is enough! Fuck the environmentalists! I want this species of pests driven past the point of extinction no later than next week. Then, I fully expect the parking lot and the sidewalks to be power washed. How in the hell can we run a successful business surrounded by such filth?"

"You're absolutely right, GeeHad. We've tried scarecrows and high-pitched noise to run the buzzards off, but now it's time to break out the poison. Consider the PETA-protected pests history," Martha replied with determination.

As Lambed HCA's chief operating officer, Martha Mulch had clawed her way into a top management post of this large hospital chain by stepping on, over, and through others. Desired results were achieved at any cost and no sacrifice was too great. However, the years of trench warfare were evident. Her round face was a road map dominated by craters and deep furrows. Accentuating her rather plump body was the hairdo from hell. It appeared as if some ill-spirited hairdresser had placed a bowl over her head and then cut her hair short at a precise angle so that it would curl underneath. With the small, oval bald patch on top, the hairdo was an exact replica of the head of a giant penis. In polite company and well out of earshot, she was lovingly referred to as "Mushroom Head," but the nickname "Dickhead" was far more appropriate for such a mean-spirited individual who ruled Lambed HCA with an iron fist.

GeeHad sneered at Johnny Cinch, Lambed's CFO. This healthy, athletic, thirty-five-year-old accounting protégé had cut his teeth at Arthur Andersen, an unfortunate career choice, made even more disastrous by his handling of the Enron audit. By virtue of the two years he subsequently spent in prison for his misdeeds, Johnny had been blacklisted by all the large and semi-reputable accounting firms. As if this was not enough misfortune, his personal esteem had been crushed by a nasty divorce and the resulting bankruptcy. GeeHad knew that this was the right man for the job precisely because Johnny's reputation was tainted. Most importantly, he had learned that Johnny was an expert at playing the corporate shell game and backdating executive stock options. Revenue and expenses were mere numbers on a piece of paper, and debt could easily be shifted from one company to the next. GeeHad felt sure he needed the talents of such a man to line his pockets.

"Johnny, where are this quarter's operating results and next quarter's revenue projections?" GeeHad demanded, finally deciding to get down to business after his tirade.

"Ah…" Johnny mumbled nervously, shuffling the profit-and-loss statement to GeeHad and each of the other executives. "For the quarter, Lambed HCA showed a profit, but relative to the same time period last year, our revenue was down ten percent, and our expenses had increased by well over eight percent. Unfortunately, it now appears that next quarter's projections will also be disappointing," Johnny concluded, as his voice started to wane. He knew GeeHad would not be pleased.

Immediately GeeHad turned beet red and began wildly beating on the conference table.

"Damn it! These results are absolutely unacceptable! We are a publicly traded company and every quarter our stockholders expect us to exceed our projections. Revenue must go up, and expenses down! Now, let's start on the revenue side. Johnny, what exactly was the problem?"

"Well, sir, we are being squeezed across the board. The percentage of self-pay patients continues to increase at an alarming rate, and they seldom pay us a dime for valuable services rendered. Additionally, Medicaid recently... Unfortunately, I can't foresee a viable solution to these problems."

"Damn it, Johnny, I'll give you a solution to this problem. I want those sorry, self-pay bastards and the worthless group of unemployed Medicaid deadbeats thrown out of our emergency rooms! Is that understood?"

"Yes, sir," GeeHad's corporate minions mumbled collectively.

"GeeHad, by federal law we're not allowed to deny anyone access to medical treatment, regardless of their ability to pay," Dr. Cornelius Lyon interrupted.

"Bullshit! Dr. Lyon, get creative! You will either be part of the solution, or part of the problem. You implement an emergency room policy denying those sons of bitches access to our quality medical care, or I will find someone who will! These thieves overrun our ERs and consume our valuable resources. Hell, we need to be pampering the paying customer. I could give a damn if the bastards end up dying in the street! However, as a humanitarian, I do have a soft side. So, if need be, we will purchase vans to deposit their dead carcasses in the slums down on Lower Third. Do I make myself perfectly clear?"

The executives around the table began to chuckle, as they all were accustomed to GeeHad's tyrannical outbursts, leaving little doubt as to his position on any issue.

"Yes, sir, loud and clear! I will find a solution," Dr. Lyon answered affirmatively.

Dr. Lyon had been very adept at meeting GeeHad's demanding expectations over the years. He had no other choice but to do so, though, because, as a convicted felon, no self-respecting hospital would give him privileges to continue practicing as an obstetrician. Convicted of Medicare fraud, Dr. Lyon had spent over a year in federal prison, but was miraculously pardoned by the governor. Now, at the age of seventy, he felt untouchable. Without question he could implement policies which, if scrutinized by federal prosecutors, would result in his underlings taking the fall. Such was the price of success. The more he thought about it, the more he relished the challenge. In his mind, there was something very exciting about circumventing the law.

"Johnny, what's our problem on the expense side of the ledger?"

"Well, sir, the cost of doing business is increasing across the board. Our labor expenditures continue to escalate at an alarming rate. Also, the drug manufacturers, citing the cost of product development and the threatened loss of patent protection, find it necessary to increase the price of their products by fifteen percent every year. Additionally, our expenditures for supplies and products keep rising, as well as the costs for telephone services, water, electricity, and sewage," Johnny replied, his voice lowering as he bowed his head.

"That's outrageous! It's clearly time to squeeze the greedy drug manufacturers and our worthless suppliers," GeeHad insisted, pounding the table yet again. Seconds later, he was calm and rational. Dead silence suddenly filled the room. Everyone gathered around the conference table felt that this was the eye of the storm.

"Now Johnny, please share honestly with me your overview of where Lambed HCA stands," GeeHad asked in a cold and calculating voice.

Johnny Cinch squirmed in his chair. He could feel the beads of sweat ooze from his pores as dozens of self-serving eyes ripped into his soul, demanding answers.

"Well, the percentage of self-paying patients continues to increase, whereas the percentage of paying customers is decreasing. The net result is the loss of millions of dollars a year due to indigents not paying their bills. For example, in the emergency room we collect only thirty-seven cents on every dollar billed. Given these facts, along with the prohibitive costs of complying with existing federal mandates, it's a miracle that any hospital is turning a profit," Johnny concluded in an ill-fated attempt to rationalize his dismal corporate report.

GeeHad took a few moments to review the quarterly profit-and-loss statements from each of the twelve hospitals he controlled. All appeared to be in line, but the numbers were extremely discouraging. His train of thought was interrupted by a thunderous explosion from a lighting bolt, which felt like it touched down only blocks from the hospital. The lights flickered but remained on. Once again, the boardroom was deadly silent.

GeeHad stood and walked toward the window. It was pitch black outside, so he could not see the street below begin to flood, but he could make out the tops of tall trees being whipped back and forth. The rain was now coming down in sheets, pounding against the glass, and the force of the wind was so strong that it caused the windows in the conference room to vibrate.

Suddenly, there was a brilliant flash of light, followed by another thunderous explosion, and then the lights went out. Sixty seconds later, the hospital's generator came online, establishing emergency lighting. In the subdued lighting, the conference room took on a sinister glow.

Somehow, GeeHad felt energized by the violence of the storm. He turned toward his executives and, with a deep, confident voice, issued the marching orders.

"We are in a war, and in this war you either win or you lose. The bottom line is that we need to increase revenue and slash expenses. Effective immediately, I want fifteen percent tacked on to each and every bill. With regard to the bad debt generated by our self-pay and Medicaid trash, I want our collection department to aggressively hound these deadbeats. I expect vigilante groups on retainer to find these bastards and beat them unmercifully for stiffing Lambed HCA. We will squeeze every last dime out of them, while at the same time discouraging repeat business. Concurrently, we will establish a policy to keep the indigent out of our emergency rooms. Now, if the government has the balls to cut Medicare reimbursement, then I expect us to pad the bills. On the expense side, the most dramatic and immediate savings will come from layoffs. Strive to cut ten percent of your labor force over the next thirty days. With Christmas so near, I would like you all to take pride in churning out those pink slips, eliminating middle managers, aids, techs, and even cleaning personnel. Also, make life so unbearable for the senior nurses that they quit. By hiring new nursing school graduates, we can save ten dollars an hour, while maintaining our unsurpassed standard of care. Additionally, the nurses sit around half the time doing nothing. Make them empty the garbage and mop the floors!"

GeeHad paused and scanned the table. Looking for weaknesses, he made eye contact with each and every person.

"Is anyone uncomfortable with my mildly aggressive policy?" GeeHad asked. No one spoke up.

"Excellent! Well then, we are all in agreement."

"Yes," the executives of Lambed HCA mumbled collectively.

"Pardon me? I can't hear you!" GeeHad shouted.

"Yes, yes, YES!" everyone in the room chanted, with ever-increasing fear-driven determination.

GeeHad was clearly pleased by their collective response, which seemed to be magnified by the fiery flashes of light and thunderous roar from outside

"Excellent. This meeting is now adjourned," GeeHad concluded.

As he stood up, GeeHad motioned to Johnny Cinch. Johnny walked over, and the two men found a quiet corner in the room as the battle-weary executives staggered out. GeeHad's personal aid, loyal confidante, and lover, Abdul, stood close by awaiting his orders.

"I certainly had fun cooking the books. Have you had a chance to review the real numbers? Our hospitals did remarkably well, exceeding all our expectations," Johnny shared enthusiastically.

"Yes, but I wanted everyone around the table motivated and fearful that heads may roll," GeeHad replied. "By the way, I noticed that Lambed HCA's debt is starting to creep up again. I believe it's time to consider offloading a portion of this debt onto one of our close affiliates. The figure I had in mind is twenty-five million."

"Absolutely, consider it done. Knowing that you're a fan of *The Little Rascals*, and that we have already chosen 'Alfalfa,' 'Darla,' and 'Buckwheat' as clandestine corporate entities, would you have a suggestion for the new corporate shell?" Johnny asked.

"In fact I do. Name the new entity 'Swanky Spanky,'" GeeHad chuckled.

"Give me the 'high sign,'" GeeHad insisted as both men cupped their hands underneath their chins and began to wiggle their fingers in a wave-like pattern.

GeeHad and Johnny erupted in laughter at their own antics. Then GeeHad abruptly stopped laughing and motioned for Abdul to come closer. Johnny realized immediately that their conversation had concluded. He turned and promptly left the conference room.

Abdul and GeeHad were now alone. GeeHad placed his arm over Abdul's shoulder. They turned to face the window, taking a minute to relish all the fury nature had unleashed.

"Our meeting went very well, Abdul. Did you notice how all the Christian infidels continuously nod their heads in agreement?"

"Allah is great, and they are very stupid," Abdul chuckled.

"Yes, Allah is great. Fear and terror are the weapons of Allah. We grow very powerful, my friend. The nonbelievers will soon be in Hell. Have you heard from Abu Bakr?" GeeHad inquired.

"Your shipment from Wonsan arrives tomorrow, GeeHad," Abdul confirmed.

"Excellent!" GeeHad replied enthusiastically.

CHAPTER 5

THE THUNDER AND LIGHTNING persisted all day, but the torrential downpour had begun to subside. The emergency generators continued to provide the basic electrical needs, but much of the hospital remained dimly lit. It was five o'clock in the afternoon, the floodwaters that had engulfed the streets for hours were starting to recede, and, like clockwork, a sea of humanity was beginning to migrate toward Carencrow Regional's emergency room. The ER waiting room was already filled to capacity. The floors were wet, and the pungent smell of damp, soiled clothing permeated the air. The sound of the thunder was soon displaced by a deafening roar of general conversation mingled with coughing, sneezing, vomiting, and the ever present moans and groans.

As the emergency room's first line of defense, the triage nurse sat undefended in the waiting room, fully exposed to the good, the bad, and the ugly. The registered nurse/target assigned a level of acuity to each patient given their respective complaint, thus controlling when they would be seen. It was the usual daily battle, with each patient who checked in at triage deliberately attempting to appear more sick than the next, thinking they would be rushed beyond the locked doors and into the emergency room. Tempers flared as the nearly dying were rushed to the back, ahead of others who had checked in earlier. Arguments erupted with increasing frequency. Soon the triage nurse would become the focus for verbal abuse and seething glares.

Debby Flat, RN, was the triage nurse this fateful day. Debby was incredibly tenacious and extremely tough. After fifteen years of brutal combat in the ER, she no longer felt the arrows of insult penetrate her middle-aged body. Perhaps it was the years of drinking Crown Royal that dulled her sensitivity to pain. Beyond the locked doors of the waiting room lay the emergency room, which was one large space divided into two sections, separated only by a large, rectangular counter. Behind the counter sat the emergency room coordinator and the admitting clerks. It was the emergency room nerve center. To the right of the counter were the even-numbered trauma rooms. To the left were the odd-numbered rooms. These rooms were separated from the counter by walkways congested with crash carts, stretchers, and various other obstacles. The ER was manned by two teams, each consisting of a physician, two nurses, and one tech. Each team worked twelve-hour shifts and was responsible for twelve rooms.

The emergency room coordinator, Sheila "Queen of the Jungle" Mafuse, RN, was on duty. She was responsible for assigning each patient to a specific room, whether they were coming in the front door or the ambulance entrance, located at the other end of the ER.

This afternoon all twenty-four rooms and the walk-in clinic were full. Four extremely sick patients were in a holding pattern, parked on ambulance stretchers in the hall, waiting for rooms to be vacated. All lay patiently with the EMS personnel in tow, watching the mayhem.

Dr. Rex "Rrrrex" Bent; Patricia "Trissy" Bent, RN; Wanda "the Splint" Bennet, RN; and Terry "Flashback" Foxxman were in trauma room eight, trying desperately to revive a young drowning victim. The nine-year-old had been swept away during the floods while standing on a boat dock, mesmerized by the raging Cajun River. The normally placid river had turned violent with the torrential downpour. The river level rose instantaneously, and the sheer volume created so much turbulence that the water appeared to be boiling. Without question, the force of the water, coupled with the mass of large, floating debris striking the thin pilings, was more than the small, rickety dock could withstand. It collapsed, launching the child downstream. By some miracle he was found quickly. His lifeless, hypothermic body was brought to the emergency room. EMS had intubated the child at the scene; one paramedic was frantically doing chest compressions while the other pumped oxygen into his lungs.

"How long had he been down?" Rex asked as he looked at the young man's pupils, which were fixed and dilated.

"He was submerged for at least twenty minutes, Dr. Bent. By the time we got to him, he was in asystole," Demetrius, one of the seasoned paramedics, replied. CPR continued while the young man was shifted onto the hospital stretcher.

"Bag him," Rex said as he listened to the boy's lungs. He could hear the distinctive snap and crackle of fluid-filled alveoli opening and slamming shut.

"Stop CPR," Rex ordered as he felt for a pulse. There was no pulse, no blood pressure, no spontaneous respirations, and the patient remained in asystole. "Resume CPR," Rex requested. "Demetrius, what have you given the young man so far?" Rex asked.

"He's had four amps of epinephrine and one amp of bicarb IV push," Demetrius responded.

"Rex, his rectal temperature is eighty-five degrees Fahrenheit," Trissy said after inserting a probe to record the patient's core temperature.

"Get the bear hugger, warm blankets, and warm fluids. Give him another amp of epinephrine IV push," Rex ordered, surveying the young man's grossly discolored body. He had sustained multiple cuts and abrasions, presumably due to swift moving debris. For all intents and purposes the boy was dead, but no one can legally be declared dead unless they are "warm and dead." The ER team continued life-saving procedures, injecting the chemicals necessary to restart his lifeless heart. All efforts proved unsuccessful, and, after forty-five minutes, the code was called.

"Time of death, seventeen-forty-five," Wanda announced.

"Great job everyone," Rex said to the dejected team, commending their valiant efforts before walking to the room where the young man's parents, brothers, and sisters were anxiously waiting. Upon receiving the horrific news, all became hysterical. The yelling, screaming, and crying that ensued could be heard throughout the emergency department. The sounds were hauntingly gut-wrenching and, as always with tragedies such as this one, unforgettable.

Suddenly, full power was restored to the hospital. As soon as the lights came back on, all hell broke loose. An eighteen-year-old male, unresponsive and slumped over in a wheelchair, was being rushed toward Debby at a dangerous speed. The man pushing the wheelchair yelled, "Help! My brother's been shot!"

Debby flung the doors to the emergency room open and shouted, "Gun shot!" She shoved the frantic brother aside, grabbed the wheelchair, and rushed toward the back.

"Trauma room ten," Sheila shouted.

A new victim, Tyroneous Washington, had arrived. As he was being rushed toward room ten, Tyroneous started to slowly slither out of the wheelchair. Given the critical nursing shortage, the usual atmosphere of semi-controlled chaos had now crossed the threshold into the realm of dangerous and uncontrolled madness.

As his wheelchair came to an abrupt halt, Tyroneous was almost hurled onto the floor. Trissy, Wanda, and Foxxman were already in the room. Together they quickly hoisted Tyroneous's limp body and tossed him onto the stretcher. His clothes were being cut off by Foxxman, while Wanda placed a blood pressure cuff on his arm, Debby checked for a pulse, and Trissy searched for a vein in which to start an IV. As soon as Rex entered the room, the unresponsive patient suddenly came to life! He began writhing in pain—a relatively good sign, considering the alternative of being pulseless and breathless.

"Where were you shot? Where were you shot?" Debby demanded as she quickly surveyed his body, finding no blood or bullet holes.

"Popeye's," Tyroneous uttered, with what appeared to be his last breath.

"Look here, Einstein! I ain't the police, and I ain't your mama. Where on your body did the bullet hit?" Debby asked very slowly and deliberately.

"Popeye's," Tyroneous responded again as he opened his eyes and looked around the room.

Everyone in the room appeared shocked. Their jaws dropped simultaneously in disbelief. Tyroneous was butt naked. Even his little drumstick was exposed, and the only visible trauma was a small abrasion on his abdomen.

"Let's roll him and check his back," Rex ordered.

"Hey, what you do-in', man?" Tyroneous complained, resisting the emergency staff's efforts.

"Just as I suspected: no evidence of any wounds," Rex growled.

"I've been shot," Tyroneous announced with a sense of pride.

"No Tyroneous, you weren't," Foxxman informed the young victim of a probable drug deal gone bad. Tyroneous immediately crossed his arms and pouted.

"I'm ready to shoot the scrawny bastard after all the theatrics!" Debby threatened before turning around and heading back to triage.

"Obviously the bullet didn't have his name on it, or maybe it struck him in the head and bounced off," Wanda concluded as she, Rex, and Trissy left the room in disgust.

"That sorry turkey buzzard!" Rex said as he sat down to write a note on Tyroneous's chart. "Foxxman, get him a gown and let him sit in the hall while I finish his paperwork."

"Will do."

"Well, I ain't eatin' at Popeye's again, that's for damn sure!" Wanda confessed in a slow, Louisiana drawl, leaving everyone in the ER laughing uncontrollably. What a cast of characters. Trissy was a feisty nurse of German descent. She and Rex had been shacked up for several years before taking the plunge. Wanda was short and built like an Ewok, but you couldn't let her stature fool you. She always told you exactly what she thought and never minced her words. Wanda was nicknamed "the Splint," after insisting upon wearing food-speckled Velcro wrist splints throughout a recent pregnancy, and beyond. Rounding out the team was Terry Foxxman, a fifty-year-old Army medic and Vietnam veteran who always enjoyed telling war stories, usually centering around Mama-san and his escapades in the local social clubs. Anytime he was startled by a loud noise, "Flashback" Foxxman would wrap his hands around his head, squat down and yell, "Incoming!" These flashbacks seemed to come with increased frequency and severity as the fine line dividing reality from these vivid images of his past continued to blur.

DR. EMANUEL "BOOM BOOM" Whitherspoon had the odd-numbered rooms and had been so busy fighting his own battles during the day that he had not had the opportunity to shoot the breeze with his comrade-in-arms, Rrrrex. Boom Boom was a handsome fifty-year-old black man with salt and pepper hair and a mustache. He was meticulous in his dress and very methodical in the manner in which he managed his patients. His favorite form of relaxation was cruising the Caribbean with his wife. While onboard these large luxury liners, he could not help but notice the voluptuous young ladies strutting about in their thongs. Upon sharing these stories with his fellow staff members, his guidance proved inspiring. "Wear dark sunglasses," he relayed with pride, "and never let your wife see your head move." What especially caught his eye was the way their cheeks bounced while strutting about the deck, and, much to everyone's delight, he was quite talented at reproducing that motion. Upon request he would smile, raise his chin high in the air, and move his head back and forth, as his wrists and hands moved rhythmically to the gluteal beat, all the while chanting in a sing-song voice, "Boom, baba boom, baba boom, baba boom."

"BOOM BOOM, I FEEL as if our position has been overrun," Rex declared to his mentor. "This has been the shift from hell! Just look at the toll it has taken on my nurses. It's as if they've been on the Corregidor Death March." Wanda and Trissy looked at Rex in disgust, the fatigue more than apparent on their faces.

"Bite me, Rrrrex!" Wanda declared without remorse. Trissy laughed, showing her appreciation for Wanda's scud-missile response.

"Stay focused, Rrrrex, and don't take it personally. ObamaCare is on the way," Boom Boom responded with the wisdom of an ancient Asian warrior.

"ObamaCare is just going to make the situation worse!" Rex surmised, suddenly finding himself overcome by the need to vent.

"You know, this ER has become extremely dangerous, given the high volume and level of acuity. If it weren't for the shortage of doctors, nurses, and techs, all would be well," Rex shared with just a hint of sarcasm.

"No doubt," Wanda replied.

"What in the Sam Hell is this hospital going to do when security in the United States is breached and terrorism returns to our shores? There will be mass casualities," Rex complained, as the hours of frustration finally came to a boil.

"Stay focused, Rrrrex," Boom Boom replied, while continuing to work.

"Stand back, Wanda! I've seen that look in Rrrrex's eyes," Trissy warned her close friend.

"I thought Carencrow Regional was out of control when those bastards from Colombia HCA owned the hospital, but since the greedy GeeHad gained control, this work environment has become unbearable," Rex argued as his coworkers looked on, nodding in agreement.

"This ain't been no magic carpet ride, that's for damn sure!" Wanda felt compelled to add.

"I tell you, it's a plot with the Wicked Witch of the South, Ms. Teresa Talon, RN, executing this hospital's evil agenda. If her father had not been president of this hospital so many years ago, she would've never become the emergency room director of nursing," Rex retorted.

"I must admit you have a good point, Rrrrex. She has absolutely no common sense, and I know for certain that she can't even start an IV!" Wanda said, adding a little more fuel to the fire.

"That's a fact," Trissy contributed.

"That self-serving tyrant sits in her glass office all day, oblivious to what is going on in the ER. If she's not busy criticizing those who work for her, she's preoccupied with plotting the demise of anyone who appears to be a threat to her little dictatorship! Hell, she's as dangerous as a great white shark, but as useless as tits on a bull!" Rex concluded.

"Stay focused Rrrrex," Boom Boom said, although he chuckled, knowing that the facts were undeniable.

"Now let me get this straight. Are you proposing a mutiny?" Wanda asked as she placed her immobilized, splint-laden hands on her hips.

"Sounds like a mutiny to me. Rrrrex, consider me onboard," Trissy added in support. Suddenly, Boom Boom became keenly aware of a large, shadowy movement to his left. He quickly turned and lifted his head.

"Oh, Christ!" Boom Boom uttered, watching Mushroom Head steam toward him. Undoubtedly, she was under full power. Only the sound of her thunder-thighs rubbing together escaped the vacuum left in her wake.

"Run deep and silent, Rrrrex," Boom Boom whispered, then winked as he canted his head and rolled his eyes to the left in a most peculiar manner.

"Boom Boom, are you having a seizure?" Rex asked, attempting to analyze his friend's bizarre facial expressions.

Boom Boom dropped his head in frustration, realizing that his subtle message had not been received. Rex looked beyond Boom Boom and immediately saw Mushroom Head as she walked past, heading toward Teresa's office.

"Damn!" Rex mumbled as he quickly turned away from GeeHad's evil, on-rushing goon.

"Having a seizure?" Boom Boom teased.

"So, what the hell. I miss one diagnosis."

"You must be joking!" Sheila suddenly shouted out loud before hanging up the phone.

"Rex, Debby called from triage. Several of the hospital managers are passing out cokes and brownies to those in the waiting room, even to the patients who presented with nausea and vomiting! It appears that several patients complained about the waiting time, and management felt that this was the way of soothing frayed nerves," Sheila reported.

"That was a rather bright idea. You see, management really is insanely humane," Rex criticized.

"I'm sure the surgeons would be pleased to know that anyone they may be taking to the operating room tonight has a full belly," Boom Boom replied sarcastically, shaking his head in disbelief.

"Rex, Mean and Evil overheard your conversation criticizing our illustrious ER nursing director and were seen heading toward Teresa's office. They look like they're up to no good," Trissy whispered.

Mean and Evil were Boom Boom's nurses. These ladies were believed to be Siamese twins joined at the head and the chest. It was rumored that shortly after birth, they were separated and neither was left with a brain or a heart. They would sell their souls for the death and destruction of a coworker, for either promotion or pleasure. These two took such great pride in their monikers that no one used their real names. Both were in their late forties, obese, pear-shaped, and ill-tempered chain-smokers. Alone, each was dangerous, but together they acted synergistically, creating a destructive force of unimaginable magnitude. Rex and Trissy were soon to find themselves down and out, courtesy of Mean and Evil.

"They were probably heading out the ambulance door for one of their countless cigarette breaks, or to graze on some dead carcass lying in the grass," Rex replied, without giving the buzzards a second thought.

"Boom Boom, you must keep a tighter rein on those feathered reprobates," Rex suggested after being made aware of Mean and Evil abandoning their post for the tenth time this shift.

"Normally I would Rex, but those two birds are so ornery that I'm afraid of the repercussions," Boom Boom replied honestly as he began tying up loose ends before his relief appeared.

"By the way, are we still on for dinner tonight, Trissy?" Rex asked as he gazed into her sparkling eyes.

"Absolutely, of course. After a day like today, the last thing I want to think about is cooking. I can already taste the Cosmopolitan," Trissy replied as she licked her lips.

CHAPTER 6

I T WAS QUARTER TO seven and, like clockwork, Dr. Hanz "Pretty Boy" Bleeker and Dr. Fred "Fast Freddie" Leadbury had arrived to relieve the watch.

Hanz was a paranoid, thirty-five-year old white male, going on eighteen. His black scrubs and dark, slicked back hair left no doubt that he was of Italian descent. He had been hired at Carencrow Regional only weeks before. He was rather reserved, so Wanda quickly decided to break the ice. She felt compelled to ask the question that everyone thought they knew the answer to.

"You're awfully pretty. You ain't gay, are you?" Wanda asked.

"Hell, no!" Hanz shot back in his own defense as he tried to analyze why this splint-sporting Ewok would ask such an insulting question.

He did, in fact, appear rather effeminate, but his preoccupation and daily ritual of chasing every pretty girl in a short skirt left little doubt as to his sexual preference.

"Wanda, how could you embarrass Dr. Bleeker like that? Pretty Boy is all dog!" Boom Boom replied in the newly hired physician's defense.

"Thank you, Boom Boom," Hanz responded with genuine appreciation before slipping away from the counter to hit on one of the hot nurses.

Several minutes later Hanz strolled over to Rex. He looked around the ER, saw the mayhem, and just shook his head. He didn't have the courage to look at the number of charts stacked on the salad bar.

"Well, what do you have?" Hanz asked in a rather discouraged tone.

"Another day in paradise," Rex replied, knowing he had one foot out the door. He was quite pleased that he had semi-survived another grueling shift.

Hanz didn't like working the night shifts, as he always had difficulty sleeping during the day. Today had been no different.

"Christ, Hanz, you look like a walking zombie," Rex noted.

"I didn't sleep a wink."

"Well, it shows," Rex chuckled. "Whenever you regain full consciousness, let me know, and I'll give you the report. However, you're not going to be pleased," Rex added.

"I can clearly see that, but it's now or never," Hanz replied while rubbing his bloodshot eyes.

"In room one... Finally, in room twelve there is a young man who ended up being the consult from hell. The patient is a five-year-old boy transferred in from an outlying hospital for a *neurosurgical consult*, a phrase that has become an oxymoron in recent months. A friend pushed him down a stairwell earlier today, and he struck his head. Clinically he looks good, but he has a large subdural hematoma, which radiology believes could possibly be an epidural bleed. I contacted the neurosurgeon on call."

"I can only imagine how that phone conversation went with that ornery SOB," Hanz chuckled.

"Not well at all—imagine that. He even had the audacity to tell me that my consult was Mickey Mouse bullshit and there was no way in hell he was going to come in to evaluate the patient. Dr. Earnest 'Hot Rod' Kelly is on for pediatrics and has agreed to admit the patient, with neuro checks to be conducted every hour. So, thankfully you don't need to get involved, unless his condition takes a turn for the worse," Rex concluded, much to Hanz's delight.

"Every day in this jungle is a battle, with danger around every corner. Be very, very careful Rrrrex. You and I are expendable. The less-than-friendly neurosurgeon, Dr. Fubar, brings this hospital a great deal of money. Carencrow Regional will do anything and everything to keep the arrogant SOB happy in order to preserve their cash flow—even if that means covering up your sudden departure from this Earth, or his medical negligence. Stay focused, and don't take it personally," Boom Boom recommended after overhearing a portion of Rex's conversation with Hanz.

"Once again you have provided sound advice," Rex replied gratefully.

"Why don't you and Trissy get the hell out of here?" Hanz suggested, knowing that it was time to buckle down and get to work before the next disaster rolled through the door.

"Sounds good; we have dinner reservations in an hour."

"To which of the two decent restaurants in the town are you going?" Hanz asked while reviewing one of the many charts piled in front of him.

"Rula's," Rex replied.

"I recommend the 'Chum Jong Il' Salmon," Hanz suggested, knowing that the restaurant was owned by an evil North Korean named Chum.

"All I want is a Mai Tai," Rex added, moments before the hair on the back of his neck suddenly stood on end. From out of nowhere Teresa Talon appeared, walking toward the coordinator's desk. Somehow this sinister ER director of nursing had escaped from the safety of her glass cage. Teresa's eyes were bloodshot, the veins in her forehead and neck engorged, and her ears were a brilliant crimson. Even her hair looked angry.

"Y'all are not seeing the patients fast enough. They are complaining, and management wants some answers," Teresa shouted, interrupting all conversations while the shift change was in progress.

"Teresa, it's been so busy that none of the nurses have even had the chance to take a lunch break. Perhaps you should consider hiring more nurses," Trissy suggested.

"That's not my fault," Teresa shot back curtly. "If you worked more efficiently you would have time for lunch."

"Teresa, may I recommend you invest in a Viking hat for Sheila and instruct her to beat a drum in a cadence reflecting the speed with which we should be seeing the patients?" Wanda suggested.

"How big do you want the drum to be?" Teresa replied sarcastically, scrutinizing all the dissenters carefully. "There are going to be some big changes around here as a result of your lollygagging. Now get to work!" Teresa shouted before rushing off in a huff.

"Lollygagging! That dingbat works four days a week, and then has the audacity to hang a 'Gone Sailing' sign on her door so she can enjoy a three day weekend!" Wanda retorted.

"No worries, Wanda," replied Trissy. "It's nice to be appreciated, but I'm lollygagging my way out of here. See ya tomorrow!"

"I'm not sure about the hat or the drum, but the thought of rough leather is rather appealing," Sheila moaned in ecstasy.

Boom Boom shook his head, then turned toward Fast Freddie to finish giving his report.

"What in tarnation has gotten into Teresa?" Fast Freddie asked.

"Who knows, but for once I can truly say that I'm not to blame," Rex assured his coworkers, although as usual they remained skeptical any time Rex ushered a defense.

"Yeah, right," Sheila chuckled.

"Well, Hanz. That's all she wrote," Rex said with a smile.

Rex and Trissy slipped out the ambulance door just as a smiling Mean and Evil were slithering back in.

"Those buzzards are looking just a little too happy for my comfort," Rex confided in Trissy, wondering if the two birds had come from Teresa's office or from one of their countless cigarette breaks.

CHAPTER 7

THE DAY'S MASSIVE STORM front had passed, but in its wake winter's first cold front descended upon the little town of Carencrow. However, on this frigid, dark night the only vestiges of Old Man Winter's violence were scores of slush puddles, downed tree limbs, and a dense, wavy patchwork of pine needles.

Rex and Trissy arrived at Rula's shortly before eight and were greeted by Rogé, a tall, distinguished Frenchman. Rula's was a quaint restaurant nestled in a dense forest of tall pine trees adjacent to the banks of the mighty Cajun River. The stone fireplace was stoked and the fire was raging. The explosions of light, along with the snapping and crackling of the wood as it burned, added to the ambiance. Old Blue Eyes was singing "I Did It My Way" overhead just loud enough to mask the conversations radiating from each table.

"Halloween night and the place is absolutely packed. Whatever happened to trick-or-treating?" Rex wondered.

"Ah, Dr. and Mrs. Bent, it's so very good to see you again. Your table will be ready shortly. Would you care to indulge yourselves at the bar?" Rogé asked, knowing full well what the answer would be.

"It's the indulging which gets me into trouble, Rogé, but, as always, I shall follow your expert advice," Rex replied to the seasoned maître d'. Rogé smiled in appreciation, leading them through the crowd toward the only empty bar stools.

In stark contrast to Rogé's French accent, the bartender, Bubba, had a thick cajun drawl.

"Ah, nice to see ya again," Bubba said with genuine fondness as his face lit up, and his eyes began to sparkle. "Have some good drink. What can I get?"

"Let me see. Oh yes, I remember: a Cosmopolitan, please," Trissy requested with her usual panache.

"Dat's good, and for you, Dr. Bent—da usual?" Bubba asked respectfully, although he had an uncanny ability to remember faces, names, and the customer's favorite libation—especially those who tipped handsomely.

"Certainly. Do you remember the recipe?" Rex asked before looking into Trissy's sparkling brown eyes.

"Of course: three healthy shots of our premium rum, two light and one dark. In fact, I'll even include da secret ingredient," Bubba responded without hesitation, adding a little suspense to what was now *his* signature creation.

"Precisely, but what exactly is da secret ingredient?" Rex inquired with some reservation.

"It's a secret, but I'm telling you dat it's da very best—guar-on-teed," Bubba assured his reluctant customer.

"You've sold me Bubba,"

"Excellent, one 'Stumbling Drunk' Mai Tai, coming right up," Bubba replied with a smile, while cleaning off the highly polished but well-worn wooden counter.

"Rex, I think I am going to start calling you Doctor Mai Tai," Trissy suggested.

"I like it. The moniker has a good ring to...." Rex suddenly paused. His eyes had caught a special news bulletin as it flashed on the TV screen behind the bar. Bubba noticed it as well and immediately turned up the volume.

"FLASH—we apologize for interrupting tonight's LSU football game. The *John C. Stennis* Carrier Strike Group was attacked early this morning, shortly after entering the Persian Gulf. Given the tension in the region, the strike group was to reinforce the fifth fleet. Information is sketchy, but our high-ranking sources tell us that several vessels have been severely damaged, and it is estimated that as many as a thousand sailors and marines have been killed. It appears that the ships were ambushed after sailing through the narrow Strait of Hormuz. Reportedly, the attack was carried out by sea and air forces originating from Tunb as Sughra, or Lesser Tunb, a small island on the eastern side of the Persian Gulf. Although the Iranians control Lesser Tunb, they have vehemently denied knowledge and/or involvement."

"Oh no," Rex whispered in disbelief.

"Iran believes Islamic radicals are to blame. After all of her recent efforts to establish peace in that part of the world, the president is reportedly outraged, but stopped short of calling this attack an 'act of war.' The military has been placed on high alert but the threat level in the United States has not been raised. Two additional Carrier Strike Groups are reportedly steaming toward the region. It is anticipated that the president will speak to the American people later tonight. Only the prime ministers of Great Britain and Australia, thus far, have openly expressed their condolences. As always, Fox News will keep you informed, as this tragedy at sea unfolds; this is Ram Reynolds reporting."

"Good God!" Rex gasped. "It's another Pearl Harbor."

"Well, so much for diplomacy in the land of Islam," Trissy complained angrily. Rex surged through denial as he struggled to come to grips with the gravity of the news.

"I just can't believe it. All those brave men and women—lost!"

"Dr. Bent, your table is ready. If you would, please follow me," Rogé requested. However, Rex did not move, and now appeared to be in a daze, along with the many other loyal Americans sitting at the bar. All were stunned by the shocking attack in the Persian Gulf.

"Rex, honey, our table is ready," Trissy whispered, tugging on his arm.

"Yes, of course," Rex replied softly as Trissy eased herself off the barstool.

"Your usual table," Rogé announced with pride as he pulled out Trissy's chair.

"Rex, snap out of it," Trissy insisted. "Perhaps the story is wrong. Reporters embellish everything."

"Doubtful," Rex replied. As he stared out the window at the Cajun River, a vision of the young man who had drowned in the river earlier in the day suddenly appeared.

"What looks good to you?" Trissy asked after a few moments.

"Huh?"

"Food," Trissy said as she pointed to his menu.

"Oh, yes. Well, after a diet of bunker buster burgers this week, the catfish," Rex concluded.

"That does sound like the safest choice. However, I think I'll stick with my usual," Trissy concluded, closing her menu.

"Good evening. I'm your waiter, Tunk. What looks good?"

"Trissy will have the salmon and a bowl of the asparagus soup. I'll have your blackened catfish and a dozen oysters on the half shell, please," Rex requested, pleased he had arrived at a decision regarding their meals without his customary two-drink minimum.

"Very good, sir, but I feel I must inform you of the recent outbreak of Hepatitis A," Tunk replied candidly.

"In that case, I believe I'll have a Caesar salad," Rex said, looking at the elderly waiter. Suddenly, Tunk's complexion turned ashen, his eyes oscillating back and forth.

"E. Coli!" Tunk replied in a deep, drawn-out monotone.

"What?" Rex asked, bewildered.

"All the lettuce has been raised in contaminated soil with an irrigation system tied into the local sewage plant," Tunk confessed.

"You must be joking," Rex replied before looking at Trissy. When he turned back, the waiter had simply vanished.

"Call me paranoid, but I'd say this place is rather bizarre tonight. Rogé treats us like long-lost friends, which is difficult for any Frenchman to do. Bubba remembers what we drink. Lastly, Tunk turns into a schizophrenic zombie before he suddenly disappears," Rex shared before taking a gulp of his Mai Tai.

"That's true but I wonder what's with the food contamination? Surely, he must have been pulling your leg," Trissy rationalized, knowing it was Halloween.

"Perhaps, but don't look now. GeeHad just arrived with two of his bodyguards," Rex observed.

Trissy felt compelled to turn her head and look over her shoulder but resisted the urge.

"Oh, imagine that," Rex blurted. "GeeHad is being seated at the table behind you with the elusive owner of this restaurant, Chum. I wonder what that damn North Korean is doing with him?"

Trissy couldn't stand it any longer. Casually, she turned her head and peered over her left shoulder, focusing on their adjacent dining companions.

"Your asparagus soup, madam," Tunk announced, startling Trissy. Suddenly, the elusive waiter had reappeared.

"Thank you," Trissy gasped.

"And for you, Dr. Bent, our fried alligator with tangy water moccasin creole sauce, compliments of the House," Tunk said, setting the appetizer in front of Rex.

"Rex, this soup is wonderful. You need to try it."

"Ah, no thanks. I'm preoccupied wondering if I have the courage to try the gator."

Moments later, the main courses arrived.

"Your salmon, madam, and our Catfish Pontchartrain, sir," Tunk announced as he struggled to find enough space on the table to land the plates.

"That looks fantastic," Trissy replied.

Suddenly, the conversation at the adjacent table became louder.

"How dare you!" GeeHad shouted, shaking his index finger at Chum, who sat expressionless as if disregarding GeeHad's emotional outburst. GeeHad's chair slammed into Trissy's as he propelled himself back from the confines of the table. He quickly stood and continued shouting.

"Please, sit down," Chum insisted as GeeHad threw his napkin on the table.

Trissy turned around just in time to see the angry chief executive officer storm off with his bodyguards in tow, protecting his flank. Chum motioned to her assistant, a short, stocky, steroid-injected Asian who kept his right hand inside his unbuttoned coat the entire time. He immediately withdrew his hand, buttoned his coat and walked over to her table. Chum whispered into his ear, and he left, presumably to carry out her explicit orders. The very mysterious North Korean then sipped on her wine and continued eating her dinner, as if nothing had happened.

Rex had seen the anger in GeeHad's face, but could not hear any of the conversation.

"What in the hell was that all about, I wonder?" Rex whispered to Trissy.

"Wow, I'm not sure. I heard something about a shipment," Trissy gasped.

"Well, perhaps in North Korea that's considered polite dinner conversation. I just can't imagine what that evil dynamic duo is up to. However, I would assume that they are either plotting to overthrow the country, discussing more innovative ways to steal from Medicare and Medicaid, or exchanging time-proven, medieval methods of successfully torturing their employees," Rex concluded as he noticed Trissy's eyes were glazed over, as if deep in thought.

"Remember, an underpaid employee who has been beaten unmercifully is more likely to fulfill your desires," Rex added sarcastically.

"I don't know, Rex, but my gut feeling is that there is something else going on. 'Shipment,' and I think I heard the word 'Korea.'"

"Well, I just can't believe the Cajuns have outsourced gumbo to Korea. Kimchi perhaps?" Rex wondered out loud.

Trissy smiled as the mysterious waiter reappeared.

"Will there be anything else? Dessert, or perhaps an after dinner drink?" Tunk inquired.

"Trissy, how does an Amarula sound to you?" Rex asked.

"Irresistible," Trissy replied.

"Two Amarulas straight up, and the check please?" Rex requested, handing Tunk his credit card. Madame Chum stood up and walked away from the adjacent table.

Moments later Tunk laid the check down and scurried off after her without saying another word.

"Well, it's been a rather unusual evening. Let's get the hell out of here," Rex suggested, finishing the sweet brown concoction derived from the South African marula nut.

"You don't have to ask me twice," Trissy replied as she stood.

Moments later, they left the comfort and warmth of Rula's.

"Damn it's cold!" Rex complained, pulling the collar of his coat up around his neck and then quickly gazing at his watch. It was midnight.

"And sobering as well," Trissy added as they dodged downed tree limbs and walked through the nearly vacant parking lot toward her car.

"With Halloween officially over, I can honestly admit that Carencrow has not lost any of its eeriness. That's for sure!" Rex emphasized, opening the passenger side door for his nearly frozen wife.

Rex jogged around to the driver's side and hopped in. No sooner had the Mercedes SL-500 engine roared to life than Trissy was searching for her favorite CD. As the car warmed up, Rex sat quietly, deep in thought, reflecting on the tragedy in the Persian Gulf.

Suddenly, both the silence and Rex's trance were broken by the blaring sound of "How Deep is Your Love."

Rex placed the car in drive, and they headed home.

CHAPTER 8

THE MORNING AIR WAS cold and still. It was 0530, and the sun was about to rise over the Atchafalaya Basin and Camp Eagle. On a rickety wooden dock adjacent to the camp, the lights had begun to dim, and people could be seen moving about, preparing for the arrival of the much-anticipated cargo ship. The camp consisted of three large Quonset huts constructed of corrugated tin, erected on stilts. The camp itself was situated on a small sand bar within Whiskey Bay, miles away from civilization.

Mohammad and Yassar stood at the dock as an age-ravaged relic of a ship approached, quietly gliding through the still waters. Suddenly, the engines seemed to come to life as they were thrust into reverse. The propeller started to dig violently into the dense, dark medium. The cold water appeared to boil, and the ship started to shudder as the engines made every effort to stop the vessels' forward momentum. Moments later, the engines once again fell silent. The ship had come to a stop. Several mooring lines were thrown over the side as deck hands scurried about to secure the lines. The cargo ship had arrived, and the name *Il-sung* was now visible. The gangway was soon lowered with a loud grinding noise as one end of the rectangular metal structure rubbed against the ship's rusty hull.

"This is a very proud moment for us, Yassar," Mohammad said.

"It has been a long time coming, Mohammad. We shall now be able to seek our revenge," Yassar responded.

In the early morning haze, two men could be seen making their way down the gangway. Shortly thereafter, they came face-to-face with Mohammad and Yassar.

"Welcome home, Raspar," Mohammad announced as the two men hugged.

"Greetings, Mohammad, from our North Korean brothers," Raspar said proudly.

"This is Captain Asaki of the North Korean Navy," Raspar continued, introducing the captain of the *Il-sung*.

Captain Asaki was an elderly sea dog. He was short and thin in stature with a scraggly gray beard and weathered skin, dressed in a beige polyester uniform and sporting an oil-smudged white skipper's cap, which appeared far too large, with the brim covering his forehead.

"Captain Asaki, we are honored to meet you and most appreciative for your services and your country's tireless efforts in fighting the infidels," Mohammad replied.

"Your battle is our battle. The Americans present a danger to us and all the Muslim people," Captain Asaki replied.

"We have had good fortune in our transpacific passage, Mohammad. The seas have been fair, and thus we made excellent time," Raspar said.

"Yes indeed, Mohammad. However, many of my men became sick in transit, due to the exposure to our cargo, I fear. Sadly, several died and each honored soul slipped into the Caribbean. Others have been vomiting for days and are severely dehydrated. They require immediate medical assistance," Captain Asaki relayed politely, but with great concern for his shipmates who were still living.

"I am indeed sorry to hear of the death and illness. Rest assured, we will get your men to the hospital immediately. Captain, this is Yassar, my second in command. He will ensure that your men are cared for," Mohammad assured him.

"I am pleased to meet you, Yassar," Captain Asaki replied appreciatively.

"I am honored, Captain. Please have your men assemble by this large oak tree," Yassar said, pointing to a tree surrounded by a circular crushed oyster shell drive.

"We shall leave within the hour," Yassar added as Captain Asaki bowed his head in respect.

"Raspar, is the shipment as ordered?" Mohammad inquired.

"Yes Mohammad, with few exceptions. I have the manifest with me," Raspar stated confidently.

"Excellent! We shall review it momentarily," Mohammad replied.

"Captain Asaki, the storage facility for the liquid death has been built to your countryman's specifications," Yassar said, pointing to the concrete structure to his right. "However, we have no protective suits," Yassar added, with little concern.

"We do, but unfortunately they do not work as well as we had assumed. Still, my men will complete the job and transfer the deadly cargo ashore. However, we could certainly use a hand offloading all the munitions," Captain Asaki requested.

"Captain, we have thirty of our freedom fighters standing by to assist. Utilize them as you see fit," Mohammad instructed before continuing. "And Yassar, take Captain Asaki's men to Carencrow Regional. But first, alert GeeHad so he is not caught by surprise."

"As you wish, Mohammad," Yassar replied without hesitation.

"Captain Asaki, please let us know if there's anything else we can do to expedite the process," Mohammad added before turning and walking away with Raspar and Yassar at his side.

The three men walked across a gravel path and into the largest of Camp Eagle's improvements. This structure served as the command post and was bustling with activity. At least fifteen men were either sitting down at computer terminals or scurrying about. There was a loud rumbling sound generated by those engaged in conversation, but the voices were indistinguishable.

There was a transparent eight-by-ten-foot map of the United States constructed of thick plastic suspended from the ceiling in one corner of the room, with a similar map of the world situated in the opposite corner. Behind each map stood two people drawing symbols reflecting the latest updates regarding the location of sleeper cells and material. The information also reflected the sources and the respective amount of funding available worldwide to fuel this deadly operation. Funds could be wire-transferred quickly, easily, and without detection from this remote post. In the center of the room stood a large table from which Mohammad could watch his evil plan unfold.

Raspar sensed an air of excitement. He was amazed that such a sophisticated command post could exist within the infidels' homeland, yet his sense of exhilaration was tempered by a sudden wave of stomach cramps and nausea. Was he just exhausted, or, as he feared, had he been exposed to the *Il-sung's* lethal cargo? Mohammad sat down with Yassar and Raspar. He could sense that Raspar was not well, but proceeded anyway.

"Raspar, the manifest please," Mohammad ordered.

Raspar unfolded the three-page document and handed it to Mohammad.

Mohammad's eyes lit up as he reviewed the document. Onboard the *Il-sung* was everything he had requested. "Raspar, you have done quite well. We can launch our deadly assault on the United States and have enough weaponry to continue our struggle," Mohammad declared.

"Absolutely, and as an added bonus, Mohammad, the North Koreans, in a gesture of kindness, recruited fifteen suicide bombers. Their families were each given ten thousand dollars for the willingness of their sons and daughters to give their lives for our cause. However, all became ill in transit. The last recruit died yesterday. Their bodies, along with those of the sailors who had succumbed to the sickness, were tossed overboard," Raspar interjected, with little emotion. This was business as usual, and death was to be expected, if not demanded.

"That is indeed unfortunate, Raspar. Yassar, wire twenty-five million dollars to the designated account in Wonsan," Mohammad ordered. "Also, email Abu Bakr informing him that our shipment has arrived. Lastly, please let our brothers in Saudi Arabia know that now is the time to generate the computer traffic necessary to misdirect and preoccupy the infidels. The Eagle has landed!" Mohammad declared with resounding strength in his voice.

CHAPTER 9

THE ALARM ERUPTED WITH an enormously sobering ear-piercing buzz.

"Oh!" Rex groaned, desperately searching for the snooze button. "Christ!" he complained after a water glass and several magazines were knocked to the floor as his hand groped in the darkness.

"No," Trissy moaned as she, too, slowly came to life.

"What did Bubba put in those drinks, and how much firewater did I inhale?" Rex asked, pleading for some rational answer from above. "Oh, does my head hurt!" he moaned as he jettisoned the pillow and slowly struggled to right himself.

Minutes later, Rex felt somewhat human once again. He was sweet-smelling and clean-shaven. He even had a spring in his step as he closed his robe and made his way back into the bedroom, where he found Trissy fast asleep.

"Trissy, I thought you were up," Rex said. There was no response. "Huh, so much for this early bird catching the worm," Rex whispered, shaking his head and walking toward the kitchen.

Rex filled two coffee cups with hot water and added spoonfuls of robust instant coffee.

"Save me, Rex!" Trissy pleaded as she stumbled into the kitchen.

"Here you are, my little Bee Gee," Rex said, stirring in the creamer and handing the stout concoction to Trissy.

"Well, let's see what additional misery has befallen the world," Rex muttered as he walked into the living room.

"I'm almost afraid to see what happened to our fleet in the Persian Gulf," Trissy said, following him into the living room and clinching the small mug, which provided life support at this obscene hour.

"Me, too," Rex concurred as the baboon box flickered momentarily before CNN came to life.

"The *John C. Stennis* Carrier Strike Group was attacked while entering the Persian Gulf. The carrier, the guided-missile cruiser USS *Antietam*, and three escort vessels were all severely damaged, while the USS *Kidd* and the USS *Jarrett* lay on the sandy bottom. Over nine hundred sailors and marines have been killed, and an additional one thousand injured. This attack reflects one of the worst defeats the United States Navy has ever suffered. Yet, the sheer devastation is hauntingly reminiscent of December seventh, nineteen forty-one, an infamous time in history," the reporter, Sid Shark, emphasized as a camera from a helicopter captured the magnitude of the death and destruction below.

The beautiful, blue, tranquil water of the Persian Gulf stood in stark contrast to the gray ships helplessly adrift. Large, glistening oil slicks could be seen for miles, and debris was everywhere. Thick, black smoke billowed from the hulls and superstructures of all the vessels, and two of the ships were still ablaze. Multiple lifeboats and small craft were in the water, while aircraft of all types filled the skies, protecting what remained of the crippled fleet. Helicopters could be seen taking off from the still-functional flight deck of the carrier, although the *Stennis* was listing twenty degrees to port, and her superstructure was engulfed in smoke.

As the camera zoomed in on each ship, it was clearly evident that all had been severely damaged and were dead in the water. Several had large, black-singed gaping holes in their hulls and were listing precariously, while two frigates were riding so low in the water that their decks were awash.

"Although the attack occurred several hours ago, a flurry of activity continues as brave sailors and marines fight tirelessly to save their ships and their shipmates. I can see exhausted crews desperately struggling to extinguish raging fires while the dead lie flag-draped on deck, and the wounded continue to be evacuated. My God, from the air, the magnitude of this disaster is incomprehensible," Sid reported, his voice cracking with emotion.

"Sid, I understand that the *Ronald Reagan* Carrier Strike Group is racing to the scene, and one additional battle group has been ordered to the region," the news anchor, Robyn Reed, added.

"Robyn, that is my understanding as well. However, what do all these ships do when they arrive? Surely they're not going to steam into the confined waters of the Persian Gulf? Furthermore, the *Reagan* is ten days away from this region—too late to have any dramatic effect on rescue operations," Sid replied frankly.

"Sid, once again it appears that our military might has been spread too thin. Have you had any opportunity to talk to any high-ranking naval officers?" Robyn asked.

"No, but you can see the shock and horror on the faces of the military commanders and sense the tremendous personal loss. I, as well, feel an overwhelming surge of anger," Sid Shark added without fact or basis, something he was very good at doing.

"Sid, have you heard any rumors regarding the United States launching an attack on Iran?" Robyn asked, cleverly planting the possibility.

"Yes, I did in fact hear that, but have not been able to confirm that rumor. However, I can say that confidential sources have emphasized how vitally important it is that we rapidly reestablish our dominance in the region," Sid embellished once again.

"Thank you, Sid. Stay safe, and keep us posted," Robyn requested. "We now take you to Qatar where Christina Cataka is standing by."

"Thank you, Robyn," Christina replied. "In the Middle East there are massive celebrations going on in the streets. In Syria, Egypt, Iran, Iraq, and Afghanistan, Muslims are singing, dancing, and firing weapons into the air. A majority of the Arabs in this part of the world greatly dislike the United States and view the Americans as barbaric invaders."

As Christina was talking, a video of the celebrations was running. Tens of thousands of Arabs were dancing and chanting. Weapons were held high and appeared to vibrate uncontrollably as triggers were pulled and held down. The sounds of the weapons discharging and the smoke drifting from the barrels seemed to invigorate the crowd in their display of defiance.

"There is optimism that, as with the French and British conquest and occupation a century earlier, this attack and the subsequent loss of life will result in the United States pulling out of this region forever. The Middle East is rich in history, and Arabs simply insist upon controlling their own destiny. Robyn, back to you," Christina Cataka concluded emotionlessly.

"Thank you, Christina," Robyn responded in an unusually upbeat tone, reflecting her excitement in covering the tragic story.

"At home, the president called this attack an act of aggression, stopping short of calling the disaster an 'act of war.' She is expected to address the nation momentarily. We will carry the broadcast live. In the meantime, the United Nations is pleading for restraint, while the French President and the German Chancellor openly and without remorse state that this disaster was of America's choosing. Of the Arab League of Nations, only Saudi Arabia has expressed outrage with regard..." Robyn stopped mid-sentence and placed her hand onto her earpiece. "The president is about to speak. We now take you to the White House," Robyn added excitedly. Rex and Trissy sat speechless, staring at the TV in absolute shock. Neither one had touched their coffee. The president was sitting behind her desk at the Oval Office. She appeared stern and in control, yet her anger was evident.

"On Saturday, October thirty-first, our fleet, while entering the Persian Gulf on a mission of peace, was attacked by forces originating from Iranian soil. The Islamic Republic of Iran has assured me that radical groups not affiliated with their government carried out this malicious and unprovoked attack. I truly believe this to be the case and have assured Iran that our anger will not be directed toward their great Islamic nation. In turn, Iran has pledged their full cooperation in apprehending those responsible for this heinous crime. Additionally, the United Nations Security Council is meeting in an emergency session to consider resolutions and mandates and implement serious consequences against any radical group seeking to destabilize the world. At home, the director of the National Security Agency and I discussed elevating the threat warning, but decided that to do so would not be necessary at this time. Concurrently, I have instructed the secretary of defense to place the military on high alert, activate all reservists, and expedite the withdrawal of our troops from Afghanistan. Lastly, the secretary of state will travel to the Middle East to help defuse this volatile situation. As I have said before, the sacrifices of our brave men and women of the armed services will never be forgotten. However, let me make myself perfectly clear: to avenge their deaths will not strengthen, but will in fact weaken, our great nation. Diplomacy, not war, is the path we should choose to ensure that the United States of America is, once again, respected around the world. I ask you to pray for those who have been lost, for their families, for this nation, and for world peace," the president concluded.

The telecast ended abruptly and the screen went blank momentarily. Robyn Reed reappeared and began discussing the president's brief speech as Rex hit the mute button.

"Well, that proves my 'Greater Political Jackass' theory," Rex grumbled.

"That's a new one to me. What, might I inquire, is your theory?" Trissy replied rather hesitantly.

"Simply that all politicians are greedy, self-serving buggers that run a narrow spectrum ranging from 'Jackass' to 'Stupid Jackass.' If you like them, they immediately fall into the Jackass category," Rex explained.

"And if you don't?" Trissy asked, already knowing the answer.

"Stupid Jackass!" Rex huffed angrily as he thought about the president's passive response to what should have resulted in a 'declaration of war.'

"Come on, sweetheart, it's six thirty. We have to get ready for work," Trissy pleaded, pulling Rex to his feet.

"The only good terrorist is a dead terrorist," Rex growled as they both walked toward the bedroom, where they quickly threw on their scrubs.

It was time to tune out world events and help those in need at home. They had fifteen minutes to make it to Carencrow Regional's chamber of horrors/emergency room. Another day in the jungle was about to begin.

CHAPTER 10

R EX AND TRISSY ARRIVED at work on time with their minds free of the early morning self-induced haze. Unlike most couples, they truly enjoyed working together and insisted on being scheduled for the same shift. As they entered the emergency room, they could see and feel the fatigue surrounding the night shift. However, the usual chaos had been replaced with a calm, eerie quiet. They immediately sensed that they were in the eye of a category-five hurricane.

Trissy walked over to Patty Carlock, RN, to receive report and relieve the watch.

"Good morning, Hanz. How was your night?" Rex barked with enthusiasm as he approached the weary physician.

"The shift was miserable, absolutely miserable!" Hanz responded, his monotone voice dry and deep. "It was out of control all night, but about five a.m. everything unexpectedly calmed down."

"Well, what patients do you have remaining?" Rex inquired, thankful that the morning would start off slow.

"Unlike the mess I inherited at the start of my shift, only two patients remain," Hanz concluded before giving report.

"Damn fine job, Hanz!" Rex said as he patted his fellow doc on the back.

Hanz attempted to generate a smile, which was accompanied by some sort of snorting sound as he walked off.

"Where's Wanda today?" Rex asked.

"She's splitting the shift with Big Dog," Trissy responded, her apprehension based in reality.

"Oh, Lord!" Rex blurted, rolling his eyes. He thought the world of the young male nurse, Big Dog. However, his tall tales of life in the country were so bizarre, Rex never knew which ones were real. In any case, what was assured was a rousing shift filled with plenty of laughter.

"I'm sure we're in for a real sumptuous treat," Trissy said with a smile, "and he's late, as usual. I'm going to buy that boy an alarm clock for Christmas."

Suddenly, the silence of the ER was broken by a loud "Yeah, boy!" There was no doubt that Big Dog had arrived.

Alan Moreau, the infamous "Big Dog," was from nearby Marksville, a town where inbreeding was considered a fashion statement. To him, everything was big. He owned the biggest dog, had shot the biggest squirrel, and damn near married the biggest, homeliest girl! However, "Big Dog" never did marry and refused to find his own pad. Always overly enthusiastic and exceedingly energetic, his mystique was only embellished with the tall stories he shared in his thick Cajun accent.

"How are you doing today, Big Dog?" Rex asked.

"I am doing well, Dr. B. But yesterday was another story," Big Dog responded.

Down the hall, Boom Boom and Dr. Leadbury were engaged in conversation. Out front, the waiting room had been quiet. Debby Flat was back at her post at triage and her keen eye caught site of an elderly gentleman apparently being wheeled in by his granddaughter. He was gagging and grabbing his chest as he moaned.

"My husband is having chest pain!" the beautiful young lady proclaimed.

The patient was pale and sweaty. Debby immediately realized the urgency of the moment. She grabbed the wheelchair and rushed the patient to the back.

"Chest pain!" Debby yelled as she passed through the locked doors and into the emergency room. Instantaneously, the patient slumped over and became unresponsive.

The morning solitude had been shattered. The brief truce with the public was over and a new day's battle for survival was now underway.

"Room six!" Sheila shouted, watching Debby struggle to keep the patient from slithering out of a wheelchair. "Dr. Bent, I believe your services are needed!" Sheila said loudly as she pointed toward the patient who appeared to have gone into cardiac arrest.

Foxxman rushed to Debby's assistance, followed by Trissy and Big Dog. All four grabbed the arms and legs of the lifeless body and struggled to lift him onto the stretcher.

"He so sweaty that I can't get a good grasp!" Big Dog complained as the patient kept slipping from his hands.

"Here we go, on three!" Rex instructed, reaching over the stretcher and grabbing the patient by the belt buckle. "One, two, three!" Rex shouted as the team provided enough lift. The unresponsive elderly gentleman landed on the stretcher with a thud.

"He's not breathing!" Trissy shouted as the patient suddenly became cyanotic.

"Get an ambu bag," Rex instructed, feeling for a nonexistent pulse. "Foxxman, get the crash cart. Trissy, start bagging him. Big Dog, get us a line," Rex ordered as he began chest compressions.

Foxxman immediately turned on the defibrillator. Debby ripped the patient's shirt open and placed the orange rubber electrical conduction–enhancing sticky pads over his heart. Rex grabbed the defibrillator paddles and placed them on top of the sticky pads as Big Dog and Trissy rushed to carry out their tasks. Rex looked at the monitor as the electrical signal from the patient's heart came into view.

"He's in V-tach. Charge the defibrillator to two hundred joules," Rex ordered. A high-pitched whining was heard as the machine began to charge.

"Stand back!" Rex shouted. The machine beeped, announcing that it had been fully charged to the requested power of two hundred joules. "Everyone clear?" Rex increased the pressure on the paddles placed on the patient's chest.

"Yes!" Big Dog, Trissy, and Debby shouted in unison, stepping back from the stretcher.

Rex immediately depressed the discharge buttons and a loud thump could be heard as a high-voltage electrical shock was delivered. The patient's limp body was momentarily lifted from the stretcher and his arms flailed.

"Charge to the defibrillator to three hundred joules," Rex ordered, pressing the paddles against the patient's chest, ready to deliver an even greater amount of power in a desperate attempt to restart his heart.

"Three hundred joules it is," Debby responded calmly.

Again, the machine started to whine as it began to charge.

Suddenly, the cardiac monitor indicated that the patient was in a normal sinus rhythm. Rex removed the paddles from the patient's chest.

"Bag the patient, Trissy. Big Dog, check for a pulse," Rex ordered.

"Yeah, boy! I have a strong carotid pulse," Big Dog announced.

"Good job, gang," Rex praised.

"We have a blood pressure of one hundred over sixty, and a pulse of one hundred thirty," Foxxman proclaimed with great satisfaction.

"Big Dog, run in one hundred and fifty milligrams of Amiodarone over ten minutes and then put him on a drip," Rex ordered. "We need an EKG *stat*. Run a cardiac workup and let's get ready to intubate," Rex barked. "Sheila, call radiology for a portable chest X-ray to confirm tube placement. Also, let the lab know we need an arterial blood gas in thirty minutes," Rex requested as he walked out of room six.

"Rex, the patient is a Mr. Kevin Barr from Healdsburg, California. He's in the wine business. His wife, Linda Barr, is in the family room," Sheila notified Rex.

"Where in the hell is Healdsburg?" Rex wondered aloud. "And what in hell is he doing in this buzzard-infested swamp?"

"I understand that he and his wife were visiting Mr. Barr's inebriated cousin," Sheila replied.

"That's possible," Rex replied, knowing the Cajuns' love of flammable fire water.

"Now, Rex, let me warn you that Mr. Barr's wife is quite a bit younger than he," Sheila said, issuing yet another warning.

"Obviously, then, Mr. Barr and I have a lot in common. We both love grapes, and we both married beautiful, younger women," Rex said, winking at Trissy.

"Aren't you nice?" Trissy replied, kissing her husband on the cheek.

"That's where you're wrong. He's a billionaire gentleman farmer, and you're a decrepit, debt-ridden, dirty old man," Sheila giggled in a very sinister manner.

"Sheila, there just happens to be a fine line between being a billionaire and being penniless. I just happened to have grown up on the wrong side of the tracks," Rex uttered in his own defense.

"Yeah, right," Sheila chuckled.

"Bed six's EKG," the technician said, handing Rex the electrical tracing.

"Thank you," Rex said. "Sheila, get in touch with the cardiologist on call. Mr. Barr is having an MI. There are tombstones in all leads," Rex said with urgency.

"Big Dog, get Mr. Barr ready for a trip to the cath lab. Bolus him with five thousand units of heparin and start a drip at one thousand units per hour."

"Yeah, boy," Big Dog replied, springing into action.

"Rex, please go see Mrs. Barr. And remember, she's his wife and not his granddaughter!" Sheila yelled as she issued her fourth warning.

"Alright, alright, stop nagging!" Rex insisted as he continued on his mission.

"I'm not nagging," Sheila growled. "Trissy, please go with your husband and see that he doesn't put his foot in his mouth again!" Sheila shouted.

Minutes later Rex and Trissy left Mrs. Barr and stepped back into hell.

"My God!" Rex gasped as he observed the pandemonium in the ER.

In the blink of an eye, the ER had crossed the fine line dividing controlled chaos from uncontrolled madness. A sea of humanity had suddenly descended upon Carencrow Regional's emergency room. Rex and Trissy successfully dodged their way through the traffic and made their way back to the counter.

"For God's sake, Boom Boom, this place is out of control," Rex complained.

"Stay focused, Rex," Boom Boom replied. "Your mission is to survive the shift, and the shift is now half over."

"What a miserable morning, and the afternoon will probably be worse," Rex moaned.

"Cardiology is on line two!" Sheila shouted.

"Don't worry about the mule, just load the wagon," Boom Boom muttered as Wanda arrived to relieve Big Dog.

"Rrrrex, surgery is coming down to examine the patients with cholelithiasis and acute appendicitis. Also, our bipolar plastic surgeon is aware of the young man with the thumb amputation," Sheila reported, adding, "I think his lithium level is low."

"Great."

"Also, Rrrrex, Debby called from triage and needs help. She has six very sick patients with nausea and vomiting that need beds. Debby must be low on Crown Royal and hallucinating, because she describes the patients as being distant cousins of the blue-footed boobies," Shiela announced.

"I'll bring them to the back, Rrrrex," Trissy insisted, jogging toward triage.

"Big Dog, help Trissy fetch the patients," Rex requested.

"Yeah, Boy," Big Dog responded enthusiastically as he raced to catch up to Trissy.

"Rrrrex, I'm here to relieve Big Dog," Wanda announced.

"Great, we could use the extra hands."

"Wanda, Foxxman, we need your help, pronto!" Trissy shouted, as she and Big Dog wheeled what looked like a lifeless body toward room fourteen. The patient was mumbling incoherently. He was so weak that he had to be lifted onto the stretcher.

Suddenly the smell of death permeated the room.

"He's still breathing, but his pulse is weak and thready," Trissy announced after a quick assessment, before slapping electrical leads onto the patient's chest and starting an IV as Big Dog wrapped the blood pressure cuff around the patient's arm, and Foxxman placed a pulse oximeter on his finger.

"We need all hands on at triage ASAP. Debby has five more critical patients!" Trissy shouted.

"Oh, that smells like a GI bleed. Trissy, what in the world did Debby tell you about this patient?" Rex gasped, and gagged as he entered the room to examine the patient.

"She said that a van pulled up to the entrance and unloaded six patients, all with the same complaint of nausea and vomiting. Whoever dropped them off spoke in broken English and quickly took off. Debby believes she understood that the patients were crew members on a ship, which recently arrived from Asia," Trissy replied as Rex felt for the man's radial pulse.

"I'm Dr. Bent. What is your name?" Rex asked, but the patient only moaned.

"Are you hurting anywhere?" Again, there was no response.

Rex then rubbed the patient's sternum with his knuckles hoping that this physical irritation would elicit a response. The patient moaned a little louder and appeared to move his arms and legs but otherwise did not respond.

"What in the world could have happened?" Rex asked as thick layers of skin sloughed off wherever he touched.

The patient's skin was blue with large blisters and massive denuded areas.

"Damn sure looks like a snake crawling out of his skin," Big Dog observed as Trissy connected the IV tubing and bolused the fluids.

"His pupils are round and reactive, but his eyes are divergent and keep oscillating back and forth," Rex said as he continued his exam. "Wow, even his lips are blue, as is his entire mouth. Mucus membranes are dry, no JVD, trachea is midline, heart tachycardic without murmurs, lungs are wet, abdomen distended and tense, extremities cool and pale without palpable pulses," Rex added.

"What a bizarre presentation," Wanda whispered.

"Bolus him with two liters of normal saline, start bagging him, and get ready to intubate," Rex ordered while pumping up the bed, depressing the red handles that enabled the head be tilted downward, ensuring an increased blood flow to the patient's brain.

"Already in progress," Trissy replied, and she hung a second liter of fluid.

"The patient has large blisters on the palms of his hands but not on the soles of his feet; now that's an unusual finding," Wanda noticed.

"Maybe he burned his hands while trying to extinguish a fire onboard his ship," Trissy suggested as the automatic blood pressure cuff cycled, struggling to determine a blood pressure.

"His blood pressure is seventy-over-forty, heart rate one-sixty, respiratory rate thirty and O-two saturation eighty-five percent," Trissy announced.

"Wanda get me a hemocult card," Rex requested as he checked the patient's rectum. "Belay that order!" Rex shouted. His finger was coated in a thick blue/black tar-like gel with a smell that would wake the dead. *There was no doubt he had a GI bleed, but why the blue color on his lips and in his stool,* Rex wondered.

"His rectal temp is one hundred and four," Trissy said moments later.

"Trissy, get two blood cultures and order three-point-three-seven-five grams of Zosyn IV. Foxxman, get us a Tylenol suppository, place ice bags to the axilla, and find a cooling blanket," Rex ordered.

"Yes, sir."

"Sheila, we need four units of O-negative blood *wikiwiki*, and call an ER Code *blue*. We have five other patients fighting for their lives!" Rex shouted. "Big Dog, start two more lines with normal saline wide open," Rex ordered.

"If you're waiting for me, you're already behind, and I've already sent all the appropriate labs," Big Dog replied with great pride.

Suddenly, the patient started retching uncontrollably. Massive amounts of blue vomit gushed several feet in the air.

"Oh boy, it looks like Old Faithful just erupted," Big Dog said as Rex turned the patient onto his side, while Trissy suctioned his mouth to prevent the sailor from aspirating.

"Code Blue ER, Code Blue ER, CODE BLUE ER" loudly reverberated throughout the hospital.

Seconds later the patient was intubated.

"Good God, I've never seen anything like it. Call the code. Great job, everyone." Rex said fifteen minutes later.

"Time of death, nineteen-eleven," Wanda announced sadly.

Within minutes all of the patient's shipmates had met the same fate.

CHAPTER 11

I T WAS FIVE IN the evening, and the sun was starting to set on the Atchafalaya Basin and Whiskey Bay. The moss-shrouded trees were bathed in a golden hue, the silhouettes of which were reflected in the calm, glassy water of the marsh. The air was still and cold. Camp Eagle appeared to glow peacefully in a magnificent amber light.

The terrorists had nearly completed offloading the weapon of mass destruction from the *Il-sung*. The lethal cargo had been pumped from compartments deep within the rusty container ship into a small, domed concrete structure adjacent to the dock. Thirty thousand gallons of liquid death were now on American soil. As Yassar made his way toward the dock, he could see puffs of condensation being expelled with each breath. The exhausted men struggled with the remaining crates. Yassar was looking for Captain Asaki and spotted him next to the gangway talking with the first officer, Wasabi.

"Captain, it has been a long day. How are we progressing?" Yassar inquired, oblivious to the fact that he had just interrupted a conversation. Lieutenant Wasabi turned and took two steps to his right.

"The work has progressed well, Honorable Yassar. I am terribly sorry that my men fell ill. Without the help of your freedom fighters it would have taken us days to unload your valuable cargo. I estimate that we shall be finished in another three hours," Captain Asaki responded with pride.

"Mohammad has word of the health of your crew and wishes to speak with you. He's in the command center. Please, come with me," Yassar requested, without injecting any emotion.

"Very well," the captain replied before turning to his first officer. "Lieutenant, I will be back shortly. Tell the men to knock off. We will resume the work in the morning."

The two men started toward the command center. As they made their way along the gravel path, Yassar pulled up the collar on his coat to ward off the cold.

"I have not seen Raspar all day. How is he feeling?" Captain Asaki asked as he turned toward Yassar.

"Raspar is quite ill. He has the same symptoms of sickness which your crew exhibited. He cannot stop vomiting and continues to run a high fever," Yassar explained.

"Oh, no!" the captain replied.

"When I last looked in on him, his entire body was cherry red and swollen to twice its normal size. His eyes were drawn and he was on the floor screaming incoherently, writhing in pain. Thus far, he has refused to go to the hospital, but his condition is so serious that Mohammad has insisted. One of our men shall be transporting Raspar to the hospital within the hour," Yassar responded, with little genuine concern.

"I'm indeed very sorry to hear that. I had grown quite fond of him on our long voyage. There is no doubt that he strongly believes in your cause," Captain Asaki said.

"His sacrifice is greatly appreciated, for the same fate awaits millions of the American infidels," Yassar replied with anger in his voice as the two men walked up a short flight of wooden steps.

Mohammad immediately noticed Yassar and Captain Asaki as they stepped into the warmth of the command center, which was vibrant with activity.

"Captain Asaki, have you completed the offload?" Mohammad inquired.

"No, Mohammad, we have a few hours of work remaining. I left instructions for the men to knock off for tonight and resume work in the morning."

"Excellent, Captain, but we're expecting another vessel tomorrow afternoon. The work must be completed, and the *Il-sung* underway by noon," Mohammad insisted.

"Yes, sir, but I cannot leave without my men," Captain Asaki replied.

"Captain, I am afraid that your men will not be making the return voyage; all are dead," an emotionless Mohammad informed the North Korean captain.

"No!" the stunned captain blurted. As he stared into Mohammad's cold, dark eyes, Captain Asaki realized it was not a joke. His strong, stoic sea-worn face was suddenly transformed, reflecting shock and despair. He was proud of those who had served with him. The news was gut-wrenching.

"I am indeed sorry, Captain," Yassar interjected. "I understand that every attempt was made to save their lives. We have taken the liberty to notify Colonel Chum of this terrible loss."

"Your brave men are now the honored dead in our Holy War," Mohammad added. "Now, Captain, I must ask you to leave, for we have much work to do."

Yassar escorted the emotionally drained Captain Asaki out of the command center. While standing on the porch, a gold Bentley could be seen traveling toward them at an excessive rate of speed, trailing a plume of dust. As the brakes were applied, the vehicle slid. Small stones were slung violently in all directions as the tires attempted to dig into the loose gravel. The Bentley came to a rumbling halt and, before the dust had settled, out stepped GeeHad.

"Where is Mohammad?" GeeHad angrily demanded to know.

"He is inside," Yassar replied curtly, concerned with GeeHad's threatening tone.

GeeHad stormed past the two men, flung open the door, and entered the command center.

"I will see you in the morning, Captain," Yassar said, turning to follow GeeHad into the building.

Mohammad had his back to the entrance and was leaning over a computer terminal evaluating valuable incoming data. He did not hear the commotion or feel the vibration as GeeHad's massive body approached.

"Mohammad, what in the hell are you doing?" GeeHad screamed.

All conversations in the room suddenly came to an abrupt halt. The freedom fighters quickly turned and stared in silence at this imposing creature. The only sound that could be heard was some form of grotesque snorting emanating from the outraged GeeHad.

Yassar positioned himself behind GeeHad, placing his hand on the handle of the large knife he carried in a leather sheath on his belt. Somehow he resisted the urge to cut GeeHad's throat right then and there.

Mohammad turned to see GeeHad hovering over him. With his eyes bulging and nostrils flaring, GeeHad appeared possessed. Mohammad was caught by surprise but soon regained his composure. As he stood, he shook his finger violently at GeeHad.

"Don't you ever, don't you EVER, talk to me in such a threatening tone, GeeHad! How dare you barge into this command center and demand anything! You work for me, remember? Now, what is the meaning of this intrusion?" an enraged Mohammad shot back.

There was a moment of silence as GeeHad and Mohammad stared at one another. After realizing the importance each held to this operation, both men began to calm down.

A disappointed Yassar took his hand off his knife and the freedom fighters in the room resumed their duties.

GeeHad took a deep breath. "I'm indeed sorry, Mohammad," he said apologetically. "However, I am very worried that the six Asian sailors you sent to Carencrow Regional for treatment will jeopardize our years of hard work. The condition in which they presented and their subsequent deaths have already aroused suspicion. There is an American emergency room physician, Dr. Rex Bent, who has contacted the National Security Agency and the Center for Disease Control. But rest assured, his curiosity will cost him his life. Hours ago, I ordered his execution."

"Cancel that order immediately, GeeHad!" Mohammad shouted. "Dr. Bent's death will only arouse more scrutiny," Mohammad concluded.

GeeHad appeared bewildered, given the curt reprimand.

Mohammad thought for a moment as he stroked his beard. "No, we must create the illusion that Dr. Bent is indeed the terrorist who has betrayed his own country for personal gain. Yassar, find out where this infidel lives and plant a dozen or so vials of anthrax and the Ebola virus we have remaining in storage. Also, purchase stock in his name with the companies who are either manufacturing or attempting to develop antidotes to our weapons of mass destruction. Then, have our brothers in Saudi Arabia send an email thanking Dr. Bent for his contribution to Al Qaeda and our Muslim cause," Mohammad insisted enthusiastically.

"That is a brilliant plan, Mohammad," GeeHad responded, his eyes all aglow.

"Absolutely," Yassar said in agreement. "I can just visualize Homeland Security salivating upon the interception of the message. The CIA, the FBI, the DEA, and local law enforcement will descend upon Dr. Bent like rabid, bloodthirsty animals. He will be so preoccupied fighting for his reputation from a jail cell that he will not have time to disrupt our noble activities."

"If there is any constant in the universe, the media will turn this journalistic coup into a celebratory circus. All the while, the National Security Agency will briefly drop their defense as they bathe in the glory of their perceived victory," Mohammad chuckled. "Now, GeeHad, with regard to our communication problem, I had requested that you be notified of the need to send the dying North Korean sailors to your hospital. Yassar, did we not inform GeeHad in advance of the arrival of the sick crew members?" Mohammad asked.

"Absolutely, Mohammad. I spoke with Abdul, GeeHad's personal confidant," Yassar replied to his leader before turning his attention to GeeHad. "I am sorry you never received my message, GeeHad." His tone reflected a hint of sarcasm, which the Lambed HCA founder ignored.

GeeHad was clearly appalled. *How could so critical an error have been made from within my organization?* He thought to himself. "I will have Abdul flogged for his oversight," GeeHad responded in disgust.

"Well, I have good news for you, GeeHad. We are shipping one more patient to your hospital, your cousin, Raspar. He is in critical condition, and we do not have the means to care for him. I trust you will not object," Mohammad insisted in a very calm, yet unyielding manner.

"Not at all," GeeHad responded slowly, although he never did care for Raspar.

"Good," Mohammad shot back with an upbeat tone, reflecting his appreciation that GeeHad had received his message loud and clear. "Now that you are here, GeeHad, we need your latest financial data. It is time to transfer the funds necessary to begin the assault on America," Mohammad requested, as GeeHad reached for his Blackberry.

"Let's download the information on this computer," Yassar suggested.

As the vital information began to download, GeeHad looked at Mohammad and smiled. "It's been a very good year, Mohammad," GeeHad announced with immense satisfaction.

An audible beep was heard, signaling that the download had been complete. Suddenly, a map of the United States appeared on the large screen behind the computer terminal. The display indicated the location of all businesses and banks affiliated with the account with the sums available on demand. All the information was color-coded and easy to evaluate at a glance.

"As a tribute to the infidels, we have established our primary account at the Bank of America. As of yesterday, we had three hundred fifty million on hand. This figure does not reflect the recent wire transfer of twenty-five million dollars to Wonsan, which you had authorized," GeeHad announced.

"You have done quite well indeed, GeeHad," Mohammad replied.

"Yes," Yassar added as Mohammad thought for a moment.

"Now, with our assault on America poised to commence, I believe it is important to protect our assets. GeeHad, transfer two hundred million dollars to our Swiss account," Mohammad ordered.

"Yes, Mohammad. May I suggest that we capitalize on new opportunities, which take advantage of the death and destruction that is about to unfold? I would like to invest in drug companies that manufacture antidotes to our lethal gift," GeeHad requested.

"Do as you wish. I realize you gain great joy, and have been quite successful in manipulating the American stock market," Mohammad chuckled.

"Surely the SEC wouldn't consider my investments to be insider trading," GeeHad laughed.

"Yassar, contact our friends in India. It is time to release the pregenerated email traffic tomorrow, as arranged," Mohammad ordered, as his tone suddenly turned very serious. "You will see, GeeHad, the value of disinformation. At o-nine-hundred, two hundred thousand messages will be sent over the Internet from India, via Saudi Arabia, to the United States, Europe, Canada, and Mexico. The infidels will believe that an assault is imminent and the attacks will be launched from North and South America. They will frantically attempt to defend thousands of miles of borders, while protecting the United States infrastructure and the targeted nuclear power plants referenced," Mohammad announced.

"After the destruction of the prized American fleet in the Persian Gulf, the infidels will have no doubt that the information is true," GeeHad said.

"As you can see, GeeHad, we believe in out-sourcing to India," Yassar added appreciatively.

Suddenly, one of the freedom fighters approached Mohammad and whispered into his ear.

"Thank you," Mohammad replied softly. "Well GeeHad, it appears that Carencrow Regional will be spared from any further scrutiny—Raspar is dead," Mohammad reported, with little emotion. GeeHad remained expressionless. He said nothing.

"Yassar, it is now time to launch our embargo of the United States of America," Mohammad announced.

"Yes, Mohammad," Yassar responded enthusiastically.

"GeeHad, I believe you will be pleased with our Muslim-style embargo. America will be attacked from land, sea, and air.

The infidels will soon be in a state of panic, trapped within a dying nation isolated from the world," Mohammad proclaimed victoriously. He gazed around command central, his jet black eyes settling on Yassar, his trusted second in command. "Commence Operation Uncle Slam. Activate all cells!" Mohammad shouted for all to hear.

CHAPTER 12

I T WAS 6:00 A.M., and twelve bleary-eyed physicians staggered into the emergency room lounge for their monthly meeting. A pungent caffeine cloud engulfed the small room. The physicians sat at a large, rectangular glass-topped table, sipping on rot-gut hospital coffee and exchanging polite conversation while awaiting the arrival of Dr. Gonzo "Speedy" Gonzalez, the emergency room medical director. Rex sat next to Boom Boom, inhaling the vapors emanating from the toxic brew he had just poured.

Suddenly, the door to the lounge flew open. Dr. Gonzalez, Dr. Lyons, and Mushroom Head rushed into the room.

Boom Boom remained silent so as not to draw unwanted attention on himself. He was well aware of the wrath management could unleash.

Dr. Gonzalez was a fifty-year-old Hispanic male who had worked in the emergency room for many years. The external damage caused by this grueling profession was more than evident. However, his body language, along with his ever-present anxiety and paranoia, revealed the extent of the internal damage.

Dr. Gonzalez stood at the head of the table, his hands trembling violently as he passed out copies of the last month's performance in the emergency department and the day's agenda, which outlined the topics to be discussed. "As you all can plainly see, the results of last month's performance were dismal…"

"Same old BS," Rex whispered to Boom Boom. Suddenly, Rex felt his feathers ruffle and knew instinctively it was time to share his opinion. But before he could mount a response, Dr. Lyons decided to take control.

"In the past, no one would have questioned the manner in which you practice medicine, but times have changed. As you know, medicine is a business, and, as with any business, if you don't turn a profit, you might as well lock the doors. Gentlemen, this hospital has limited resources and is presently operating in the red. Thus, we have no choice but to become more efficient and to do so immediately. This not only requires that we expedite patient care but also that we do so with less staff. Furthermore, it is important for you to review the patient's ability to pay prior to you rendering those expensive services. In other words, the self-paying and Medicaid patients need to be run off and given the lasting impression that they are not to return!"

"Well, sir, yours would be an unwise policy for three reasons: number one, it would jeopardize our medical licenses; number two, the hospital would clearly be in violation of federal law; and, most importantly, number three, it's not in the patients' best interest," Rex responded, pointing his finger at Dr. Lyons to emphasize his position.

"Let me convey my position in more succinct terms. We can have a new emergency room physician group onboard in a matter of days. So, you either conduct business in the manner with which I desire, or you will be fired. Do I make myself perfectly clear?!" Dr. Lyons growled with ever-increasing intensity in his voice.

There was no response, only the look of shock on the faces of the physicians who had sheepishly gathered around the conference table for their monthly beating. Dr. Lyons looked into the eyes of each and every physician present, watching for signs of weakness. Clearly, it was evident that heads were going to roll. "Dr. Gonzalez, is this your position as well?" Dr. Leadbury inquired.

Dr. Gonzalez responded with a grunt and an affirmative nod of his head.

"This meeting in now adjourned. You all have your orders," a dusky Dr. Gonzalez gasped in a raspy, wheezing voice.

Dr. Gonzalez, Dr. Lyons, and Mushroom Head then stood up, abruptly leaving the room without another word.

"Well, Boom Boom. that was one hell of a dog and pony show. I am pleased that Speedy and management see things our way," Rex commented in a rather chipper but sarcastic tone. "Ah, well, that's enough excitement for one day. It's time to relieve the beleaguered night crew," Rex said as he stood up. However, there was no response from his colleague, Boom Boom, or the other subdued physicians. All remained seated and silent.

CHAPTER 13

As soon as Rex left the conference room, he looked down the short corridor leading to the emergency room. He could see the pandemonium.

"The jungle appears rather busy," Rex concluded, his eyes focusing on what appeared to be a sea of humanity madly scurrying about.

The moans, groans, and complaints generated a deafening roar, with the only discernible words coming as Rex passed a specific patient's room.

"Ya killing me, ya killing me!" a young boy screamed in a blood-curdling, ear-piercing pitch as he received a shot in the booty.

"I'm Tammy Tequila, and it's not last call," an inebriated restrained patient proclaimed as she violently rocked the stretcher back and forth.

"Well, it looks as though your shift has been rather interesting, Hanz," Rex said with a smile, shaking his hand.

"I should say," Hanz replied curtly.

"Pretty Boy, you're not wearing new cologne are you?" Rex asked, sniffing the air.

"Hell, no!" Hanz shot back without hesitation, while sniffing himself to see if he had ripened over the last twelve grueling hours.

"Then what's that smell?" Rex asked, looking around the emergency department.

"Oh no, it's not me," Sheila said as Rex started to sniff in her direction.

"Aha, there it is!" Rex shouted, while pointing. There on the floor in close proximity were three dark black tarry footprints, which were obviously the source of the obnoxious aroma.

"Rex, that's feces from a drunk with a GI bleed," Pretty Boy replied as he looked at the soles of his shoes. "Damn!"

"Oh, so it's not Al Gore's carbon footprints," Rex chuckled. "What do you have?"

"I though you would never ask. In room two... The ER was such a mess this morning that I couldn't attend our meeting. Was there anything of importance discussed?"

"Well, I wouldn't say that it's important, but you have the choice of either being fired or losing your medical license. But not to worry, I get the feeling that Mushroom Head and Dr. Lyons have me, and only me, in their gun sights," Rex added.

Hanz looked confused but walked off without saying another word as a shouting match erupted between a skinny dude and a man the size of gorilla.

"You two, knock it off!" Sheila demanded as the men started shoving one another. "Security!" Sheila shouted, but no one appeared. "Wan, where is the security guard?"

"He is in the lounge eating and watching TV," Wan, the tongue-tied Thailander, responded nonchalantly as he proceeded to carry out his daily restocking chores.

"Wan, could you please retrieve our brave security guard, 'No Nuts' Nolan, from the lounge?" Sheila insisted.

"C'est si bon," Wan replied as he shuffled off aimlessly in the opposite direction, mumbling, "I don't eat cats. I'm Baptist."

"That boy worries me," Sheila growled, clenching her fists and grinding her teeth in frustration.

"I'll get him, Sheila," Foxxman assured the coordinator before scrambling to the lounge.

"Ahhh!!" Rex shrieked as he came face-to-face with a large alligator foot surrounded by a flock of feathers. This rather unique calling card attached to a stick had been thrust into his face.

"Me Big Chief Thunder Chicken need to powwow now, Pale Face," a disheveled little man with a deep voice declared.

Rex felt his heart begin to race uncontrollably. Several moments went by as he struggled to control his breathing.

"Ha, that's the first time you've ever been speechless. Was the big bad pussy frightened by the dirty little chicken?" Sheila asked sarcastically in a cartoon-like voice.

"Very funny, Queen Sheila; now, would you be so kind as to locate a padded room for Big Chief Thunder Chicken?" Rex requested, while attempting to regain his composure.

"Oh, certainly, put the chief in room eight," Sheila announced after a moment of hesitation.

Wanda escorted the disheveled, elderly, defrocked chief to his room.

"Nice back scratcher, Chief," Wanda commented, examining the bizarre ornament before placing it back onto the counter.

"Speaking of flightless birds, those two ornery, goony birds on the stretchers look mighty familiar," Rex noted as his eyes wandered the hall.

"Be nice, Rrrrex," Boom Boom said. "Mean and Evil are not feeling well. It's probably the flu. Sheila is attempting to call in two nurses as relief. But for now, it's Foxxman and me against the world."

"What in the Sam Hell are you two doing laying down on the job? This is an emergency room, not a Holiday Inn," Rex admonished the nurses with delight, until he realized that they were really not feeling well.

Mean and Evil moaned in response while writhing uncontrollably on the stretchers. Each had received antiemetics by IV for nausea and had a liter of normal saline going wide open. Rex noticed that their normally shriveled, pale-gray, pasty skin now appeared edematous and beefy red. *This is an obvious improvement,* he thought. For a brief moment, Rex wondered if their illness was a result of caring for the now-deceased sailors who presented to the emergency room yesterday. However, Rex's train of thought was soon interrupted by Sheila's calm, soothing voice.

"Rex, get your rump over to your side and stop terrorizing Mean and Evil. We put a new patient in room two."

"All right, all right, don't rush me," Rex responded as Sheila shook her head in frustration.

"Dr. B, forgive me, I had intended to tell you earlier," Foxxman apologized. "The sailor who died yesterday, I went through his belongings and found this empty wrapper in his pants pocket."

프 러시안 블루

"Interesting, but what does it mean? Probably Tylenol. But I'll tell you who does know, our confused Cajun-Buddha buddy from Thailand. Wan, where in the hell are you?" Rex shouted.

"C'est si bon," Wan replied loudly as he shuffled out of a patient's room.

"What does this say?" Rex asked as he handed Wan the wrapper.

"Russian Screw" was Wan's translation, after chuckling for several minutes and rubbing his chin, while struggling to remember the language his South Korean mother had been so insistent that he master in his youth.

"Russian Screw!" Foxxman howled.

"Good God. Are you sure?" Rex asked as he shook his head in disbelief, convinced more than ever that Wan was not all there.

"C'est si bon," Wan replied confidently before shuffling off, mumbling, "Dem-o-rat, Dem-o-rat, he, he, he…"

"Dem-o-rat, what in the world is he babbling about?" Rex wondered.

"Ha, either he is talking about tonight's dinner or he is a card-carrying Republican," Sheila concluded.

"Oh, now that makes sense," Foxxman agreed, although he had a bewildered look.

Trissy noticed Wanda's head resting on the countertop. It had been a long, arduous morning, but the shift was still young, and now was no time to throw in the towel.

"Wanda, are you all right?" Trissy asked.

"No. I was doing well earlier, but now I feel very weak, dizzy, and nauseous. I'm burning up, and it feels like I'm being cooked from the inside out," the normally energetic nurse moaned.

"Wanda, you look like hell," Rex said candidly. "You're not pregnant again, are you?"

"Buzz off, Rrrrex," a feverish and physically exhausted Wanda whispered quietly.

"Sheila, Wanda is out of commission. Do we have a room free?" Rex requested.

"Room four; and Rex, don't expect me to find you another nurse. Everyone I've called to replace Mean and Evil has refused to come into this jungle on their day off," Sheila responded.

"Well, we need to go on *diversion* before this situation becomes any more dangerous," Rex demanded.

"That's just not possible, Rrrrex. You know the rules— management refuses to acknowledge the D word," Sheila replied.

"Ah yes, the old tradeoff between patient safety and revenue. The patient always looses," Rex complained.

"Stay focused, Rex, and don't take it personally," Boom Boom advised.

"Foxxman, help Trissy get Wanda to room four," Rex ordered.

"Will do!" Foxxman replied, taking Wanda by the arm and escorting the fallen nurse to her room.

"What the hell is going on, Boom Boom? The nurses are starting to fall like flies. Do you think this illness has anything to do with the disease that struck the sailors?" Rex suggested.

"Rex, you're starting to exhibit signs of paranoia. This is nothing more than a simple stomach virus," Boom Boom responded.

"Perhaps, Boom Boom, perhaps," Rex replied, as he began to vividly recall the details related to the doomed sailors.

"Trissy, I know this time of year we're seeing a great number of patients with the flu, but there's no way in hell that this is a simple gastroenteritis," Rex noted, as his suspicion of a biological or chemical attack began to intensify.

"I agree. Let's just hope terrorists haven't released some bizarre strain of virus," Trissy replied quietly, wiping the perspiration from her forehead.

"Trissy, are you feeling all right?" Rex asked with the utmost concern.

"Well, now that you ask, I'm feeling a little run-down, Rex, but I think it's because the morning has been so hectic," Trissy rationalized.

Rex then noticed that Trissy's beautiful, soft, bronze complexion was starting to take on an eerie red glow, and the ever-present sparkle in her eyes was beginning to fade.

"Oh, Christ!" Rex shouted. His wife was starting to exhibit the same life-threatening symptoms.

CHAPTER 14

IN THE SHADOW OF Cadillac Mountain on Mount Desert Island in Bar Harbor, Maine, stood a magnificent estate built at the turn of the century by Major George McMurtry. Surrounded by the Germans in World War I, the highly decorated American soldier was one of the few survivors of the *Lost Battalion*. His estate, the Bayview, was as spectacular and as colorful as his reputation. Situated high on a rocky cliff overlooking Frenchman's Bay and Bar Island, the majestic thirty thousand-square-foot-mansion stood as a proud symbol of an expanding and prosperous nation. The Bayview had been shuttered for years but was kept in pristine condition by a little old lady named Gladys. As the new headquarters for the National Security Agency, the Bayview offered both security and seclusion. With the ever-increasing concern of nuclear attack by terrorists, it became more apparent that this valuable national agency should be situated far away from prime East Coast targets. Once again, the majestic Bayview had been brought to life.

It was a dark, dreary day, and a nor'easter was blowing hard. Beautiful coach lamps marked the path, as National Security Director William "Andy" Anderson's vehicle slowly made its way down the windy private drive to the Bayview. The evergreens and the limbs of the barren birch, maple, and oak trees whipped violently back and forth. Even the heavy vehicle swayed, as if in the grasp of the fierce arctic winds. The vehicle soon came to a stop. As the director stepped from the warmth of his town car, he felt the frigid air immediately penetrate his layers of clothing.

"Good God, it's cold!" he complained to his driver. But his words were lost in the howling wind and the sound of rustling leaves.

"What jackass in Washington decided to headquarter this agency so far north?" the director muttered while trouncing through the deep foliage toward the front door. As soon as Director Anderson set foot on the porch, the winds suddenly swirled, increased in intensity, and whisked away the condensation from his breath.

"Whooo!" the director moaned as the door slammed shut. He shivered in an attempt to ward off the cold, as a stoic butler helped him off with his heavy overcoat.

Director Anderson was an energetic man in his mid-eighties who had had several illustrious careers. He had been a submarine captain, a congressman, and later held several cabinet posts in Republican administrations. Now, as a seasoned diplomat, he was serving a new administration. Although the commander-in-chief was a Democrat, Anderson remained loyal, driven by the need to meet new challenges. The director was a class act whose warmth and charm were truly unique.

"Mr. Director, welcome back," Chief-of-Staff Earl Vassar announced. "How was your flight, sir?" he asked politely, although he already knew the answer.

Earl had boundless energy and an ever-present smile, rumored to be the result of the many decadent years he spent at the Subic Bay Naval Base in the Philippines chasing young native girls. He had met Director Anderson by chance, when his submarine had pulled into Subic Bay during the Vietnam conflict. As a rambunctious supply officer, Earl was able to expeditiously resupply his sub, while ensuring that her captain and his crew enjoyed their stay in tropical paradise.

"Scary; at one point, I thought the wings were going to snap off," Director Anderson complained, recalling the terrorizing flight, while rubbing his nearly frostbitten hands together.

"I'll bet it was quite a bumpy ride," Earl acknowledged.

"Yes, indeed," the director agreed. He extended his chilled hand, offering a broad smile. "Now, how have you been?"

"Excellent, Mr. Director, excellent," Earl replied, shaking the director's hand.

"My, Bar Harbor has changed in the few months since I was last here," Director Anderson remarked.

"I should say. The summer flew by and fall is nothing more than a distant memory. As soon as the temperature started to drop, Bar Harbor turned into a ghost town. Virtually overnight, ninety-percent of the storefronts were boarded up and sealed with thick plywood. Even the hordes of tourists quickly migrated south. That is, those who were smart enough to escape Old Man Winter. As for the townsfolk, the few who are not in deep hibernation, permanent or otherwise, can be found at Chowder Head's Pub."

"Is that the rather lively establishment overlooking the harbor, where we had that wonderful lunch?" the director inquired as memories of that warm summer day came rushing back.

"Yes, sir," Earl replied, remembering how much the director had enjoyed his rather succulent butter-drenched crustacean.

"Ah, a lobster dinner at Chowder Head's later tonight sounds awfully tempting, Earl. And, after that rough flight, I could certainly use a drink," Director Anderson suggested rather emphatically.

"Absolutely, Mr. Director, consider the reservation booked. In the last few frigid weeks, the owners and I have had the opportunity to become close friends. I'll ensure that we get the finest table," Earl said with unassuming confidence.

"Excellent," the director replied, placing his hand on his old friend's shoulder.

"Besides, that would give us the perfect occasion to share old war stories," Earl said with a smile. "Now, let me show you the changes we have made in your absence. Ken, please take Director Anderson's luggage up to the Major's room," Earl requested politely.

"Very well, sir," Ken replied dryly. "I just hope Gladys found time to clean the room," Ken mumbled sarcastically, attempting to lift the extraordinarily heavy suitcase.

"Please follow me, Mr. Director," Earl said.

A few moments later, the two men entered a magnificent three-story atrium surrounded by stunning marble columns. The lighted Tiffany ceiling bathed the large, open area in vibrant colors, while the massive chandeliers and several large fourteenth-century tapestries completed the rich majestic ambiance. All this warmth was in stark contrast to the inhospitable scenery, which could be viewed out of partially frost-covered windows overlooking Frenchman's Bay. Director Anderson couldn't help but notice that the bay appeared to be possessed, as treacherous waves were whipped into a frenzy and whitecaps made every attempt to leap from the confines of the turbulent body of water.

The atrium was bustling with activity as several men and women scurried about gathering and analyzing the latest intelligence from twenty-seven domestic agencies and countless international sources. The room was partitioned and furnished with dozens of desks, as well as numerous computers and flat-screen display monitors.

"Mr. Director, this area was under construction when you were last here."

"My word," Director Anderson whispered as he looked around the room. "You have done a remarkable job in just a few months, Earl. I am quite impressed."

"Thank you," Earl responded enthusiastically.

"Um, um," a young lady mumbled, gently nudging Earl.

"Oh, Mr. Director, this is Leslie Valentino, our chief-of-operations," Earl said, introducing the young woman who had mysteriously appeared at his side.

Leslie Valentino was a strikingly beautiful thirty-five-year-old who was a brilliant analyst. Born and raised in New Orleans, she knew how to let the good times roll. Leslie was the consummate professional who never let her guard down, until behind closed doors with her secret lover, Earl. A true perfectionist, she worked tirelessly day and night. No one doubted her voluptuous figure, or the accuracy of her analytical figures.

"I'm pleased to finally meet you, Mr. Director," Leslie responded, shaking the director's hand forcefully. "I feel as if I know you. In fact, every time Earl starts to reminisce, your name comes up, and he starts to chuckle rather uncontrollably," Leslie said with a smile as Earl suddenly became uncomfortable.

"Thank you, I think," Director Anderson replied slowly and cautiously.

"Yes indeed, those were wonderful times," Earl said, clearing his throat and looking at Leslie with a desperate facial plea, requesting that she use moderation in relaying his version of unforgettable and, undoubtedly, over-embellished stories.

"Earl, when it comes to issues of national security, which obviously include our escapades so many years ago, it is most important that we run deep and silent," the director whispered, as Leslie looked on with a gleam in her eye.

"My apologies, Mr. Director," Earl replied humbly, while regaining his composure.

"Mr. Director, Chief-of-Staff, we are about to start the five o'clock briefing in the parlor if you would like to attend," a feisty Miss Valentino offered.

"Absolutely, Leslie, please lead the way," the director responded without hesitation.

Leslie preceded the men into the main hallway. Picking up her pace, she could feel their eyes penetrating her body. Yet, she continued swaying rhythmically as the two men followed her cat-like strut. At the end of the hall, they scurried down a small flight of stairs, through two large doors, and into a spectacular parlor.

The parlor was situated at one end of the mansion. The room itself was thirty feet in width by forty feet in length and was surrounded on three sides by large, glass-paned windows that overlooked the bay and the grounds. The twenty-foot ceiling supported two glorious chandeliers. On the walls, the handcrafted woodwork was painted in a rich green with gilded accents, framing oil paintings from eighteenth-century masters. The light radiating from several gold sconces added mystery to the alluring artwork, which had been so effective in capturing moments in time. On the outside wall, centered in the room, was a large fireplace trimmed in marble, above which loomed a magnificent mosaic depicting a glorious victory from a war long, long ago. The crackling sounds of burning logs and the intermittent flashes of brilliant light projecting from the roaring fire made the atmosphere warm and inviting.

"My, you're speedy," Director Anderson remarked, taking a moment to catch his breath.

"It's those long legs," Earl joked as Leslie took off to the far end of the room.

She had clearly chosen to ignore Earl's comment. Moments later, she stood impatiently at the head of a large oak conference table waiting for the two men to catch up.

"Mr. Director, please," Leslie requested, pulling out an ornate chair in a chivalrous manner.

"Thank you, Leslie," the director replied as he slowly sat down.

Earl and Leslie took seats on either side of Director Anderson. Leslie looked at her watch, as the various department heads quietly strolled into the great room. They represented both the off-going and on-coming shifts. Given the sheer volume of information and the magnitude of the decisions regarding national security, it was of the utmost importance that all of these intelligence officers attend the briefings, in order to ensure continuity of thought and direction. Minutes later, all were present and seated.

Earl stood and addressed the group. "Ladies and gentlemen, we are honored to have Director Anderson with us today. It is important that he see exactly how we function as a team in our war against terrorism. So, please don't pull any punches or sugarcoat your analysis, but always remember that Leslie and I know where you live. Furthermore, rest assured that there are only a few places to hide in this frozen tundra." All smiled and there was a brief moment of laughter.

"Mr. Director," Earl announced, prior to taking his seat.

Director Anderson scooted his chair back and slowly rose to his feet. The speed of his ascent was not reflected by either his age or his height, but by the degree of pain elicited from the grinding and popping sounds coming from his knees.

"I am indeed honored to be back in Bar Harbor, the tropical oasis that it is," he said, as all those present chuckled. "Stepping from the plane this afternoon, I immediately knew how Birds Eye food felt to be flash frozen, but at my age it just takes so damn long to thaw out."

A gifted speaker who could read his audience, the director felt that he had identified with the group and had their full, undivided attention. Now it was time to get serious.

"This is certainly a tough, unforgiving environment in the winter, but not as tough or as unforgiving as our enemies. As you all know, terrorism exists throughout the world, and the terrorists are cold and calculating in their mission. In order to advance their cause, they have chosen to target innocent civilians and have had the audacity to take the battle to our shores. Thus, the importance of your efforts cannot be underestimated. Freedom and democracy will be preserved at all costs and we will remain committed to protecting Americans, both here and abroad," the director assured the dedicated group, before pausing for a moment to make eye contact with each man and woman sitting around the table.

"Earl, from what I've seen, you have done an excellent job in establishing the much-needed infrastructure, and in gathering the talent necessary to fight this battle against an evil people. I commend you all for your heroic efforts and dedication, but request that we all remain extremely vigilant," he concluded, taking his seat.

"Thank you, Mr. Director," Earl replied. "Now, Leslie, let's proceed with tonight's briefing."

"Very well," Leslie acknowledged, depressing a silver button on a small remote-control device lying in front of her. She stood and began walking toward a massive screen that lowered from the ceiling. On the screen was a map of the world displayed in brilliant color and stunning resolution. In her left hand, she held a small laser pointer needed to highlight areas being discussed and, in her right hand, the device used to manipulate the map.

"As of o-two-hundred yesterday, there has been a sudden and dramatic surge in computer traffic originating from the Middle East, more specifically, Saudi Arabia. Normally, from this purported ally, there would be approximately ten thousand messages on any given day," Leslie said.

"However, in the past twenty-four hours, over one hundred thousand messages have been sent, primarily to addresses in Mexico and Canada," Leslie stressed as Director Anderson suddenly appeared concerned. He listened intently while Leslie continued.

"Unfortunately, we have only been able to scrutinize a fraction of the traffic. However, the computers have analyzed each and every message looking for keywords and/or phrases. Ninety percent used the word 'attack,' and seventy-two percent reference Al Qaeda. Of those messages, only three methods of attack were mentioned: suicide bombers, commercial aircraft, and dirty bombs. What is so highly unusual is that these methods of attack were all referenced in equal percentages, as were the selected targets, which included the White House, the Capitol, and New York City."

"What exactly does this mean, Leslie?" Director Anderson interjected.

"Mr. Director, the statistical significance of these findings appears to be far beyond the realm of probability. On the surface one would assume that an invasion of the Unites States is imminent and will originate from our porous borders to the north and south. However, upon closer examination of the addresses to which these messages were sent, we determined that the same emails were forwarded to the same address on multiple occasions throughout the day."

"How unusual," Director Anderson whispered.

"This made us even more suspicious, so we then decided to swim upstream to examine the point of origination for all the traffic. As anticipated, ten percent of the messages did indeed originate from Saudi Arabia. However, all others were forwarded via Banda Computer Associates in Mumbai, India, and routed through Saudi Arabia," Leslie revealed, much to Director Anderson's astonishment.

"Leslie, what's the bottom-line?" the director insisted.

"The bottom-line, Mr. Director, is that, quite frankly, I smell a rat! We believe that this sudden surge in high volume traffic was instigated to divert our attention and resources. What concerns us now is the timing of this misinformation, which we believe will coincide with the intended plan of attack," Leslie concluded.

"Good God! Leslie, surely our allies have monitored this surge in correspondence. What exactly do our foreign intelligence sources make of this increased traffic?" the director asked with great concern.

"Unfortunately all of them, with the exception of Israel, believe the messages are genuine and the threat real," Leslie replied frankly.

Everyone around the table looked gravely concerned but sat quietly. For a brief moment, only the roar of the fire and the crackling of the wood broke the silence.

"Now, let's review the intelligence gathered over the last eight hours," Leslie requested. "Shawn, is there anything new from the Middle East that we have not yet discussed?" she asked, before taking her seat.

"Yes, just moments ago the Arabic station, Al Jazeera, while covering a story on the atrocities suffered by their Muslim brothers in Iraq, suddenly flashed the American flag at the end of the piece. The flag had Arabic writing scrolled across the stars and stripes. Translated, the ominous verbiage reads, 'ACTIVATE ALL CELLS.' But we don't know if this command is in reference to the United States, Iraq, Afghanistan, or other American interests abroad. Furthermore, there has been no corresponding communication to reinforce this order. Obviously, we take this threat quite seriously and will follow this situation very closely," Shawn Novak stated emphatically.

Leslie appeared quite concerned, as did Director Anderson, Earl, and the other intelligence experts gathered around the table.

Leslie thought for a moment before continuing. "Diane, what is the latest intelligence from Asia?"

"North Korea, over the past few days, has become quite defiant and appears to be taunting the United States through all forms of communication. It's as if they know something we don't. Also, there seems to be more activity originating from Jakarta, Indonesia. The communication from this refuge for radical Muslim scoundrels appears to be referencing Hong Kong and Singapore. Without question, either city would prove to be an ideal target given the worldwide flow of goods originating from their respective ports. However, at this time we have nothing more specific," Diane Croft concluded.

"Very well," Leslie replied, turning her attention to the director in charge of Europe. "Michael, what new developments have you uncovered?"

"Leslie, we are receiving intelligence that suggests that the United States Embassies in Berlin and Paris may be targeted," Michael Hardin replied.

"Don't sit on that information, Michael. Let the CIA, Army Intelligence, and the respective embassies know of our concern," Leslie ordered.

"As per your standing order, we have already done so, Leslie," Michael assured her.

"Excellent," Leslie replied, activating the display switch, focusing in, and selectively enlarging the North American continent. "Now, with regard to the United States and our borders, there seems to be a great deal of activity. What have you and your team been able to put together, Waleta?"

"There are several new developments. With regard to communication, we are all aware of the recent surge in computer traffic, but what is interesting is the dramatic increase in cell phone usage over the last week. Unfortunately, those we have under surveillance are changing cell phone numbers and telecommunication carriers quicker than we can draw a bead on them. Also of importance is the money trail. There has been a significant increase in fund transfers from the United States to Switzerland and Saudi Arabia over the last two days. The third issue of importance to relay is that yesterday, it appeared that several ambassadors, representing nations in the Middle East, were recalled," Waleta Moore relayed, much to everyone's dismay.

"This is more than mere coincidence," Director Anderson concluded, looking at Earl.

"Without question, the slimy sons-of-bitches have something planned and, unfortunately, it appears to be going down soon," Earl concluded.

"There's no doubt that we are quickly running out of time," Leslie said, reflecting on the information she had just heard.

"Is there anything else you would like to share, Waleta?" Leslie asked.

"Regrettably, I do. It pertains to the dead Asian sailors. We have followed this rather bizarre story closely over the past few days. As you recall, one body washed ashore on the beach in Galveston, while three others were recovered from the Caribbean. All had a deep blue skin discoloration, the significance of which has not yet been determined. However, the autopsy results should be available tomorrow. Of the five hundred ships leaving Asia for the United States in the last two weeks, only forty-five have crossed through the Panama Canal. Forty-four of those ships have been accounted for and their ports of destination confirmed. The one vessel unaccounted for is the *Il-sung*, a one-hundred-eighty-foot cargo ship registered in Libya, but reportedly sailing from South Korea. However, we have thus far been unable to confirm the *Il-sung* embarking from any port in South Korea. Furthermore, there is no indication of what was on the ship's manifest. Therefore, until proven otherwise, we must assume that the *Il-sung* is laden with weapons of mass destruction," Waleta concluded confidently.

"Of greater concern," Leslie added, "is that yesterday, an emergency room physician from Louisiana reported to the CDC the violent deaths of six Asian sailors, all of whom exhibited the same deep blue skin discoloration."

"It appears that the *Il-sung* has somehow eluded our defenses and reached our shores," Earl interjected.

"Have we notified the Navy and the Coast Guard?" Director Anderson asked.

"Yes, sir, it was done early this morning. We've insisted upon an aggressive search by land, sea, and air for the vessel," Earl assured the director.

"Also, Mr. Director, the FBI and the CIA are scheduled to descend upon Carencrow Regional Hospital tomorrow morning to investigate the physician's claim," Leslie added.

A junior analyst then entered the parlor. He whispered in Waleta's ear before handing her a note.

"We have just intercepted an email to the physician in Louisiana from an unknown source in Saudi Arabia, praising him for his efforts in the Holy War," Waleta reported.

"Christ, obtain a search warrant on this rogue physician's house and businesses immediately!" Earl demanded.

"Absolutely, I'll take care of it personally," Waleta assured Earl before quickly leaving the room.

"Perhaps this is the element of luck we needed to unravel this mystery," Earl added.

"My gut tells me you're right. However, it's hard to ignore all the other pieces of the puzzle and focus solely on a little town in Louisiana," Director Anderson replied.

"Does anyone else have any additional issues that need to be discussed?" Leslie asked as she raised her voice over the independent conversations, which had suddenly erupted.

"Now that I think of it, there is one additional concern, which we are attempting to substantiate. Israeli intelligence reports that the submarine *Hugo Chavez* recently left port in Venezuela bound for the United States. However, we have been unable to verify this information through other sources or via satellite," Brian Joyner shared.

"What type of submarine?" Director Anderson asked with great interest, given his background as a submarine captain.

"Reportedly a diesel boat."

"Well, I'm not sure how much damage an old diesel boat could inflict, but keep us abreast of any new developments, Bryan," Earl requested.

"Now, one last time, does anyone have anything else to share?" Leslie asked, looking around the room. "Very well then, let's get back to work."

The meeting was now formally adjourned. As the intelligence officers left the room, Earl, Leslie, and Director Anderson stayed behind.

"You have done an excellent job, Leslie. The intelligence gathered and evaluated has been timely, accurate, and of enormous value," Earl praised.

"Yes, but this is no time for kudos. Our battle group was decimated in the Persian Gulf three days ago, and we lost nearly a thousand brave men and women. We have hundreds of active terrorist cells operating quietly within this nation, an unscrupulous physician on the loose who has sold out his country, and now, it would appear, an unaccounted for South Korean vessel," Director Anderson reminded Earl and Leslie.

"Mr. Director, let me assure you that we all share your concern. However, for the first time, I feel as if we are closing in on the enemy," Leslie replied.

"Absolutely, and when we catch them, I intend to skin the beady-eyed, towel-draped buggers alive," Earl assured the director with a gleam in his eye.

"As with life, timing is everything," Director Anderson reminded his top intelligence officers. "We may be closing in, but do we have enough time to stop the terrorists from unleashing weapons of mass destruction on the United States? You both have my utmost confidence. However, in light of the new intelligence, I think it's important that I brief the president. Perhaps she would consider elevating the national threat level, although the overwhelming concern is creating a state of panic," Director Anderson shared.

"Mr. Director, may I suggest that after your conversation with the president we stick to our game plan and head out for a quick bite to eat?" Earl recommended, attempting to lighten the mood.

"The lobster and a cold blueberry beer is an irresistible combination," Leslie suggested.

"Unquestionably," Earl emphasized.

"As tempting as a blueberry beer sounds, I believe that I'll have to pass on anything that's cold. However, I'm surely not going to turn down a steaming hot Maine lobster. Leslie, would you care to join us?" Director Anderson asked.

"Possibly later, Mr. Director. However, I must warn you that if I have to endure the stories of Earl's escapades in the Philippines one more time, I might feel compelled to bop him in the nose," Leslie replied with a smile as she made a fist.

"She's serious! Thus, a hasty tactical retreat to the pub is definitely in order," Earl said with a snicker and a wink, intended to proclaim his innocence and reflect his boyish charm.

CHAPTER 15

ANOTHER SHIFT FROM HELL had ended, but not without taking its toll. Trissy had been inflicted with the same mysterious illness that had victimized several other emergency room nurses who were now in critical condition. Rex was gravely concerned. His beautiful wife had received two liters of fluid in the emergency room, and her vital signs remained stable. Yet she continued to look rather puny, although she insisted that she felt better. He had pleaded with her to stay in the hospital overnight, but his feisty, hardheaded German adamantly refused.

"Hanz, enjoy your stint in the jungle," Rex chuckled after giving report to the rather dejected but well-rested physician.

"Foxxman, would you and Wan please assist Trissy out to our car? I'll meet you out back at the ambulance entrance," Rex requested.

"Will do!" the two men replied simultaneously, before helping Trissy into a wheelchair.

As Rex left the hospital and walked toward the Mercedes, his thoughts turned to Trissy's friend and coworker, Wanda, who had not fared as well. She remained hypotensive and had to be admitted to the intensive care unit. Unfortunately, Wanda always complained that admission to Carencrow Regional was a fate worse than death—a sentiment shared among the staff. However, in this case, Wanda had no choice. The Grim Reaper was giving her the evil eye.

"Wan, Foxxman, thanks for your help," Rex said.

"Thank you," Trissy whispered.

"You're more than welcome, Dr. B. Take care, Trissy," Foxxman added, while Wan mumbled something incoherent and shuffled off.

Rex gave the former Vietnam veteran a hand salute, in a final gesture of gratitude, before placing the car in drive and speeding off.

What modern medicine could not do for Trissy, Rex felt certain that the Bee Gees could. Surely, the high-pitched wailing would cheer her up. As much as he dreaded their squeaky voices, Rex turned on the radio and depressed the CD play button. Moments later, "I, I, I'm stayin' alive, stayin' alive…" was blaring over the speakers. Spontaneously, Trissy's eyes began to glow, and she started to perk up.

"I hope that Wanda is OK, but I'm not so sure that I could muster the same concern for Mean and Evil," Rex said, driving home through the darkness.

"Rex, Wanda is a tough lady. She'll be fine. With regard to the other two, they're ornery old birds who will most likely outlive both of us," Trissy replied softly and slowly.

"You know, there is something unsettling, if not sinister, about this town," Rex said, taking his eyes off the road momentarily to reevaluate Trissy, even though the passing street lights provided very little illumination.

"Rex, I have never had the courage to tell you, but Carencrow is the French word for 'buzzard,'" Trissy remarked candidly, much to Rex's surprise. Rex had always been very easygoing, unfazed at any turn of events or startling news. However, this revelation was truly shocking.

Suddenly the events that had unfolded over the past few days raced through his mind.

"Oh, that's comforting. Trissy, I can't help thinking about those dead Asian sailors. What a bizarre clinical presentation. Although their skin was blue and sloughing off in thick bloody layers, each man appeared to have been severely burnt," Rex said as the wheels in his mind started turning.

"I thought the autopsy was to be completed today?" Trissy inquired.

"That was my understanding as well. I just hope we're notified of the cause of death immediately, because I'm convinced that whatever took their lives has made you and the other nurses extremely ill."

"Rex, with so many patients coughing on us all day, we were most likely exposed to the same virus. I agree that there was something very unusual about the sailors, but there is no sinister plot. I'm confident that the coroner will have some simple explanation," Trissy replied.

"Well, you could be right, but we're missing something, and it's right in front of us. I can't prove it, but I believe that the sailors are probably North Koreans and are somehow related to Chum."

"Now, that's a stretch," Trissy replied.

"Furthermore, now that I think about it, the heated argument between GeeHad and Chum that we witnessed several nights ago at dinner was highly unusual. GeeHad and his booty buddies are most likely also involved in this scheme."

"Rex, I think you're chasing the wind and starting to exhibit a wee bit of paranoia, as Boom Boom so openly concluded!" Trissy said.

"Now, that diagnosis is highly likely, my love, given my close proximity to the multitude of certifiable patients and psychotic managers who stroll through the emergency room on a daily basis," Rex agreed. "Nonetheless, when we get home, I intend to email the National Security Agency and the CDC once again," Rex declared, attempting to justify his thoughts and proposed actions.

"Rex, you never received a reply from the first message you sent to the respective bureaucratic bunglers, informing them of the little blue men," Trissy joked.

"They weren't little blue men, they were dying, blue-tinged Asian sailors. Perhaps I didn't express my concern forcefully enough," Rex complained. "I just don't understand why, in today's security-conscious environment, neither the CDC nor the NSA has contacted me," Rex argued.

Trissy turned slowly toward Rex, somehow finding the energy to muster a smile. However, Rex didn't notice her shaking her head, conveying the subtle message that the male species may never be understood. "Well, perhaps they realize that you…" she stopped mid-sentence when, from out of nowhere, a blinding bright light emanating from behind the Mercedes illuminated the interior of their vehicle.

Rex reactively looked in his rearview mirror and was momentarily blinded. Suddenly, as he reached to flip the mirror down, there was a loud explosion. Glass shattered and the Mercedes was thrust forward violently, as the sound of twisting steel grew louder. Rex resisted the urge to hit the brakes, instinctively stepping on the accelerator. Concurrently, he looked in his side mirror, only to see the reflection of a massive tubular chrome grill. Again, there was a loud explosion and the Mercedes was thrown forward.

"What in the Sam Hell is going on?" Rex screamed as he pushed the accelerator to the floorboard.

Trissy found the energy to turn around, only to see the outline of a black Hummer riding their tail. "Faster, Rex, faster!" Trissy shouted.

"Chasing the wind, huh?" Rex uttered sarcastically, hitting the high beams.

"Well, perhaps I underestimated the gravity of the situation!" Trissy responded apologetically after being recharged by a sudden and unexpected adrenaline rush.

The lights appeared to be getting brighter, and Trissy turned around again to see if they had gained any distance. Unfortunately, the monstrous vehicle appeared even closer. "They're on us, Rex!" Trissy shouted as their speedometer passed eighty miles an hour.

Suddenly, a multitude of fiery flashes shot forth and metal projectiles struck the Mercedes. The bullets that struck the vehicle squarely erupted with a loud, deep thud, while those that glanced off the car created a high-pitched ringing sound.

"Oh, Christ!" Trissy screamed, sitting back in her seat. "They're firing at us now! Rex, this is no time to dillydally!"

"Dillydally?" Rex mumbled in disbelief at Trissy's choice of words, while death loomed. "Keep your head down!" Rex insisted.

"What?!" Trissy shouted back.

"Duck!" Rex gently nudged Trissy's head down before looking over his shoulder. The chrome-ridden black box of death was not far behind.

"Rex, get us out of this mess!" Trissy screamed, her survival instincts suddenly overcoming her physical exhaustion.

"I'm working on it!" Rex shouted back.

As the Mercedes continued to accelerate, Rex struggled to keep the car on the road. His eyes strained to see what lay ahead in the darkness as the speedometer continued its rapid swing to the right. Rex could feel the car sway and hear the screeching of rubber, as the tires clawed the black asphalt while rounding the curves.

Again, there were several large pops, and a spray of bullets struck the Mercedes. Instantaneously, there was a loud explosion. One of the deadly metal projectiles had struck the back windshield. The force of the impact shattered the glass, sending deadly shards forward into the cabin. A cold, violent wind was suddenly sucked into the vehicle, creating a noisy, twisting turbulence.

"Are you all right, Trissy?" Rex shouted.

"Yes!" she yelled, giving Rex a thumbs up. As her beautiful blonde hair whipped about, she unexpectedly sat up in her seat. *Clearly, there is no way to outrun the Hummer,* Trissy thought to herself. Then, leaning toward Rex, she shouted, "I think I have an idea!"

She pointed to the center console and the switch that operated the retractable metal roof. Trissy was a perfectionist who was not only detail-oriented but also extremely creative. She had read the Mercedes owner's manual dozens of times, and the threatening, highlighted words suddenly appeared to be an invitation: "Do NOT Operate While This Vehicle Is Moving."

Rex understood her plan and shot Trissy a thumbs up. The Mercedes was traveling at well over a hundred miles per hour while being aggressively pursued by a Hummer intent on their demise. It was clearly time for a new strategy. By now, the two vehicles had raced miles out of town. The blacktop had narrowed and an expansive, murky bayou now hugged both sides of the desolate country road. Rex slowed down, allowing the Hummer to quickly close the distance between the two vehicles. Trissy had her hand firmly on the switch that operated the retractable roof, while Rex fought to maintain control of the vehicle.

"Steady, steady, brace yourself, Rex!" Trissy shouted. The Hummer then slammed into the rear end of the Mercedes. Simultaneously, Trissy activated the switch. For a few seconds, it appeared that the roof was not moving, and she felt an immediate sense of despair.

Maybe the mechanism was damaged in the collision, or by one of the bullets, she thought to herself, pulling on the switch with even greater force. Then, slowly, the roof rose above the forward-locking mechanism. Suddenly there was a thunderous snap. The heavy metal roof broke free, striking and embedding itself in the front windshield of the Hummer. The monstrous, black, boxy beast started to swerve dangerously, quickly losing speed. Rex took the opportunity to pull alongside the vehicle. In the dim light, Rex could see that the metal roof had penetrated deep enough into the cab to strike the driver, severing his neck. It almost appeared as if his head was mounted on a shiny silver platter. His face was bloodied and contorted, yet the killer of Middle Eastern descent looked hauntingly familiar. As his white turban began to unwind in the wind, the far end started whipping in the breeze, slapping against the side of the Hummer. Suddenly, the passenger in the Hummer lowered the window and Rex could clearly see the barrel of an AK-47. He was sure that the gunman's vision was briefly obstructed by the wild gyrations of the driver's possessed turban. However, time was now of the essence; he had to act quickly.

"Hang on, Trissy!" Rex screamed.

Trissy looked on in disbelief as Rex unexpectedly and aggressively turned the steering wheel to the right. There was a loud *BOOM* as the Mercedes struck the driver's side of the Hummer, rocking the giant vehicle.

Trissy screamed after being tossed about by the forceful collision. "Rex, what in the hell are you doing?"

"Trying to avoid being shot," Rex yelled, watching the barrel suddenly thrust upwards. The gunman had been jerked back into his seat.

Again and again, Rex rapidly turned the steering wheel to the right. Each time, the Mercedes found its target with a loud, horrendous *BANG*. Yet the persistent gunman was once again in position. As the barrel of the AK-47 was lowered, Rex rammed the Hummer one last time. Suddenly, there was a rapid succession of brilliant flashes of light and a thunderous roar as the weapon discharged. Trissy looked on in horror, fully expecting the high velocity projectiles to rip through their bodies any moment, but the killer had squeezed the trigger prematurely, and the bullets flew high of their mark. Almost immediately, the Hummer veered to the right and flew off the road. Rex and Trissy could see a massive splash as the big, black, gnarly beast struck the dark, murky water several yards from shore.

They began screaming uncontrollably with joy while Rex applied the breaks on Trissy's rather expensive battering ram. The celebration continued as the Mercedes came to a stop in the middle of the dark, deserted road in Nowhere, Louisiana.

"Wahoo!!!" Rex shouted, shaking his fist into the cold night air.

"Thank God!" Trissy gasped. "For a moment there I thought we were destined to be buried in some wretched crawfish pond," she added, looking at the ominous waters of the bayou.

Rex gazed into Trissy's sparkling eyes. He released his seatbelt. Sweeping the glass fragments off the console, Rex leaned over and they embraced. Rex brushed Trissy's hair to the side and gave her a deep, passionate kiss, which lasted several minutes. All the while, the thought of their near-death experience raced through his mind. He could not fathom life without his beautiful wife. As their lips parted, Rex looked into Trissy's eyes once again.

"Trissy, you're an absolute genius. We were running out of road, gas, and time. You saved our lives," Rex whispered as he held her closely.

"Thank you, Rex," Trissy replied. "However, you were the one who talked me into purchasing the sports package on the Benz."

"Well, you do have a good point. It was a rather wise investment, because the German sports car handled impeccably under very demanding circumstances. However, our next car is going to have bulletproof glass and a reinforced steel body," Rex declared, while gazing over the hood. White smoke was now trickling from the engine and the car's magnificent lines had been converted into large folds of charred, twisted metal.

Rex slowly turned the Benz around, ever mindful of the deep, treacherous embankments on either side of the narrow road. However, as he turned the steering wheel to the left, the car refused to move, as if the parking break was on.

"Christ, not now," he complained, placing car into park and stepping out to examine the damage. "Just as I thought," Rex complained.

"What?" Trissy asked, attempting to step out of the car, but the frame had been pushed well into the cabin, and her door wouldn't budge.

"The metal was rubbing against the front passenger tire." Rex took off his shirt, wrapped it around his hands and pulled on the fender with all his might, moving the warm, contorted metal outward, away from the wheel. "There, that should do it."

"Well, do you think the service department at the dealership can replace my beautiful panoramic roof?" Trissy asked as Rex shivered in the cool night air and quickly placed his scrub top back on.

"Certainly, my love, but I'm afraid that the rest of the car is kaput!" Rex confessed, leaning over the passenger side door and giving his wife a kiss.

"What do you mean?" Trissy asked as Rex hopped back into the driver's seat.

"I mean that the car looks as if it lost a battle with an Iraqi land mine. There is no way in hell that the body shop would consider salvaging the Mercedes."

"Well, knowing what responsible drivers we are, I'm sure they will probably insist upon giving us a fancy new loaner car," Trissy surmised.

"Now, that's a real possibility," Rex chuckled, knowing that Trissy was having trouble coming to grips with the extent of the damage her Mercedes had suffered. Holding Trissy's hand, Rex gave the car a little gas and successfully made the tight turn.

Moments later Rex came to a halt, at the point close to where the Hummer had left the road. He situated the Benz so the headlights penetrated the darkness, illuminating the once-dangerous threat. The Hummer was standing on end in the water, with the nose of the vehicle embedded in thick bottom sediment. Large plumes of steam billowed skyward, but cleared on occasion, revealing the brackish water lapping at the front door. There were no lights on, and there appeared to be no movement. Rex and Trissy looked on as the stillness of the evening was broken by an eerie hissing sound as the cold water rapidly cooled the overheated engine of this man-made serpent.

"Trissy, with the exception of Governor Schwarzenegger, why do you suppose that, by and large, short little pricks with big egos are attracted to Hummers?" Rex asked.

"It's a visibility issue, Rex," Trissy replied.

"Well, visible or not, I sure as hell have no intention of calling nine-one-one for these evil bastards."

"I honestly don't blame you, Rex. And, by the way, we are nine-one-one," she reminded him.

"Excellent point. I hereby pronounce these maggots. Time of death, unknown," Rex announced gleefully.

A chill suddenly overcame Trissy. "Sweetheart, I'm frozen. Please, let's get out of here," Trissy requested, as more steam began to escape the confines of the Mercedes, modified engine compartment.

"Will do, let's just hope we can make it home," Rex replied, turning up the heat and stepping on the gas.

"By the way, now that I think about it, how are we going to explain all this damage to the USAA?" Trissy asked.

"Good question. We're going to have to get creative."

With the heat maxed out, it was rather comfortable driving on this rather brisk evening. Trissy appeared fully recovered from her earlier ordeal, and, with the stars above shining brilliantly, all appeared to be right in the world for one brief moment.

CHAPTER 16

ITT WAS EARLY EVENING when Director Anderson and his Chief-of-Staff, Earl Vassar, drove through the desolate streets of Bar Harbor on their way to Chowder Head's for dinner. The local watering hole was located adjacent to a large park on the main square, which sloped down to the harbor and the town's pier. As they exited the vehicle, Director Anderson shivered, as the merciless arctic wind attacked savagely. With each breath, he endured a painful stinging sensation as the cold air threatened to freeze the warm, moist alveoli lining his lungs. Likewise, each exhalation billowed forth clouds of condensed crystals, which were quickly whisked away. To his right, he could see several lobster boats being violently tossed about in the turbulent waters within the poorly protected harbor. Each boat clung to its respective mooring in an attempt to avoid utter destruction on the jagged rocky shore.

"Earl, I must say that you did not embellish your description of Bar Harbor in the winter. The streets are absolutely deserted!" Director Anderson shouted as they quickly scurried across the park to Main Street.

With the exception of the sign, Chowder Head's, shining brightly, there were no cars to be seen, and all the business fronts were concealed behind thick sheets of plywood. To Director Anderson, it appeared that no one had lived in this ghost town for years.

"They say that on any given day in January, you can even lie down in the middle of the street and not be concerned with anyone running you over!" Earl shouted, stepping down from the curb.

"I'm about to freeze to death, so we just might get a chance to test your theory!" the director shouted back into the wind as they approached the narrow, icy sidewalk on the other side of the street.

The director had only eaten at Chowder Head's once last summer, but the experience was so satisfying that he anxiously looked forward to returning. The pub had atmosphere. The well-worn, creaky wooden floor, along with all the whimsical and historic artifacts hanging from the walls and ceiling, created this uniquely inviting environment. Furthermore, the succulent lobster, along with an ice cold blueberry beer, proved to be a truly memorable meal. However, what made this pub so unforgettable were the patrons. Their honesty, hospitality, and quirky down-home sense of humor was intoxicating.

As they approached Chowder Head's, a dull light could be seen radiating from within. However, there appeared to be no movement. The eerie gray shingles, the overhangs supporting dangling daggers of ice, and the frost-covered windows created a cold, unwelcoming facade.

"Christ, Earl, do you think they're even open?" Director Anderson shouted, his teeth chattering as he stomped his feet on the sidewalk, trying to encourage the warm blood to flow to his extremities.

"Undoubtedly," Earl replied, opening the front door to the historic establishment.

Neither the director nor Earl wasted any time entering. They were immediately consumed by the warmth and overwhelmed by all the activity. The pub was jammed, and damn near every square inch of real estate appeared to be occupied. People of all sizes and shapes were cutting up, obviously enjoying an evening on the town. There was shouting, laughter, and smiles all around as each patron fought to resist the dismal effects of the ever-present cabin fever. Waitresses squeezed through the crowd with trays of drinks held high. Earl glanced at all the libations destined for thirsty patrons. Only whiskey and beer could be seen on the flying wooden tray. There were no umbrellas or garnishes. This was obviously a hard-drinking, fun-loving crowd.

"Good gosh!" Director Anderson proclaimed, as a tall, slender woman made her way toward him through the sea of humanity.

"Welcome back to Bar Harbor, Mr. Director," Nieve said with a big smile and a thick New England accent.

"Thank you," Director Anderson replied, grasping her outstretched hand.

"Earl, I assume you and Leslie made it home alright last night," Nieve inquired, after giving Earl a hug.

Earl did not want the director to think that he was out carousing every evening. So, his response appeared to be somewhat delayed.

"Ah…yes," Earl replied, searching for the proper words that only a seasoned diplomat could muster.

However, the damage was done. The director shook his head, pretending not to have heard the conversation. He realized Earl's zest for life and his need to find some escape from the confines of winter.

Nieve looked at Earl with a sense of bewilderment, given what appeared to be a brief moment of confusion.

"Gooood," Nieve replied in a slow but playful manner, mimicking Earl's delayed response. "Johnny has reserved the most unusual table in the house. By the way, where's Leslie tonight?" Nieve asked as she motioned for the two men to follow her toward the table.

"She had to work late," Earl shouted as he and Director Anderson squeezed through the crowd.

At last, the nerve-wracking, twenty-foot journey through the sea of humanity had been completed.

"What would you like to drink?" Nieve asked, as the two men sat down.

"Mr. Director, may I suggest we start the evening with two pints of the finest blueberry ale in all the land," Earl recommended.

"Earl, as much as I enjoyed that ice cold beer last summer, my bones are still frozen, so I'm going to have to decline. Nieve, do you have any single malt whiskeys? Oban, perhaps?" the director inquired.

"Absolutely, straight up or on the rocks, Mr. Director?" Nieve asked.

"Straight up with a splash of water, please. I don't even have the courage to look at an ice cube," the director replied as he briefly considered taking off his heavy overcoat.

"One blueberry beer and one scotch, neat, coming right up," Nieve confirmed, before scurrying off to the bar.

The director took off his glasses and looked down. With his thumb and forefinger, he began massaging his closed eyes adjacent to the bridge of his nose, as if to remove the fatigue from the long day's travel.

Earl couldn't help but notice how exhausted the director appeared. Not only were the physical demands of the job overwhelming, but the emotional strain of being responsible for the nation's security was beyond comprehension. Hopefully, Chowder Head's would provide a much-needed moment of relaxation. As Earl looked around the pub, making every effort not to be caught staring at an exceptionally beautiful blonde, the director put his glasses back on.

"Ha, ha, ha!" the director suddenly roared uncontrollably.

"Mr. Director, what's so funny?" Earl asked although he just knew that he had been nabbed, given his sudden visual indiscretion.

The director then pointed toward Earl. Self-consciously, Earl looked at his clothing and then nonchalantly tugged at his nose, in an effort to release any large visible bats clinging to the thick tufts of hair protruding from his cavernous nostrils. Yet, all efforts to find the source of the director's amusement failed, and the director kept laughing. Earl then realized that the director was not pointing at him, but above him and toward the wall. Earl turned and came face to face with a smiling stuffed wart hog.

"Ooof!" Earl snorted, after being caught by surprise. He had seen the pig on several occasions, but had never had the opportunity to get up close and personal. He then focused on the sign hanging beneath the swine's neck, which read: *Please don't try to teach the pig how to sing. It's a waste of your time, and it annoys the pig!*

Earl howled with laughter after reading the warning decreed on the scraggly beast.

"Now that's funny," Director Anderson chuckled, struggling to regain his composure.

"I should say," Earl said, wiping tears from his eyes. He was pleased that the director was so tickled, and quite relieved that his old friend had not been laughing at him.

"Mr. Director, welcome to Chowder Head's, where most of the women are as large as a moose, as buxom as May West, and as warm as your wallet is thick," a swaying Johnny Croft proclaimed with a grin, his Cuervo Gold sloshing over the rim of his glass.

Johnny and his wife, Gala, owned and ran this infamous pub. Johnny was a jovial forty-year-old transplant from Austin whom time and the harsh elements had ravaged.

"Johnny, that wasn't nice," Gala scolded in a playful tone as she placed her arm around his waist in a gesture that reflected her acceptance of her husband's antics. Gala was a strikingly beautiful thirty-five-year-old native of New England with classic Scandinavian features. Her skin was soft and radiant and whenever she smiled, her whole face lit up. This glow was even more evident after downing a cocktail or two.

"Earl!" Gala shouted, swaying rhythmically in cadence with Johnny. She leaned over and gave him a big hug, followed by a kiss on the cheek.

"Mr. Director, this lovely lady is Gala, Johnny's wife," Earl announced.

"That's wife and wild-husband tamer, Earl," Gala clarified with a big smile. She then made a gesture that left no doubt that she was the one cracking the whip.

"Well, if I were sober, I would probably take offense at your comment," Johnny slurred affectionately as he grabbed his wife from behind.

"Mr. Director, as you recall, Johnny and Gala are the proprietors of this watering hole," Earl reminded his boss.

"Come, my little lobster, we go upstairs. I put your naked body in boiling pot. Jacuzzi just right temperature," Johnny proclaimed lustfully.

"Must watch pinchers and feelers," Gala cautioned, snapping her hands in a claw-like manner.

"We need many babies. Most exciting—we go quickly!" Johnny announced with a snicker and a gleam in his eye as they scurried off without another word.

"My, Earl, I would say that Johnny and Gala are rather colorful characters," the director observed as he took another sip of scotch. "You must forgive them, Mr. Director. Come winter in this northern latitude, the air becomes thin, the nights dark and cold, and the mating rituals follow tribal lines. If they had not been in heat, I feel certain they would have said goodbye," Earl confessed.

"Well, I am not sure what tribe those two are from, but I get the feeling that Johnny is going to show Gala his happy crab," the director joked.

Earl laughed at the director's unexpected remark.

"Gentlemen, may I get you another round?" Nieve asked.

"Absolutely," Earl and the director responded in unison.

"How about something to eat?" Nieve queried.

"Lobster," they replied in unison again. Nieve gave each a strange look, as if she was having trouble understanding the customs of those who hailed from the southern United States.

"Oookaaay, may I recommend two one-and-one-half pounders each?" Nieve suggested.

"That sounds irresistible, Nieve," the director said.

"I agree. Please make it two orders, Nieve," Earl confirmed.

As promised, the second round of drinks arrived in short order. Earl took a swig from his ice cold beer and then looked at the director. Suddenly, Earl looked past the director and began squinting, as if attempting to focus. He was mesmerized by the elk behind the director. The massive twelve-pointer was so low on the wall that it appeared to be grazing on the director's head. Earl could actually make out one small, light gray, lichen-like tuft clinging to the director's barren, shiny scalp. As Earl's powers of observation appeared to be improving, he attributed this aberration to the hops. He looked down at his bottle of ale and thought, "Damn, this is good beer!"

"Earl, are you all right?" the director asked.

Earl appeared startled at first and then slowly responded. "I'm not sure, Mr. Director. Forgive me for staring, but it appears that the elk behind you is nibbling on your head."

"Earl, have you lost your mind?" the director asked, resisting the urge to turn around. Instead, he blindly reached above his head, only to encounter the broad, cold, fuzzy nose of a giant elk.

"Well, obviously we're both losing our minds. I trust that snout belongs to an elk and not our waitress," the director chuckled.

Earl was so shocked by the director's humorous comment that he choked on his beer after the swig went down the wrong pipe. As he coughed, struggling for air, frothy ale shot out of both nostrils.

Unbeknownst to them, Nieve had emerged from the crowd with their dinners and had undoubtedly heard the comments.

"Gentlemen, you must realize that the female species is endowed with alluring charms and blessed with excellent hearing. So, let me assure you both that any similarities between me and that elk are purely coincidental," she huffed. "Now, here are your damn lobsters!" Nieve added rather sarcastically, as she pounded the metal seafood platters down on the table.

Earl and the director suddenly looked sad. It was as if they had been caught misbehaving at school, and the evil Catholic nun had just slapped their hands with a heavy wooden ruler.

Earl immediately sprang to his feet and placed his arm around Nieve, squeezing her tight.

"Nieve, you are breathtakingly beautiful. We would never say anything to hurt you, or the elk for that matter," Earl apologized as he handed Nieve a one hundred dollar bill, which was most likely compliments of the TARP slush fund.

"That's right," the director chimed in as Nieve quickly stuffed the charitable contribution into her pocket.

"Besides, we were talking about the rather plump waitress at the Thirsty Whale and not you, my love," Earl assured Nieve.

"That had better be the case gentlemen, or snip, snip," Nieve smiled, making a Bobbitt-like scissor motion with the index and middle finger of her right hand. The symbolic gesture made it abundantly clear that any dangling appendages were vulnerable to attack. Earl and the director cringed at the thought. "I know you were. Enjoy the lobster," Nieve conceded enthusiastically before strutting off, happy as a clam.

"Good recovery, Earl!"

"Thank you, Mr. Director. With the threat of castration a real possibility, one must become quite creative in short order," Earl sighed with a sense of relief.

"Without question, creativity is an absolute necessity in our profession, Earl."

The gloom surrounding the table suddenly lifted and both men smiled as they stared at the cherry red, piping hot crustaceans. Steam billowed from the bottom feeders and a salty aroma filled the air. There was no time to attach the funky plastic bibs that came with each meal, clothing be damned! All conversation ceased, and for minutes all that could be heard was the cracking of shells, followed by the splash of the sweet meat hitting vats of drawn butter. As soon as the tender, succulent morsels hit the palate, the taste buds triggered the pleasure centers in the brain, eliciting subtle, yet uncontrollable *ums* and *ahs*.

"Just look at all the meat on this claw, Mr. Director," Earl said, holding up his prize. "There's nothing like a Maine lobster. The meat just melts in your mouth."

"I can't tell you how much I've looked forward to this meal, Earl, but I am stuffed," the director said, shoving away the platter piled high with empty shells.

"Mr. Director, you must find room for the blueberry pie," Earl insisted.

"Earl, I just can't," Director Anderson replied as he cleaned his hands with a lemon-soaked cloth provided for such an occasion.

"Excellent job, boys!" an enthusiastic Nieve commented, retrieving the remnants of the cold-water shellfish. "May I get you anything else?" Clearly, the misunderstanding from earlier in the evening had been forgotten.

"Two B&B's straight up and two blueberry pies a-la-mode, please," Earl requested politely.

Nieve was off like a shot before the director had a chance to respond. "Oh no, Earl, I'm ready to pop."

Suddenly, the loud music, which had been blaring overhead, began to fade, and a guitarist appeared on a small stage in the corner of the pub.

"Welcome to Chowder Head's!" he said, the microphone screeching in an ear-piercing tone. "For those of you who don't know me, my name is Rick," the performer said in his raspy, tobacco-ravaged voice. "For those of you not from Baaa-Ha-Baaa, let me be the first to inform you that you're probably lost. The reality is that there is no reality, especially in this town. So drink hardy and tip well. Now, here's a sea chantey for all you thirsty lobstermen in the crowd," Rick announced, before taking a swig of beer.

High, high up she rises, high, high up she rises, high, high up she rises early in the morning.

What do you do with a drunken sailor, what do you do with a drunken sailor, what do you do with a drunken sailor early in the morning?

Throw him in the brig until he's sober, throw him in the brig until he's sober...

"Now there's a catchy tune that reminds me of our rather unruly days in the Philippines," Earl declared as Nieve placed the desserts and the after-dinner drinks on the table.

"Please don't go there, Earl," Director Anderson begged as Leslie suddenly appeared.

"Hello, Leslie," Nieve said enthusiastically.

"Leslie, thanks for coming," Earl said as he stood and gave his chief-of-operations a kiss on the cheek.

"Yes, what a pleasant surprise," Director Anderson added, standing as well.

"May I bring you anything?" Nieve asked.

"No, no thank you, Nieve. I have to get back to work, but thanks anyway," Leslie responded politely.

"Personally, Leslie, if I were you, I would consider sitting at another table. These two have not been on their best behavior," Nieve whispered.

"Somehow, I can believe that, Nieve," Leslie replied with a smile before Nieve faded into the crowd.

"Leslie, please reconsider. Get something to eat or a drink, perhaps," the director pleaded.

"No, thank you, Mr. Director; by the way, how were the lobsters?" Leslie asked in a rather monotone voice, which was unusual for the vivacious young lady. It was as if she was struggling to be polite. Earl sensed immediately that Leslie was distracted.

"Excellent," the director said cheerfully.

"Good," Leslie responded unenthusiastically.

"Leslie, I know you very well. There is something on your mind. What is it?" Earl inquired.

"Well, I didn't want to ruin your evening," Leslie said, before briefly pausing. "The autopsy results are back."

"I knew it!" Earl shouted as both men leaned forward across the table.

The sobriety was instantaneous, and the enjoyment from the previous few hours, a distant memory. Earl and Director Anderson focused on Leslie's every word.

"The blue skin discoloration was due to a color pigment, ferric hexacynanoferrate, which was discovered by a German painter, Heinrich Diesbach, in seventeen-o-four. It was prized for its intense blue color and subsequently used by artists in paintings for hundreds of years," Leslie explained.

"Leslie, what's the bottom-line?" Earl insisted.

"It is essentially a combination of cyanide and iron which goes by the name 'Prussian Blue,'" Leslie continued.

"I still don't understand the correlation," Earl complained.

"More specifically, Prussian Blue is the key ingredient in a cocktail that binds to radioactive isotopes and draws these deadly elements from the body, thus providing the maximum protection from the devastating effects of a dirty bomb," she declared, much to Earl and the director's astonishment.

"Good God!" Earl gasped, suddenly realizing the implications.

"Of course!" Director Anderson exclaimed. "Earl, just as potassium iodide pills were used to protect the Russians against radioactive iodine emitted from the Chernobyl meltdown, Prussian Blue offers some degree of protection against Cesium-one-thirty-seven and, I believe, thallium, both of which would be prevalent after either a nuclear reactor accident, or the explosion of a dirty bomb," Director Anderson recalled, reflecting back to his nuclear engineering days.

"In other words, the terrorists have reached our shores with one, if not several dirty bombs!" Earl declared.

"It would appear so. Most importantly, we have to assume that these dirty bombs are leaking," Director Anderson surmised.

"But if the Asian sailors died of radiation poisoning, why didn't the Prussian Blue antidote save their lives?" Earl asked.

"Simply because of the proximity to and the time spent near the weapons," the director explained.

"Exactly. In fact, Prussian Blue was used successfully in the nineteen-eighties on several hundred nuclear power workers in Brazil who were accidentally contaminated with cesium," Leslie replied.

"Leslie, what exactly was in the report?" Director Anderson inquired.

"The forensic pathologist concluded that each man had absorbed well over six thousand rads. The description of his findings and the events surrounding their deaths was quite graphic. In his words, their skin was scorched, and all suffered third-degree burns. As their bodies oozed precious fluid from the open wounds, they experienced intractable vomiting and excruciating pain as all the internal organs were roasted. Shortly thereafter, blood vessels ruptured and began to bleed into the belly, lungs, and out of every orifice. As the sailors cooked from the inside out and the outside in, massive amounts of tissue died. Each became septic and oxygen-starved. Apparently, all were conscious and most likely aware of the impending doom as they gasped for air, like fish out of water, dying," Leslie relayed in horrifying detail.

"It appears that our worst nightmare is unfolding. The terrorists now have the means to destroy cities and kill millions of Americans. Now, without question, the national security level must be elevated to Red. I need to inform the president immediately," Director Anderson insisted.

CHAPTER 17

REX PULLED THE FORMER pride of the German automotive giant into the carport. An intense, metallic grinding sound emanating from the engine was amplified as it bounced off of the ceiling and walls in the confined space.

"I never thought we would make it home," Rex shouted just prior to turning off the ignition.

"I had no doubt; the Benz has always been reliable," Trissy replied as the engine kept chugging with such force that the vehicle rocked violently, as if in a death roll.

"I'm tempted to shoot the beast, just to put it out of its misery," Rex offered as he and Trissy were jerked back and forth by the possessed motorcar.

"That's not funny, Rex," Trissy scolded while holding tightly onto the door handle with her right hand and center console with her left.

Suddenly, there was a loud pop, followed by one last clunk. Without question, the Mercedes had come to a rest. Now, all that could be heard was a horrendous hissing sound as steam billowed from underneath the contorted hood. The engine had finally died, and by all accounts it had been a horribly agonizing death.

"Well, too late," Rex announced, opening his door and stepping out of the vehicle.

Trissy eased herself up and onto the passenger car seat. She put one hand on her crushed, nonfunctional door and leaped over it and out of the vehicle.

"Oh—my—God!" Trissy gasped in disbelief, as she swiftly moved her hands to her face while surveying the damage her beautiful car had sustained. The sleek, powerful sports car had been reduced to a molten, twisted, rectangular block of steel.

"Well, I think we should call this code. There's no way that the automotive gods could save this patient," Rex surmised, shaking his head in disgust as he unlocked the side door to their modest, ranch-style home.

"Well, at least we're alive. If the terrorists had caught us, they would've chopped us up into little pieces and fed us to the crawfish," Trissy replied as Rex slammed the door behind them and bolted it shut.

"There's no doubt we would have met with an untimely demise if it weren't for your quick thinking," Rex concluded as he turned on the lights. Out of habit, he threw the keys to Trissy's deceased pride and joy onto the kitchen table.

"Trissy, check all the windows and doors. Make sure they're locked and that the locks haven't been tampered with, while I search the house for any unwanted guests," Rex requested, pulling Trissy's .38 from the kitchen drawer. He immediately opened the chamber and spun the barrel to ensure that the weapon was fully loaded. With the weapon leveled, Rex cautiously surveyed the entire house, while Trissy verified the internal safety and drew all the curtains shut. Satisfied that their home was secure and that no intruders were lurking within, Rex walked into the master bathroom and opened a shallow linen-lined door revealing a hidden closet. In this closet was the security system, with monitors and a recorder, as well as a large safe, which housed a small arsenal. He quickly reviewed the images that the outside cameras had captured over the last twenty-four hours.

"No visitors," Rex concluded, turning his attention to the safe. He quickly twisted the combination dial to the left and then the right until a loud click was heard. Rex turned the long, thick metal handle clockwise, and the massive steel door swung open, revealing an impressive array of weaponry, which had been collected over a lifetime.

"Ah, yes," Rex whispered with great satisfaction. There were his father's old hunting rifles and the Winchester his dad had given him for his twelfth birthday. There were knives, pistols, numerous semi-automatic weapons, and enough ammunition to withstand an assault from a small army.

"Come to Papa," Rex insisted, reaching for a black waterproof bag and a backpack. Stowed within these items were toys from his Navy SEAL days. The waterproof bag contained night vision goggles, his wearable from 5VS, which would not only continuously monitor but also relay all five vital signs, a fourteen-inch razor-sharp Bowie knife concealed in a black plastic holster with leg straps, and a Beretta with a silencer and one hundred rounds of ammunition. However, the most impressive items were contained within the small backpack. They included ten pounds of plastic explosives with frequency-specific detonators, a Doppler radar with GPS, a heat-recognition scanner, and a laptop-sized computer, which housed communication equipment so sophisticated that it afforded a quick and easy satellite uplink. Rex's eyes lit up as he surveyed the collection. His joy was suddenly tempered as old memories of special operations came rushing back. He could visualize each mission and the faces of his fallen comrades who had given their lives in defense of our great nation.

Rex shut his eyes. Moments later, the visions were gone.

"Christ," he whispered as he wiped beads of sweat from his forehead. "I'm getting as bad as the Foxxman with these damn flashbacks."

The black waterproof bag and backpack would remain hidden for now. However, he reached for his favorite assault rifle and a fully loaded magazine clip, slamming the clip into the rifle until he heard the familiar snap.

"It feels so good to be able to defend yourself," Rex whispered as he grabbed the heavy metal door to swing it shut. Surprisingly, as the door began to move, it emitted a hauntingly deep growling sound. It was as if the vault was resisting closure. However, after a loud thud and a spinning of the dial, his arsenal was once again secure.

Rex had returned to his roots. The doctor had reverted back into a warrior. The healer now found it necessary to take lives in order to protect Trissy.

"Rex, are you alright?" Trissy shouted from the living room.

"Yes, dear!" Rex shouted back, closing the door that concealed the hidden closet.

"Are you sure?" Trissy shouted as Rex placed Trissy's .38 under his pillow.

"Absolutely," Rex replied, entering the living room where he found Trissy sitting on the sofa.

"What took you so long?"

"I thought we could use a bit more firepower," Rex replied as he gently slapped the palm of his hand against the butt of his assault rifle.

"Good thinking. Well, I'm happy to report that my mission has been accomplished. All doors and windows are secured, and I set the house alarm," Trissy stated emphatically.

"Excellent."

"By the way, where's my gun?" Trissy asked.

"I stashed it under my pillow, just in case any radical Muslim night crawlers come calling tonight," Rex replied.

"Rex, there's no way in the world that tonight's encounter was road rage. Those men were trying to kill us. Why? I don't know, but I would assume that it has something to do with you contacting the CDC and the NSA," Trissy concluded.

"Well, those goons were certainly not trick-or-treaters, because Halloween was last week," Rex joked.

"Rex, be serious," Trissy cautioned.

"Unfortunately, I agree. And, that reminds me, I need to check my email to see if those bureaucracy-burdened agencies have had a chance to respond. If not, I intend to bird-dog them until they do," Rex assured his wife, as he walked toward his office.

"Please, not tonight Rex," Trissy pleaded. Recognizing the concern in her voice, Rex stopped immediately and turned around.

"Personally, I believe Mean and Evil turned us in to the local Al Qaeda."

"You do rather enjoy picking on those two, don't you?" Trissy questioned, already knowing the answer.

"There is absolutely nothing I would enjoy more than roasting those two buzzards. And that's exactly what I intend to do, once they're feeling better," Rex threatened.

"Speaking about feeling better, I surely hope Wanda is all right," Trissy confided as her thoughts suddenly turned to her dear friend and fellow nurse.

"I'm sure she's fine," Rex replied, in an effort to ease her fears. "Now, it's been a rather harrowing day, my love. Given the fact that the Benz was demolished and we nearly lost our lives, I'd say a good stiff nightcap is in order. May I get you a drink?" Rex asked, walking toward the bar nestled within the butler's pantry.

"Rex, I still don't feel one hundred percent, but a small glass of Yellow Tail might help calm my nerves," Trissy replied, while turning on the TV.

Rex returned with a glass of Chardonnay and a Wild Turkey on the rocks. He handed Trissy her drink and plopped down on the sofa next to her.

Rex swirled the whiskey in his glass as Trissy settled on the news channel.

"Ah, I like Blitzkrieg Bob," Rex said, voicing his approval. "Could you turn up the volume please?"

"This is BB reporting from Dover Air Force Base. As you know, the *John C. Stennis* Carrier Group was decimated in the Persian Gulf three days ago."

As the battle-hardened reporter spoke, the images on the screen reflected video shot earlier in the day. The footage gave a dramatic account of the massive destruction and reflected the tremendous loss of life. From the air, a fast frigate could be seen in the crystal clear water, totally submerged, resting on the seabed, while several other ships lay on the ocean floor, only their masts penetrating their watery grave. Three other ships, including the carrier *Stennis*, had run aground. Black smoke was trickling skyward from the carrier and one of the frigates.

Rex and Trissy watched in silence, horrified at the sight.

Blitzkrieg Bob, "BB," continued with his analysis as the cameraman scanned the hangar and the runway.

"This unprovoked attack represents the worst defeat our naval forces have ever suffered, with the exception of Pearl Harbor. Nearly a thousand lives were lost. Tonight, the first wave of our brave servicemen returned to American soil. Four C-one-thirty transport planes landed approximately one hour ago. Each flag-draped casket was ceremoniously taken into the large hanger behind me as the band played 'Navy, Blue, and Gold.' It has truly been a gut-wrenching sight. In all, there were seven hundred and ninety-four sailors and one hundred and nintey-eight marines killed. Fifty-four sailors are still missing, and are presumed dead. This is indeed a very sad day for all Americans. This is Blitzkrieg Bob reporting live from Dover Air Force Base in Delaware. Now, we take you back to Wendy Wolf," the reporter concluded.

"This story, just in. The president intends to raise the threat level to Red in the morning. Fox News has uncovered that the NSA is concerned with regard to a sudden increase in communication that contains specific references to targets in the United States. Also, an influential source has revealed that pathology and infectious disease experts at the CDC remain troubled by the six Asian sailors who were found dead in the Gulf of Mexico several days ago. An eyewitness who found one of the bodies that had washed ashore stated that the body was bloated and had an eerie blue tinge, although most of the skin appeared to have been eaten away. She also added that the man's features were grotesquely distorted."

Rex and Trissy leaned forward and listened intently to the story.

"It now appears that there may be six additional sailors who were afflicted by the same disease. Apparently, they were evaluated and treated in a small hospital in Louisiana. All died shortly after admission. The CDC and the National Security Agency, along with both federal and local authorities, are aggressively pursuing this lead," Wendy Wolf concluded, before Trissy turned off the TV.

"Wahoo!" Rex shouted with joy.

"Yes, the cavalry is coming!" Trissy screamed, jumping from the sofa. "I'd say that your correspondence has certainly stirred Carencrow's pot of ill repute," Trissy announced with pride. "Oh

Christ, Rex, look at the time. It's almost twelve o'clock and we have to work tomorrow."

"Come on, Cinderella, your carriage awaits," Rex said, grabbing his assault rifle. He took Trissy's hand and they danced toward their bedroom.

CHAPTER 18

THE NIGHT AIR WAS cold and unusually still. GeeHad and Martha Mulch were at Rula's finishing dinner. All was going according to plan, and GeeHad was confident that Allah and the Islamic State would be pleased with his contributions. The logs in the fireplace had been reduced to ash and were smoldering as the last of the patrons put on their coats. The ever-present Chum was behind the bar, counting the night's take. When she was satisfied that every dollar had been accounted for, she poured herself a large snifter of Louis XIV brandy.

"Ah," she sighed as her favorite nightcap saturated her taste buds and trickled down her throat. "My, that's good." However, her satisfaction was short-lived, because she could see GeeHad's grossly distorted image through the curvature of the glass.

"Damn he's ugly, even by Asian standards," Chum moaned.

However, looks and manners be damned; it was time for their volatile relationship to be set aside, for there was much to do. As she slowly made her way over to GeeHad's table, Chum reminded herself that they had a common goal—the destruction of the United States of America.

"The meal was acceptable, Chum," GeeHad remarked, with little sincerity as he picked food from between his snarly teeth, wiping the remains on the white linen tablecloth.

"Thank you, GeeHad, but next time you use napkin or shirt sleeve," Chum insisted angrily in broken English, looking at mounds of saliva and splatterings of partially digested food littering the table. She knew that this desert rat was never one to chew with his mouth closed.

"Hum," GeeHad growled.

"The meal was excellent, Chum," Martha quickly added, in an attempt to help defuse the rapidly escalating tension, although kindness and compliments made her stomach churn.

"GeeHad, would you care for an after-dinner drink?" Martha asked, as an angry Chum took another sip of her brandy.

"Yes, I believe I would," GeeHad replied arrogantly.

"Ping, two brandies for our guests," Chum shouted. "And, make sure you use the good stuff," she added, with a hint of sarcasm.

"As you wish, Madame Chum," Ping replied, knowing full well that he was to pour the rotgut Louisiana Bayou Brandy from Bubba & Bubba Embalmers, Limited.

"Pong, place another log on the fire," Chum ordered as the young muscular Korean busboy nodded respectfully.

"What in the hell are you running here, Chum, a restaurant or a panda farm?" GeeHad asked sarcastically. Chum wondered what he had meant by the snide remark.

"Um, um," Martha chuckled. "Yes, a brandy sounds wonderful," Martha added, struggling to hold back her laughter.

As Ping walked quickly toward the bar, Chum felt she had to struggle, once again, to forge a truce.

"Your cause is great, GeeHad. How is your work progressing?" Chum asked the clandestine Muslim terrorist. She awaited his response with keen interest. As a colonel in the North Korean army, Chum was tasked with not only gathering intelligence, but also implementing the plans envisioned by her government. And, in this case, her orders were clear. America must pay dearly for the embargoes and the multitude of crimes committed against her people.

"All is well. The liquid death that your countrymen provided will be put to good use. With all the pain and suffering the United States has inflicted upon your people, rendering the Atlantic seaboard and the entire west coast uninhabitable should prove just retribution."

"Excellent," Chum said, her cold, dark eyes making a futile attempt to glow.

"Islam is great, for we have the power to control the destiny of millions," GeeHad raged, raising his voice to emphasize his words.

Martha smiled and held her chin high. GeeHad's ruthless follower felt empowered by his declaration of death. Although an infidel herself, she had every intention of riding this Muslim power train to glory.

"I admire your commitment, GeeHad, but you must never forget the contributions which Buddhism has brought to the world. Our religions face an evil enemy. Together we will rise and become even more powerful. Christians and Jews will be slaughtered and, eventually, we shall rule the world," Chum predicted as Ping placed the after-dinner drinks on the table.

Not in my lifetime, Chum. Even Buddha is on borrowed time, GeeHad thought to himself as he took a sip of brandy before spitting it out.

"Damn what in the hell are you pouring? This is nasty," GeeHad complained.

"It's an acquired taste," Chum replied as Martha wisely shoved her glass to the center of the table just as GeeHad's phone rang.

"GeeHad," he answered, at first in English but then, unexpectedly, continued in Arabic. Chum was unable to speak the language but listened intently, studying GeeHad's facial expressions. Arabic, she felt, was such a harsh language, but the inflection in GeeHad's voice was now clearly one of anger. Moments later GeeHad hung up. His face was expressionless. It was clear he was collecting his thoughts.

"Abdul and Repulse are dead," GeeHad announced without emotion. "Their bodies were retrieved from the Marksville Bayou on the outskirts of town only moments ago."

"Oh no!" Martha gasped.

"They were instructed to follow Dr. Bent and his wife home from the hospital, and then keep his residence under surveillance. Each was well aware that I had retracted the death sentence," GeeHad replied, coming to grips with the reality that his men had defied his explicit orders.

"How unfortunate," Chum said, before polishing off her brandy.

"They could have jeopardized our plans and years of work. But their deaths pose a new problem," GeeHad said, slowly stroking his chin. He remained silent for a few moments, assessing his options. "Chum, it appears that we are going to need your help once again," GeeHad announced.

"In what way?" Chum asked suspiciously.

"I need two of your men for an operation, which will take place early tomorrow morning," GeeHad requested politely.

"And just what is the objective of this mission?" Chum inquired, her tone clearly reflecting her doubts.

GeeHad looked at her, sensing her apprehension. He was not sure how much information he should reveal. However, given the importance of this mission, he felt it was imperative to give her the chilling facts.

"As you know, six of your honorable countrymen from the *Il-sung* were brought to Carencrow Regional several days ago. Their deaths have aroused much suspicion, and Dr. Bent has been adding fuel to the fire by contacting the CDC and the National Security Agency. It is only a matter of hours before officials from these agencies and the local authorities descend upon our peaceful town," he shared candidly as Chum's weather-beaten face took on an air of concern.

"That bastard could jeopardize everything my country has worked so hard to achieve! Get Bent! The doctor needs to die!" Colonel Chum growled decisively, clenching her fists.

"No, absolutely not!" GeeHad shouted, recalling how his position on this issue had changed since his meeting with Mohammad in Whiskey Bay several days ago.

"We would all like to see him dead. However, his death would arouse even more suspicion, and probably result in an expanded search, which would surely disrupt, and, most likely, uncover our operations," Martha emphasized.

"Dr. Bent is a thorn in our side, but our best strategy in dealing with this threat is to implicate him as the mastermind of some insidious plot to destroy America," GeeHad proposed.

"Just what are you suggesting?" Chum inquired.

"What we have in mind is planting several vials of last season's unused WMDs in his home."

Chum's jaw dropped at the implications of this diabolical plot. Her mind raced to evaluate the benefits and the risks of such a plan as GeeHad continued to sell her on his scheme.

"In fact, our brilliant engineers successfully combined anthrax with the Ebola virus. I just happened to have access to several thousand vials," GeeHad announced with pride.

"My God!" Martha blurted.

"Unfortunately, the tremendous success we had in the laboratory did not translate into the number of deaths in the field that we had desired. Still, uncovering this weapon will be the shot heard around the world. The effect will be devastating," GeeHad assured Colonel Chum.

"Dr. Bent will be thrown into a small, dark cell where he will rot," Martha said with a smile.

"Yes, as the infidels tremble, praying for mercy," GeeHad laughed.

"Where in the world did you get your hands on anthrax?" Chum asked, more and more fascinated with the plot.

"If you must know, it was obtained from our Russian friends via Iran. However, we were disappointed with the results. Hundreds of pounds of the spores were distributed via the U.S. Postal Service, but only a few buildings were evacuated, and only a handful of Americans killed," GeeHad disclosed.

"So our intelligence was right! We always suspected that your group was behind the release of the anthrax," Chum replied.

"Ultimately we increased the virulence of the strain in order to create a more effective means through which to inflict terror. However, although much improved, last year's creation also fell short of expectations. I have in my possession the only remaining vials. I believe the Americans would refer to this as an end-of-year clearance sale," GeeHad responded without emotion.

"It's going to be tough convincing the authorities that the few small glass vials you plant were collected and are to be distributed by some obscure renegade physician. What if the authorities realize it's a frame-up?" Chum remarked, playing the devil's advocate.

"The Americans are not very smart. Give them a few bits of information and they will create a story which fits the facts and justifies their analysis. Yesterday, emails were sent to our operatives in Canada and Mexico from Saudi Arabia thanking Dr. Bent for all of his efforts in our struggle. We know that the traffic to these addresses is closely monitored. It is only a matter of time before the National Security Agency links our email with his correspondence and the reported deaths of the sailors. Our parting gifts need to be planted in Dr. Bent's home first thing this morning, after he and his wife have left for work," GeeHad rationalized with unwavering confidence.

"With the unexpected deaths of GeeHad's freedom fighters, we need to recruit a few of your men," Martha explained.

"I see. I assume they will provide security and other means of assistance for your raid," Chum rationalized.

"Exactly. Furthermore, from his own computer, correspondence will be returned to our friends in Saudi Arabia, and funds transferred to named and numbered accounts he controls. The hunter will soon become the hunted. Dr. Bent will be captured, tried for treason, and hung by the neck until dead," GeeHad concluded with great satisfaction.

"GeeHad, the plan sounds brilliant, but what if the authorities already have his house under surveillance, and your deception is uncovered? Furthermore, what if Dr. Bent knows more than we think, and the search for local coconspirators is initiated?" Chum wanted to know.

"Chum, the what-ifs are a crock of shit! We must be aggressive if we are to salvage our mission, which is to unfold only days from now. Can't you see that?" GeeHad shot back, his tone belittling.

One could feel the tension in the air as Ping brought Chum another glass of brandy. Just then, GeeHad's cell phone rang again.

"Yes," GeeHad answered with a heavy Middle Eastern accident, followed by a brief conversation in Arabic. It was clearly evident that he was pleased as he flipped the phone shut and placed it back into his coat pocket.

Chum swirled her brandy and made every effort to control her anger. As she lifted the glass to her lips, she promised herself that when this mission was complete, she would strongly consider cutting GeeHad's throat. She smiled as she thought of the dumb expression he would have on his hideous face as her knife sliced through his windpipe, severing major blood vessels, before sawing through his cervical spine.

"Martha, ensure that Dr. Bent's fingerprints, which Teresa has gathered for us, are on each vial. And make sure Johnny Cinch has the CD with all the prearranged, verifiable communication and financial information. Let's not leave anything to chance."

"Yes, GeeHad, it will be done. Rest assured that all aspects of the operation will be executed with precision. Additionally, Dr. Lyons is standing by to ensure that Dr. Bent leaves his house promptly. If all goes well, we shall be in his home by o-six-forty-five and out by o-seven-hundred," Martha replied.

"Excellent."

"Now, Chum, we need two of your best men to stand guard as Martha and Teresa complete their assigned tasks," GeeHad again requested. He was now confident that he had made his point and Chum would cooperate. Yet, she hesitated before responding.

"Very well, GeeHad," Chum uttered, her tone subdued. "Ping and Pong will assist Ms. Mulch on this mission."

"Thank you, Chum," GeeHad muttered as Martha Mulch jotted down Dr. Bent's address.

"We will meet them at this location tomorrow morning at o-six-forty," Ms. Mulch said as she handed Pong a cocktail napkin with the necessary information.

As GeeHad stood to leave, Ping handed him a check.

"I suppose you would not want to consider comping this meal, Chum?" GeeHad asked, opening the small black folder and examining the bill.

"Nothing is free," Chum replied coldly as GeeHad placed his credit card inside the small black rectangular folder.

"I see that you even charged for the poisoned brandies," GeeHad remarked.

"Thank you, Colonel Chum. It was a wonderful evening," Martha said as GeeHad signed the bill and retrieved his credit card. There was no response. Chum sat silently at the now abandoned table, enjoying her drink.

"Although she reluctantly agreed to help us tomorrow, I believe Chum is rapidly outgrowing her usefulness," Martha whispered as she put on her coat.

"I fully agree," GeeHad announced with great pleasure before turning around to take one last look at Chum, who appeared to be deep in thought, staring at the fire.

Moments later, the beauty of the dying embers had been enhanced by the flames from a newly placed oak log. However, Chum's concentration was soon broken, as she was momentarily startled by the ominous shadows cast on the walls as her Arab guest and his companion departed.

"Ping, let GeeHad proceed with his plans, and then kill Dr. Bent," the North Korean field operative ordered.

CHAPTER 19

THE ALARM ERUPTED PRECISELY at 0530. However, the rude awakening had little effect.

The incessant *beep, beep…* seemed to drag on for an eternity before eliciting any response.

"Oh, Christ," Rex moaned, struggling to hit the snooze bar several minutes later. "Where in the hell is that damn thing?"

Beep, beep… slowly started to fade as Rex left the bedroom and staggered down the hall.

With one swift twisting motion, the crystallized Colombian Gold was unleashed. He never knew how much of the robust grounds to put into the cup, and his recipe changed frequently. However, this morning two rounded scoops seemed appropriate, and he knew that Trissy would never complain.

The hot water hit the condensed grounds, and the aroma instantaneously overwhelmed his senses with surreal pleasure.

"Wow," Rex exclaimed as the escaping vapors slapped him in the face. "What a wake-up call!"

He inhaled deeply. Rex always enjoyed the smell of coffee more than the taste.

With the stimulants mixed to his ever-changing specifications, Rex took two sips. As he walked down the hall toward the bedroom, he could hear the time beast buzzing.

"Trissy, wake up honey," Rex whispered, setting the coffee on her nightstand before turning off the alarm. "Trissy, wake up," Rex requested as he gave Trissy a gentle nudge.

"Ummm," she moaned quietly, not stirring. Slowly, the pillow she had so carefully positioned over her head began to move. "Rex, I think I've relapsed. I don't feel very well," she groaned as her face emerged from underneath the down-filled sanctuary.

"Cover your eyes," Rex insisted, turning on her nightlight.

"Oh, that's bright," Trissy moaned as her eyelashes fluttered. She squinted, then immediately sought refuge under her pillow. Although his glimpse was brief, Rex could clearly see that Trissy's face was a fiery red, her eyelids quite edematous, and the whites of her eyes injected with engorged blood vessels.

"Your color looks bad," Rex added, feeling for the radial artery on her wrist. Thankfully, her pulse was strong and bounding, but not racing.

"Thanks, Rex," Trissy mumbled.

"Trissy, you're burning up. Are you nauseous?" Rex asked, becoming more concerned.

"Yes, in fact, if I had the strength to make it to the bathroom, I think I would toss my cookies," Trissy gagged.

"Trissy, let me take you back to the hospital. You need to be admitted," Rex recommended, gently rubbing her back.

"No."

"Please."

"No," his stubborn German wife answered emphatically.

"I think you'd bounce back much quicker with some fluids," Rex added as a last-ditch effort to convince Trissy of the most prudent medical course.

"No means no!" Trissy growled in frustration.

"I assume that 'perhaps,' or even 'maybe,' are also out of the question," Rex replied, wondering why his wife would not heed his advice.

"No means, HELL no!" Trissy emphasized with increasing conviction as her body started to shake and beads of sweat rolled down her forehead.

"Well then, I'll call Sheila and let her know that you're not going to be able to make it in this morning," Rex conceded, knowing he'd lost this skirmish.

"Rex, tell them that I'll try to come in later if I'm feeling better," Trissy said, lifting her pillow briefly to look at her husband.

"Trissy, I think you're out of commission for today. It's bed rest, Tylenol, and fluids for you, young lady. Now, would you care for a shot of Phenergan to relieve the nausea?" Rex asked.

"Please," Trissy moaned.

"I'll be right back," Rex insisted, before scurrying off toward the kitchen.

He soon returned with a large glass of ice, a thirty-two-ounce bottle of Gatorade, and twenty-five milligrams of Phenergan he had drawn up into a syringe.

"Here you go, Trissy," Rex said as he poured her a cold glass of the red liquid teeming with electrolytes. "Unfortunately, this stuff looks better than it tastes."

"Now, which cheek shall it be?" Rex asked, setting the glass and the plastic bottle on the nightstand.

"Rex, I'm dying. Shoot first and ask questions later," Trissy pleaded.

The covers came down, exposing her gorgeous body.

"Even your backside is warm and red, Trissy," Rex said, his thoughts suddenly flashing back to the similarities in the physical findings Wanda, Mean, and Evil had displayed.

As difficult as it was to visualize Wanda, Mean, and Evil at this time in the morning, Rex felt that there just had to be a simple explanation. Trissy and the other nurses became sick at virtually the same time. Clearly they had been exposed to the same substance, which left their skin fiery red and edematous. Each nurse ran fever and complained of myalgias and arthralgias, in addition to experiencing intractable nausea and vomiting. However, unlike the Asian sailors, the symptoms and physical findings were not as severe. There were no bullous or weeping lesions, and no denuded areas reflecting where thick sheets of skin had sloughed off, exposing bleeding subcutaneous tissue. There had to be a common denominator.

"Rex, are you still there?" Trissy moaned as her nausea intensified.

"Yes, sorry. I drifted off for a moment," Rex apologized as he wiped the alcohol pad over Trissy's gluteus minimus.

"What were you thinking about?" Trissy moaned, her voice muffled.

"I was thinking about what you, Wanda, and the buzzards had in common with the sailors. Either you all have been exposed to a bacterial or chemical agent, or possibly some genetically modified virus," Rex replied, uncapping the needle and clearing the air from the syringe.

"Rex, it's a simple virus."

"Well, not that I'd want to cause any alarm, but simple viruses have been known to launch pandemics, killing millions over the centuries. Okay, Trissy, here comes the stick and the burn," Rex said, burying the needle deep into her muscle. The potent medicine was injected quickly and the needle retracted. Trissy never moved.

"Burn," Rex whispered as the graphic word kept reverberating through his mind, like an echo in an endless canyon. Rex pulled back Trissy's beautiful hair and kissed her on the cheek. "Sweet dreams, my love. I'll check on you later. Your pistol is under my pillow, and the rifle is leaning against the night stand," Rex reminded her.

"Don't forget to lock the doors and set the alarm," Trissy reminded him.

"Yes, dear," Rex replied reactively, although he had not heard what she had said.

Within twenty minutes Rex was showered, shaved, and dressed. As usual, it was green scrubs and Nike sneakers. *What a dress code*, Rex thought, as he walked toward his office.

"Ah, Mala Mala," Rex whispered with great satisfaction as he sat down in front of the computer and smiled. The screensaver, a bull elephant charging their jeep, quickly faded. Rex double-clicked on the mail logo. There were fifteen advertisements and one message, entitled "patriot."

"Hmm, this could either be a virus, or the reply that I've been waiting for from the bureaucratic bunglers," Rex whispered, opening the mail.

"*The country is very appreciative for the information, which you have provided. We intend to closely evaluate these issues of concern in due time.*" Rex read and reread the response, signed by a Leslie Valentino.

"Son-of-a-bitch," Rex grumbled, realizing that the response was canned and that no thought had gone into the importance of the facts he had brought to light.

"There!" Rex shouted with satisfaction after pounding the keyboard into near submission. His reply was complete. Undoubtedly, this message would be received loud and clear.

Dear Ms. Valentino,

Enough with complacency—now is the time to be concerned, and here are five reasons why the end may be near:

1. *Three days ago, the bodies of several Asian sailors washed ashore after drifting in the Gulf of Mexico.*

2. *Two days ago, six blue-tinged Asian sailors mysteriously appeared in Carencrow, Louisiana, a small town thirty miles inland from the coast. The sailors checked into Carencrow Regional Medical Center's Emergency Room, where they all died violently within hours from causes unknown.*

3. *Yesterday, several nurses who had been treating these sailors the day before became deathly ill. Here again, their life-threatening illness is from causes unknown.*

4. *Carencrow Regional is owned and operated by a rather suspicious Muslim-controlled entity headed by a maggot who goes by the name GeeHad Bin-Sad.*

5. *Last night my wife and I were nearly killed while driving home.*

I strongly suggest that you reevaluate your intelligence and expedite your timetable. Once again, our great nation is under attack!

Regards,

Dr. Rex Bent

Rex, satisfied that he had expressed the urgency of the situation, clicked send.

"There you go, Leslie, stuff that in your damn bureaucratic bimbo bonnet," Rex whispered defiantly.

"Ah, o-six-fifteen," Rex said, looking at his watch. "I've just enough time to catch the news and enjoy another gut-wrenching cup of joe." Last night's cobwebs suddenly started to clear, and the TV came into focus

"Oh, no!" Rex gasped.

Although the audio was difficult to understand, the message was loud and clear: *Grand Central Station Attacked* flashed across the lower screen. Suddenly, both the visual and audio were lost, but they returned momentarily, both with superb quality. Razorback Ralph stood with his back to the camera, observing the devastation and chaos reminiscent of 9/11. He held onto his earpiece, not yet aware that he had just gone live. However, no words were necessary. The picture revealed the death and destruction in graphic detail.

"It's not possible. This can't be happening," Rex whispered, in an attempt to convince himself that the United States of America would never again fall prey to any murderous terrorists.

Rex continued looking on in disbelief. Flames were leaping hundreds of feet into the air as thick black smoke rolled skyward and ash billowed onto the street. Glass and twisted steel were everywhere. Those morning commuters who had survived the explosion scrambled from the burning structure in a state of panic. Thousands of men and women, all determined to survive, ran for their lives. Each appeared to choose different directions in which to flee certain death. Those with their clothing ablaze soon fell and remained motionless. Others were tripping over a multitude of obstacles, including the dead and dying, and, as with any stampede, the slower ones were pushed to the ground, crushed under a sea of humanity. Only a series of small explosions covered the shouting, the bloodcurdling screams, and the pleas for mercy. As Razorback Ralph turned to face the camera, his facial expression revealed the horror of the moment. As the seasoned reporter gathered his thoughts, a multitude of sirens could be heard as ambulances, fire trucks, and police vehicles rushed to the scene. Soot-laden and exhausted, many survivors could be seen in the foreground. Some had stopped and were bent over with their hands firmly placed on their shaky thighs, gasping for air, while others helplessly stumbled forward, clearly in a state of shock and oblivious to the surrounding mayhem.

"This is Razorback Ralph reporting live from New York City. Effective at o-eight-thirty the national alert status was to be upgraded to *red*, but the increased level of security came too late. At approximately o-seven-eleven, magnificent Grand Central Station and the adjacent historic MetLife building were rocked by several massive explosions, which were felt several miles away. We understand that at any given time during the morning commute, ten thousand people are within Grand Central station. Furthermore, the adjacent office building is home to an additional two thousand workers. The dead and the dying are everywhere, and the survivors..."

Suddenly, there was a deep rumbling sound, followed by a thunderous snap. Ralph broke off his commentary and turned to see the fifty-nine-story MetLife building collapse and tumble onto the glorious old train station. Seconds later, a massive wave of cement dust and flying structural debris shot into the street. Ralph and his crew were instantaneously overcome by a fierce wind propelling deadly structural remnants and dust so thick that it sucked all the oxygen from the air. Moments later, the screen was a brown haze through which it was evident that Ralph was fighting to keep his balance as he was being bludgeoned by deadly projectiles. Oddly, the sounds of the reporter choking and gasping for air were mysteriously magnified in intensity.

"I can't breathe! I can't breathe! My God! This is like Pompeii after Mount Vesuvius erupted," the reporter exclaimed as he bent over, slowly lowering his left knee to the ground. "The fallen, the fallen are everywhere!"

The hard-nosed, battle-tested journalist gasped before collapsing into a plume of ash, which, in a flash, engulfed his breathless body. Moments later the screen went blank.

"My God!" Rex shouted. "The terrorists have struck again!" The anger resonated in his voice as he looked down at his watch. It was 0650.

"Oh, Christ, late again. Well, Pretty Boy will just have to understand," Rex rationalized as he scurried to the bedroom to check on Trissy one last time before leaving. "I love you," Rex whispered, sitting on the side of the bed. He pulled Trissy's beautiful blond hair to the side and kissed her on the cheek. His stricken wife remained motionless but appeared comfortable. Her respirations were non-labored and her pulse strong and regular.

"No worries, my love, no worries," Rex said softly, feeling a renewed sense of determination. He now had the strength to face whatever challenges lay ahead.

Rex scrambled back into the kitchen, grabbed the keys to his Mustang, and opened the door leading to the garage. His soaring spirits plummeted as he came face to face with what remained of Trissy's beautiful Mercedes.

"So much for German engineering. Daimler should really consider reviving the indestructible Panzer," Rex quipped while opening the door to his pride and joy.

The key easily slipped into the ignition and, with a slight twist, the Mustang came to life. As the engine warmed, he reached for his cell phone and dialed the ER.

"Emergency room, Sheila," the buxom nurse coordinator answered with authority.

"Sheila, Queen of the Jungle, this is Rex. You won't believe it, but I'm running late."

"What else is new, Rrrrex? I'll tell the rather agitated Dr. Bleeker that you will be here at Standard Bent Time, ten minutes after the hour," Sheila replied with a chuckle. "By the way how is Trissy?"

"Not well. She's looking rather puny and will not be able to make it in."

"Well, we'll just have to work short. I can only hope that she's doing better than the others who fell sick yesterday"

"By the way, how's Wanda?" Rex asked.

"Rex, she is still in guarded condition, and no one is sure she is going to make it. As for your concubines, Mean and Evil, they were moved to the ICU last night because their blood pressures kept dropping."

Rex shook his head after hearing the concerning news about Wanda.

"Rex, did you hear me? You'd better get your butt in here to fight the forces of evil before Dr. Bleeker throws one of his famous temper tantrums," Sheila suggested in a stern tone.

"Will do," Rex replied enthusiastically, flipping the cell phone screen down and tossing it onto the passenger seat. With the engine warm, Rex hit the gas. The Mustang leaped forward. As the dark blue sports car continued to accelerate, his thoughts started to race.

"The Asian sailors who had suffered such agonizing deaths and the fallen nurses all had something in common, but what kind of weapon of mass destruction would cause high fevers, fiery red skin with such extensive blistering, and severe gastrointestinal symptoms?" Rex wondered, while shifting into second gear. He was too engrossed in thought to notice the danger lurking at his doorstep. Two large dark vehicles with tinted windows were parked on his street.

CHAPTER 20

IT WAS EARLY MORNING on the Atchafalaya Basin. The moist, cool air concealed Whiskey Bay in a hazy mist rising from the warmer, murky water. Just as the lights at Camp Eagle began to dim, the solitude and peacefulness was pierced by celebration. The terrorists had been watching CNN, patiently awaiting the results of their first of many diversionary assaults on America. The cheering started as soon as it was evident that Grand Central Station was ablaze and intensified as each explosion ripped the historic structure apart.

"You see the dead and the dying, but do not overlook the fear in the eyes of the survivors, my fellow Soldiers of God. All of America will come to either understand the wisdom of Islam or die by our hand," Mohammad proclaimed as the MetLife building collapsed.

"Allah, Allah, Allah!" the terrorists shouted with joy, jumping up and down in a rhythmic chant.

"Allah is indeed great, Mohammad. Your crusade against the infidels is unfolding as planned," Yassar announced with pride, holding his head high.

"You see, Yassar, one call to the spineless Christian reporters shortly before our plan was executed, and we can view the greatness of our work, live. The media's greed in being the first to report breaking stories even outweighs the concern for their people," Mohammad said with a chuckle.

"I am honored to serve you, Mohammad," Yassar proclaimed.

"The years of planning have yielded the results we so greatly desired. It has been far too long since Osama first brought our battle to the infidels. Abu Bakr and the warriors in his cell should be commended for the success of their mission, Yassar, for they created and then executed their plan brilliantly!" Mohammad shouted over the celebration.

"As you desire, Mohammad, I will inform Abu of your pleasure!" Yassar shouted back.

The floor of the small wooden structure began to vibrate as the celebration intensified. Mohammad motioned to Yassar to step outside. Moments later, Mohammad stood on the porch in silence with Yassar at his side.

"What was the secret to Abu's success, Mohammad?" Yassar inquired, gazing over the placid lagoon.

"Abu had the patience, the determination, and the audacity to fight for and subsequently obtain multiple vending leases within Grand Central Station and the MetLife building," Mohammad shared openly with his number two man and most trusted friend.

"But that must have been an extremely difficult undertaking given the hundreds of locations available," Yassar replied.

"Only those leases adjacent to key structural elements of the massive buildings were obtained," Mohammad disclosed.

"Brilliant. Therefore, a relatively small amount of explosive was necessary to topple those decadent symbols of American pride," Yassar concluded.

"Yes, and as an added bonus, the explosives were set off by activating twenty-nine-dollar cell phones with roll over minutes! The activation number dialed was U-four ISLAM," Mohammad chuckled. "You must make sure that this attention to detail is injected into our forthcoming operations."

"With certainty, Mohammad. The attacks you envisioned on Washington DC, San Francisco, and Los Angeles are proceeding, as planned and on schedule," Yassar assured his great and revered leader.

"Of that I am certain, because no aspect has been overlooked," Mohammad replied.

"And, we will continue to closely monitor the progress of each operation. The only concern I have is America's level of alert. It has been elevated to Red given today's success. Hopefully, this will not interfere with our plans," Yassar said, expressing a shadow of doubt.

"Yassar, do not concern yourself. I have lived in this country for years and trained at one of their finest universities. I know the Americans. They lack the heart and the spirit of their forefathers. The fear we have created will soon result in fatigue. In their pity and self-doubt, they will not only question their leaders, but also the wisdom of fighting a battle they cannot win. Within twenty-four to forty-eight hours, America's readiness will be at its lowest level, and phase two of our Holy War will be executed."

"In a matter of hours our next phase of Operation Uncle Slam begins. By targeting the East Coast and the West Coast, America will experience the shock and awe of our unyielding strength. The attacks launched by land, sea, and air will destroy financial and political strongholds, forcing America to watch its pagan symbols of pride crumble before its very eyes," Mohammad growled gleefully.

"Of course, once again this death and destruction will be brought into living rooms courtesy of our good friends at CNN," Yassar said with a smile.

"This reality will be followed by fear, panic, and the overwhelming need for self-preservation. Millions of spineless Americans will remain secluded in their homes, trembling. All travel will grind to a halt, and the streets will become desolate. At this point, the timing will be appropriate to launch our final assault, which will effectively drive men, women, and children from their homes and into the streets. There will be a mass exodus from coastal communities as the infidels scurry inland," Mohammad assured Yassar.

"Excellent!" Yassar replied.

"As panic turns into hysteria, the American nonbelievers will leave their dead unburied and their dying unattended. The United States of America will be in financial ruin, isolated from the world with its coasts uninhabitable. Most importantly, this evil empire, which had the audacity to occupy Arab soil and kill our brothers, will be humiliated. All will soon come to understand the power of Islam," Mohammad said with unmistakable determination.

Mohammad stood quietly and continued to stare at the Whiskey Bay. He was beeming with pride and suddenly felt an overwhelming sense of power. The future of Islam was in his hands, and he felt invincible.

The sun was just starting to rise. At this time in the morning, the Atchafalaya Basin appeared magical. The celebration suddenly became louder as the door of the command center was flung open.

"Mohammad, GeeHad is on the phone. He wishes to congratulate you on the success of the operation in New York!" one of the freedom fighters shouted.

"Tell GeeHad that greater victories will soon be realized. I am preoccupied with launching our next assault but will call him later this morning," Mohammad responded.

"Very well, Mohammad," came the reply as the door swung shut.

"It is time to end our celebration, for we have much work to do. Come, Yassar, our reign of terror continues," Mohammad said, before walking back into command central.

CHAPTER 21

REX ARRIVED AT WORK at 0710. Although late, he slipped into the lounge to grab a cup of coffee prior to relieving the watch. There he found many of the emergency room personnel glued to the TV, watching the tragedy unfolding in New York City.

"Sorry I'm late, Hanz. Trissy and I had a rather bad evening," Rex confessed, realizing that his humbleness would be met with a cold reception. And cold it was, for Rex could sense that Dr. Bleeker was not pleased with his tardiness.

"Rex, I have three patients to turn over to you," Dr. Bleeker blurted. It was clearly evident that there would be no small talk this morning. Within seconds, report had been given, and Dr. Bleeker was out the door.

"Beemer and Big Dog, thank God I'm working with you two today. As you both know, Trissy and Wanda are out of commission. Please keep me out of trouble," Rex insisted as he shook hands with the two nurses he would be working with on the shift.

"Yeah, Boy!" Big Dog howled.

"You're working with the first team, Dr. B," Beemer assured Rex.

"Ha, yeah right," Sheila chuckled, overcome with the need to add an element of doubt. "That's like saying the brains of this operation is Wan."

"By the way, where is that boy?" Rex inquired.

"No doubt wandering around aimlessly."

"Stop flapping your jowls and get to work" the administrative clerk Holly Hardin barked after noticing how slowly Rex was moving.

"Yeah, get the lead out," her sister, Linda Croft, huffed as she defiantly folded her arms.

"Now you've gone and done it Rex. You had better do what they say. They are much bigger than you and have friends in high places," Sheila whispered.

"My apologies, ladies," Rex replied, knowing from past experiences that this was a battle he would never win. Holly and Linda looked alike, dressed alike, spoke in the same monotone voice, and exhibited absolutely no flexibility—every action had to be by the book.

"You have a fifty-eight-year-old male going to room two when he gets back from CT," Shiela announced. "He was hit over the head with a hammer tonight after refusing to give his drinking buddy a beer."

"'Hammer Head' in room two, gotcha," Rex confirmed, filing the information away within the deep recesses of his atrophied memory bank.

"Oh, and just to make your morning complete, you have a young male psych patient heading to room six. He states he has a history of 'skips-o-phrenia.' He's worried that his antenna isn't up all the way and is convinced that he needs to be admitted for poor reception," Shiela chuckled as Rex flashed her an oh-Lord-why-me look.

"Well, perhaps he should switch to satellite," Rex responded as he reviewed the chart of a patient Dr. Bleeker had handed over to him.

"C'est si bon—*Prussian Blue,* PRUSSIAN BLUE! He, he, he..." Wan shouted his translation correction from the day before as he shuffled past Rex.

"Huh, what?" Rex asked after being startled by the Thailander, who had suddenly appeared out of nowhere.

"Code Blue ICU, Code Blue ICU!" the voice over the hospital loud speaker shrieked.

"Now what?" Rex moaned, shaking his hands toward the ceiling.

"Your turn to run Rex, I'll hold down the fort," Boom Boom conceded as Rex walked out of the room.

"Rex, that could be Wanda," Sheila emphasized while leaning over the counter.

"Oh, Christ, I surely hope not," Rex shot back while scrambling toward the intensive care unit.

CHAPTER 22

ITT HAD BEEN TWENTY days since the container ship *Mecca* left the port of Aden in Yemen. The vessel was 330 feet in length and displaced well in excess of 30,000 gross tons. She had traveled through the Suez Canal to Istanbul, Turkey, where additional cargo was loaded. The *Mecca* was now on her way across the Atlantic, bound for the United States. The ship was one of hundreds of ships tracked daily by satellite, under surveillance by the National Security Agency, Naval Intelligence, the CIA, and the Coast Guard. All that was known about this vessel was that she had been registered in Libya, the point of embarkation and her last port of call. The manifest was not available, nor was her final destination. Thus, the *Mecca* raised enough suspicion that the vessel warranted further investigation. The various agencies came to the conclusion that this investigation should take place at sea, far away from America's shores. The Coast Guard Cutter, *Freedom*, had been dispatched from her home port in New York to intercept the ship. At first this appeared to be a routine mission—one of the dozens, which were carried out each day on the high seas.

The commanding officer of the *Freedom*, Commander Adam Flaaten, stood on the bridge as his ship steamed at thirty knots toward *Mecca*. His mission was to evaluate the threat level the ship posed to the United States. This required that the container ship be boarded in order to determine her destination, to ensure that the captain and her crew were legitimate, and to ensure that all required documentation was in order. Additionally, he was to review the ship's manifest and examine the goods being transported. Most importantly, his orders were clear. Under no circumstances was the ship to come within twenty miles of United States without first being inspected.

Freedom's navigator, Lieutenant Paul Paski, had plotted and was continually updating the intercept course for this routine mission.

"Captain, I recommend that we come right to a heading of one-eight-five degrees."

"Very well, helmsman, come right five degrees to course one hundred and eighty-five," Captain Flaaten ordered.

"Aye, aye, Captain," the helmsman announced.

The captain walked to the navigation table at the far end of the bridge where Lieutenant Paski continued to work on the navigational chart.

"Paul, how far are we from the *Mecca*, and what is our time to intercept?"

"Captain, we are fifteen miles from the vessel and should intercept her at eleven-o-five, approximately forty-five minutes from now."

"How far from shore will we be at the time of intercept?"

"Seventy-five miles," Lieutenant Paski replied after using his compass to determine the distance.

"Excellent. The ship is well within our territorial waters and must now comply with our laws," the captain announced with confidence before stepping out onto the flying bridge. He lifted binoculars to his eyes and, with minor adjustments, was able to quickly focus on his quarry.

"Paul, have Combat Information Center raise the *Mecca* and inform her that the United States Coast Guard Cutter, *Freedom*, requests that she stop and be boarded. Also, please ensure that Lieutenant Mossy and his boarding party are prepared," the captain ordered.

"Aye, aye, Skipper," the navigator replied as the captain paced the bridge.

The Mecca *has to be in excess of four hundred feet in length*, Captain Flaaten thought to himself. There were forty-foot containers stacked three-fold above the deck from the bow to her stern, and the vessel was lying low in the water. There was no doubt that the ship was fully loaded. *But with what cargo?* he wondered.

A large bow wake could be seen as the massive vessel plowed through the dark blue waters. It was clearly evident that the ship had not complied with his orders to stop all engines.

"Paul, what is the *Mecca's* course and speed?" the captain asked.

"Captain, she is traveling on a course of two-five-zero at a speed of eighteen knots."

"There is no doubt she is headed for New York Harbor," the navigator added.

The *Freedom* was now less than ten thousand yards from the rogue ship, and closing rapidly.

Captain Flaaten picked up the growler and rang the CIC. The XO, Lieutenant Commander Michael Frachtman, answered.

"Mike, have you had any luck raising the *Mecca*?" the captain asked.

"No, sir, we've tried several frequencies but have not yet been successful."

"Continue making every effort to contact that vessel. I want those engines stopped," the captain ordered in a tone reflecting his growing impatience.

"Helmsman, decrease your speed to eighteen knots. Right standard rudder, make your new course two-five-zero," the captain ordered, and the helmsman confirmed.

Freedom listed heavily starboard as the vessel turned.

Minutes later, she was one thousand yards off the *Mecca's* port beam. Both vessels were on a parallel course and traveling at eighteen knots. Again, Captain Flaaten peered through his binoculars. There was no one on deck. Suddenly, the *Mecca* turned to port, and in an instant the distance between the two vessels closed to less than six hundred yards. The massive container ship now cast a shadow over the smaller Coast Guard cutter.

"Left standard rudder, come to course two-three-five," Captain Flaaten barked. The distance between the two vessels slowly widened to 1,200 yards.

"Captain, the *Mecca's* new course is now two-six-zero and her speed has increased to twenty-four knots. She's now heading for the Chesapeake Bay and Washington DC," the navigator announced.

"Quartermaster, sound general quarters," Captain Flaaten ordered.

"Aye, aye," the quartermaster responded, picking up the 1MC.

*Ding, ding, ding, ding…*the deafening alarm rang.

"General quarters, general quarters, man your battle stations, man your battle stations. This is not a drill. I say again, this is not a drill," the quartermaster announced.

"Helmsman, increase your speed to twenty-four knots and come right to two-four-zero," the captain ordered.

"Aye, aye, Captain," the helmsman responded as the captain picked up the growler.

"CIC, Lieutenant Commander Frachtman."

"Mike, as you are aware, the *Mecca* is now heading toward Washington DC."

"Yes, sir, Captain."

"I'll be damned if we are going to be caught by surprise, as we were in the Persian Gulf. When the five-inch gun is manned and ready, I want two shots fired across *Mecca's* bow," the captain ordered in a calm, deep voice. "This should grab their attention," Captain Flaaten commented.

Within minutes the first of two seventy-pound projectiles roared from the barrel of the deck gun. Seconds later the points of impact were marked by plumes of water shooting twenty feet into the air. The warning shots, however, elicited no response. The ship maintained her course and speed, undeterred by the threat.

"Paul, how far are we from the mouth of the Chesapeake?"

"Thirty nautical miles, Captain."

"Captain, the lookouts report activity on deck," the quartermaster relayed.

"Very well," Captain Flaaten responded as he peered through his binoculars and observed dozens of men, women, and children on the main deck of the large container ship.

"Captain, we are now twenty-five nautical miles from our shores," Lieutenant Paski informed the captain.

As the captain continued to study the ship, what had first appeared to be a calm gathering of passengers, soon erupted into chaos. There was pushing, shoving, and fighting. Arms appeared to be grabbing at air, and bodies twisted violently. Suddenly and inexplicably, these people started to disappear from the view he had captured on full magnification. As he carefully widened his visual field, he was horrified.

"My God! These people are being thrown overboard!" Captain Flaaten gasped. "Quartermaster, have a locator beacon tossed overboard to mark this position and announce over the 1MC that lifeboats two and four are to be manned and ready for recovering multiple survivors," the captain ordered, as he rang the CIC.

"Aye, aye, Captain."

"Captain we are twenty miles from our shores," the navigator announced.

"Very well," Captain Flaaten responded as he picked up the growler and rang the CIC.

"CIC, this is the XO."

"Mike, our tactical picture has changed. We need to take out that ship's engine room. I want ten rounds fired at the waterline, aft of amidships."

"Very well, Captain. Consider it done," the XO affirmed.

Ten rounds were fired in quick succession. Some of the rounds skipped off the water before striking the hull of the ship, while others were right on target.

Multiple explosions could be seen and heard. The extent of the damage was evident. At the waterline, a twenty-by-fifteen-foot section of the hull had been ripped open. Seawater rushed in as black smoke billowed out.

With her engine room destroyed, the *Mecca* quickly lost speed. Captain Flaaten realized that *Freedom* had struck the necessary crippling blow. *Perhaps there was time to save those in the water,* he thought.

"Lieutenant Paski, what is the distance and the heading to our locator beacon?"

"Captain, the heading is zero-six-zero, and the distance is five miles."

"Very well, helmsman, all back two thirds. Prepare to launch the lifeboats," the captain ordered. Confirmation of his orders followed immediately.

Freedom shuddered, her propeller struggling to slow the ship's forward momentum.

"All stop, launch the lifeboats, and notify the Ensigns Davis and Wynn of the heading and the distance to the locator beacon. Also, let them know that they're on their own until we can complete our mission with the *Mecca.*"

"Aye, aye, Captain."

The lifeboats were launched in short order and were soon out of sight. It was late afternoon. The sun was setting, and a blanket of ominous gray clouds filled the skies. The winds were beginning to pick up, and large, rolling swells suddenly appeared from what, moments ago, had been a relatively calm sea. The *Mecca* started to pitch and roll violently as the elements played with the dying ship. There was no doubt that the seas were soon to claim the heavily damaged vessel. The container ship was now listing to port fifteen degrees, and her stern was low on the water. The angle on the bow slowly began to rise above the turbulent seas, and the ship had taken on a ghostly appearance.

Although the *Mecca* was sinking, the captain felt there was still time to complete his mission and board the ship. As Captain Flaaten eased *Freedom* closer to his quarry, a distant explosion could be heard. The captain immediately sensed that his search and recovery boats were in danger. He spun around in time to see smoke and fire on the horizon.

"Captain, the lookouts report a fire off our starboard quarter. They believe it's one of our lifeboats."

"My God!" the captain shouted, overwhelmed with anger.

"Raise the search and rescue crews."

"Captain, Ensign Wynn is on the scrambler," the XO announced, patching the voice communication into the overhead speakers on the bridge and the CIC.

There was a good deal of static which seemed to wax and wane in intensity, but the words were discernible, and the message shocking.

"This is Ensign Wynn. Captain, Ensign Davis's boat has exploded. Both he and his crew are presumed dead. We have stopped our present rescue mission and are searching for our shipmates, over."

Captain Flaaten shook his head in anguish, hesitating briefly before responding.

"Ensign Wynn, this is the captain. Do you have any idea what caused the explosion? Over."

There were disturbing moments of silence as a horrified Ensign Wynn watched Petty Officer Sims examine the body of a small child they had recovered from the frigid waters only moments before. The pale, lifeless body lay frozen on the deck of the small rescue craft. The grotesque facial expression, along with the clenched fists and the twisted extremities, made Ensign Wynn nauseous, but he continued to watch as Petty Officer Sims cut into an unusual cloth life vest the dead girl was wearing. With one stroke of the razor sharp knife, thick white blocks of what appeared to be clay were revealed, and rusty metal shards fell onto the deck.

"I say again, do you have any idea what caused the explosion?" Captain Flaaten asked. There was no response.

"Sims, carefully open her left hand," the ensign ordered after noticing a wire extending from under the girl's clothing to her fist, which was clenched in an odd manner. All the fingers were clasped while the thumb was extended. The sound of the young girl's brittle bones snapping was unmistakable as each finger was pried open, quickly revealing a small, black, cylindrical object.

Captain Flaaten anxiously paced the bridge, frequently glancing at the *Mecca*. The distance between the two vessels had closed to under five hundred yards. The boarding party was standing by, awaiting the order to launch. However, the mission would have to be delayed until he had a clearer picture of what had happened to Ensign Davis and his crew. His suspicion of the *Mecca* and her evil intentions grew with every passing moment. He would not needlessly send another crew into harm's way. For the first time in his long, glorious career, he felt torn between his mission and the lives of his loyal crew.

Captain Flaaten could no longer stand the silence. It was imperative that he have more information. He attempted to raise the rescue vessel once again.

"Ensign Wynn, this is the captain. I say again, what have you found?"

"Sims, toss this murderous pint-sized wench overboard and take great care not to touch the triggering mechanism," the ensign ordered.

"You have my word, Mr. Wynn. I will not touch the little black switch, but I must add that even the sharks do not deserve the likes of her."

"Captain, this is Ensign Wynn. We have been set up. The victims are laden with plastic explosives, which have been sewn into their life vests. Each has a hand-held triggering device. One of the survivors must have had enough strength to set off the bomb, which claimed Ensign Davis and his crew."

"Mr. Wynn, clear the area. Head back toward *Freedom*," Captain Flaaten ordered without hesitation.

"Helmsman, all ahead full, left full rudder."

"Very well, Captain," the helmsman responded.

The captain then picked up the growler and rang the CIC. "Mike, what is the bearing and range to our rescue crew?"

"Zero-six-five degrees and ten thousand yards, Captain," the XO responded.

"Cancel the boarding party," the captain insisted.

"Very well, sir."

As the *Freedom* raced to recover Ensign Wynn and his crew, Captain Flaaten picked up the growler once again and rang communications.

"Lieutenant Barnes."

"Lieutenant Barnes, this is the captain. I need a flash message sent to Admiral Chester at Central Command. The message is to read..."

From the crest of a wave Ensign Wynn could see the *Mecca* ablaze and thought for a moment he caught a glimpse of *Freedom*. As soon as the bow of his small lifeboat plunged deeply into the next trough, there was a brilliant flash of light, followed by a thunderous roar and an intense wave of heat. Most ominously, as the boat rode the crest of the next wave, no light could be seen in any direction. For Ensign Wynn and his crew, the immense ocean now appeared to be void of all life.

CHAPTER 23

As soon as Rex returned from the code in the ICU, he walked into a world of pandemonium. Wan appeared lost in some Thailander trance, nearly knocking Rex over as they crossed paths. With his head bowed, oblivious to the mayhem, Wan scurried about mumbling, "I love my job, I love my job, I love my job." But Rex didn't buy the act. There was no enthusiasm in Wan's voice.

"Sheila, what in the hell is going on here? This is what happens when you take a lunch break and leave Wan in charge," Rex joked.

"Yeah, well, just look at what the responsibility has done to him," Sheila fired back.

"Personally, I believe his present condition is a result of working for these damn Arabs for so many years," Rex remarked.

"Yeah, you got that right! Unfortunately, we are all destined for the same psychiatric facility, while management gets rich beating on their overworked and underpaid employees," Sheila complained.

"Yes, but you have to admit that they are quite talented. How many managers can bludgeon the peons and steal from their stockholders at the same time?"

As if on cue, there was the pounding of footsteps marching in unison, interrupted by the repulsive, high-pitched squeal of Mushroom Head's thighs rubbing together. The danger was real! "Oh, Lord, just when you thought it was safe to go back into the ER, here comes Mushroom Head, Dr. Lyons, and a herd of GeeHad's henchmen," Rex whispered, looking down at a chart in an attempt to blend in with his surroundings. "Boom Boom, look out! The muckity-mucks have arrived," Rex said in an alarming tone.

"Not to worry, Rrrrex. Be advised, your execution is not scheduled for today," Boom Boom responded as the high priestess and her entourage walked past the peasants on their way to Teresa Talon's office.

"Well, that's certainly comforting," Rex responded.

"Remember, stay focused and don't take it personally!" Boom Boom added with his usual Japanese samurai warrior accent.

"Hi, Boom Boom," Rex shouted back, bowing in respect to his teacher and mentor of ancient Asian customs.

"Hahahaha, al-wa-gator gumbo. Hahahaha, c'est si bon," Wan blurted out suddenly and unexpectedly.

"Wan, where are you going?" Foxxman asked his bewildered coworker. There was no response.

"You know, you can never determine if Wan is laughing with us, at us, or launching some new Cajun-Thai curse," Rex observed.

"There's no doubt in my mind that it's a curse," Boom Boom stated emphatically.

"He's probably going to turn us all into monkeys, I would suppose. However, he keeps mumbling something about alligators for some reason," Rex noticed.

"Well, we all have our problems. Personally, Dr. B, I believe all my problems can be traced to those flavorful 'Agent Orange' martinis in Saigon at Mama-san's Bar and Grill," Foxxman retorted.

"Ah, you may be interested to know that in another, less reserved lifetime I frequented that bar. As I recall, the beer was cold, and the women were hot. Thank God I never drank the martinis!" Rex confessed.

"Rex, stay focused," Boom Boom requested.

"I love my job, I love my job, I love my job," Wan could be heard saying over and over again.

"Rex, tell me. Who coded in the ICU? Was it Wanda?" Sheila inquired.

"Yes," Rex replied in a very somber tone.

"Christ, I knew it!"

"Thankfully, she never went into cardiac arrest," Rex reported.

"Well, she's a tough lady. I just know that Wanda will pull through," Sheila replied, in an attempt to lighten the mood. However, the tone of her voice reflected both concern and uncertainty with regard to Wanda's full recovery.

"Undoubtedly. By the way, what have you heard about those two gamey birds, Mean and Evil?" Rex asked.

"Rex, you won't believe it, but they both left the hospital while you were in the ICU. In fact, they came by the ER to say good-bye. And, I might add, to give you a ration of shit for kicking them while they were down."

"Well, how did they look?"

"So edematous and erythematous that you didn't even notice their super-sized wrinkles," Sheila observed.

"Ah, so that ashen gray look, earned over decades of tobacco abuse, has been replaced with something a little more fashionable."

"Perhaps, they're using a new foundation," Sheila quipped.

"I'd say it would have to be something with a cement base and large aggregate," Foxxman added.

"Yeah, boy!" Big Dog shouted in agreement.

"By the way, Rex, have you heard anything from either the CDC or pathology with regard to the Asian sailors or the mysterious illness which struck our nurses?" Sheila asked.

"Yes, as a matter of fact, I have. The CDC informed me that they will 'take the matter under consideration in due time,'" Rex replied disappointingly.

"Those sorry bastards, are you sure they got the story straight?" Sheila asked.

"Well, I wouldn't hold my breath, but on the news last night I was left with the impression that the CDC would be in Carencrow this week," Rex announced.

"No way! The CDC wouldn't stumble into this lawless, buzzard-ridden town unless they were lost," Sheila replied confidently. "By the way, earlier today, I attempted to pull up the pathology reports on the dead sailors. All information has been erased from the computer."

"Call medical records and request their old charts," Rex suggested.

"Rex, I did. The records had not been pulled, which is what happens when litigation is pending. I was told that there were no old records and the numbers I was providing had never been issued. Knowing how money hungry these Muslim vultures are, I even called the accounting office. Again, they had no records on these patients. It's as if the sailors never existed," Sheila replied.

"Well, isn't that interesting?" Rex raised his hand to his face and gently massaged his chin as the possibilities raced through his mind.

"Although it's always possible the federal government may be behind this cover up, I believe the more likely culprits are GeeHad and his mercenaries, but just what are they trying to hide?" Rex wondered. "And why were they trying to kill Trissy and me?"

"Rex, let me answer your last question first. GeeHad and his tribe of cross-dressers were trying to kill you because you're a royal pain in the ass. The nursing staff has considered placing a contract on you for just the same reason, but obviously the Arabs have beaten us to it. Your lovely wife, Trissy, just happened to be an innocent bystander."

"Well, that's all the thanks I get for stirring the pot over these many years. You of all people, Sheila, should thank me for keeping you on your toes and not on your back, as so many of your warm friends insisted upon!"

Sheila chuckled, but Rex could see the wheels turning.

"Well, ya got that right, but you must realize that there is a fine line between getting screwed and getting laid."

"I see your point," Rex replied politely, without knowing exactly what she was trying to say.

"Now, with regard to your first question, we may never know what they're trying to hide, but the combination of suspicious deaths, mysterious illnesses, and the subsequent deception can't be good. Whatever is going down is going down soon, and for some reason Carencrow appears to be the infidel epicenter!" Sheila gasped.

CHAPTER 24

I T WAS LATE AFTERNOON in Carencrow. The skies were clear for the first time in what seemed to be months. Oddly enough, the ever-present flock of buzzards that usually circled overhead was nowhere to be seen. The sun was so low on the horizon that light illuminated everything in its path with a pulsating, red-streaked glow. The air was crisp, and there was a stiff breeze that kept the falling, fluorescent autumn leaves whipping aloft. All was quiet and peaceful for the moment, but the town of Carencrow was clearly in the eye of the storm.

The FBI's crack SWAT team soon broke this eerie wintry silence as they executed the raid on the small house on Mallard Drive. Captain Richter looked at the secondhand on his watch.

"Go! Go! Go!" Captain Richter screamed into his handheld communication device.

Simultaneously the front and back doors imploded on contact as large, metal battering rams came crashing down. Within seconds, twelve agents with semiautomatic weapons were in the house. They entered a world of darkness maintained by heavy blackout curtains. However, they were professionals and well-equipped to operate in any environment. Night vision goggles were immediately flipped down and secured in place. Seconds later the men advanced from room to room aggressively and methodically. Not a word was spoken. Only hand signals conveyed orders. Heads peered around corners, and weapons swung from side to side, anticipating any threat axis. Soon, four men reached a long, empty corridor leading to an open door. This area presented the greatest danger, because there would be no place to hide should a firefight erupt. Adrenaline surged with each step. Index fingers gripped ever so tightly around the triggers of each lethal weapon. Senses were heightened, and the level of concentration intensified. What danger lay beyond the long, dismal hall? Finally, all four surged through the open door and into the large master bedroom, where each immediately detected movement on the bed. Instinctively, weapons were leveled and trained at the unanticipated threat before visualizing the target. In the split second between life and death, the men chose not to discharge their weapons. Trissy's life would be spared.

Another hand gesture commanded two of the men to check out the bathroom. They returned in short order and gave the "all clear" sign.

"Lights," Captain Richter announced in a loud gravelly voice, prompting Sergeant Kuo to fumble for the light switch.

WITH THE BARREL OF his gun, he poked at the concealed mound. Trissy moaned from deep within her cocoon as the FBI agents looked on quietly. The barrel was thrust forward again, but this time with greater force.

"Ouch!" Trissy's muffled voice shouted as the hard steel jarred her ribs. This time, the pain was so intense that it awakened her from a deep sleep. The covers came down, and she twisted to her left simultaneously. The barrel of the assault weapon came into focus before the faces.

Trissy screamed, pulling up the sheets to cover her exposed breasts. The shock of being awakened so abruptly only added to her sense of danger. Her heart raced as she struggled to remember where Rex had left his weapon.

"What—what is the meaning of this?!" Trissy demanded, fighting to clear her mind.

"Mrs. Bent, I am Captain Richter of the FBI. We have reason to believe that you and your husband present a real and present danger to national security," the captain growled while Trissy rubbed her eyes.

"That's absurd!" Trissy shot back as Captain Richter placed a folded piece of paper into her hand. "What's this?" she asked, unfolding the document and attempting to focus on the wording.

"Why, it's a warrant for your arrest," the captain answered sarcastically. As he wiped his nose on his sleeve, Trissy read the trumped-up charges.

"I see that my husband is under arrest as well," Trissy said, looking up at the captain.

"Yes, we believe in capturing the entire terrorist cell, dead or alive. Of course, I prefer to see traitors, such as yourselves, dead," Captain Richter announced with a great deal of satisfaction.

"Am I to assume that you're going to drag me outside and lynch me?" Trissy asked in disbelief.

"With the evidence against you and your husband so strong, that would certainly be my preference. Why crowd the judicial system when all you need is a sturdy rope and a tall tree?" the captain quipped, placing his foot on the bed and leaning toward Trissy.

"Perhaps we're not guilty," Trissy replied.

"And I suppose WMDs don't exist. Well, we shall see," the captain said confidently while moving to grab his prisoner's white robe, which lay over a nearby chair.

"I suggest you put this on," Captain Richter urged as he dropped her robe next to the bed.

Trissy studied the faces behind the weapons. There were three men and one woman. All were dressed in black and wore dark glasses. Their eyes could not be seen, but each facial expression was hard and cold. She knew that the antiemetic Rex had injected hours before could cause bizarre dreams, and even hallucinations, but this had gone too far.

"I'm not about to put on that robe, and I sure as hell have no intention of going anywhere with you, or these escapees from a Blues Brothers concert," Trissy growled defiantly, hoping this nightmare would soon come to an end.

"Suit yourself. Over the years, I've dragged several criminals to the station butt naked. Of course, most of those were hookers," Captain Richter chuckled insultingly while taking off his sunglasses. Trissy immediately felt violated as the stranger's jet-black eyes seemed to penetrate her soul. Yet, he continued staring. As each moment passed, his eyes moved with increasing velocity and irregular gyrations.

That's one hell of a nystagmus! Trissy thought to herself. However, there was no doubt that the evil captain was anticipating that Trissy would once again reveal her voluptuous breasts as she complied with his order and put on the robe.

"Yes, I'll bet you have," Trissy replied to the animal with a perverted personality and crazy eyes.

Trissy felt the anger within her start to surge uncontrollably.

"Captain, I want you and your men out of this house immediately," Trissy shouted, reaching for the phone to call 911.

"That's just not possible, Mrs. Bent," Captain Richter answered, ripping the cord from the wall before grabbing her arms.

"Get your hands off of me," Trissy screamed, struggling to remain covered, while attempting to free herself.

"Adding resisting arrest to the charge of treason seems somewhat excessive," the captain shouted, before shoving Trissy back into the bed. "Now, here's the warrant authorizing me to search your house," Captain Richter growled as he tossed yet another legal document in her direction.

"Captain, it would be my pleasure to assist Mrs. Bent," Corporal Lisa Carpenter blurted out in an effort to diffuse the situation.

"All right, but I want this evil bitch in the kitchen in five minutes," Captain Richter insisted, storming out of the bedroom with Sergeants Kuo and Kane following closely behind.

"Yes, sir," the stocky female agent with a closely-cropped, lavender crew cut responded smartly.

"No government agency would act so aggressively," Trissy complained as Corporal Carpenter handed Trissy her robe.

"We're just doing our job," the corporal replied with little emotion as Trissy slipped on her robe and secured the drawstring.

"I want to see some ID," Trissy demanded.

"In due time," the corporal simply replied.

"You've made a mistake. Rex and I are well-respected in Carencrow. Suddenly, for no apparent reason, our home has been invaded, and I have been assaulted and threatened at gunpoint by some stupid jackass!" Trissy complained.

"There has been no misunderstanding, but I am sorry for any inconvenience. Over the years, Captain Richter has made significant improvements in his interpersonal skills," Corporal Carpenter assured her prisoner.

"Inconvenience? Is that the politically correct buzzword for your Gestapo tactics?" Trissy fumed. "Now, just what in the hell are the little man's intentions?" Trissy asked with growing apprehension.

"To take you downtown where you will be booked and then tossed into the darkest and deepest dungeon imaginable," the corporal replied with a smirk before glancing at her watch. "You have exactly three minutes to change into something a little more appropriate."

"Christ!" Trissy shouted, scurrying toward her closet with Corporal Carpenter in close pursuit.

As Trissy slipped into a pair of jeans she wondered if the intruders were in fact FBI agents.

Anyone can obtain a black jacket with a gold insignia, she thought to herself as she put on her blouse. Suddenly, she was consumed by the thought that her survival was now dependent upon quick action. However, she remained nauseous, exceedingly weak, and unable to clear her mind.

"Let's go," the corporal insisted, yanking Trissy from a closet before giving her a shove toward the bedroom.

"All right, you don't have to push," Trissy complained, becoming more determined to go on the offensive. She knew Rex had left her pistol under his pillow, but where had he left the automatic assault rifle? As she walked past her bed, she remembered that he'd put the rifle next to nightstand. She took an abrupt left.

"Now where are you going, missy?" the agitated corporal asked.

"I need my jewelry," Trissy insisted as Corporal Carpenter grabbed the back of her shirt and jerked her back.

"You're not Paris Hilton," the corporal growled.

"No, but I'm not Rosie O'Donnell either. That distinction belongs to you," Trissy shouted as she freed herself momentarily, quickly reaching for the rifle. However, her reactions were far too sluggish. Just as she grabbed the barrel and lifted the weapon from its secure resting place, the female agent knocked it away using the butt of her gun. Rex's prized piece was sent flying. It bounced off the wall before striking and shattering the night lamp.

"I rather enjoy Rosie," the stocky female agent snarled as she placed her muscular arm around Trissy's neck, tightening the grip until Trissy began to gasp for air.

"I can't—breathe!" Trissy screamed as everything suddenly went gray.

WITHIN MINUTES, THE HOME on Mallard Drive had been secured, and the prevailing darkness lifted. Lights were on, and all the curtains had been opened. Thirty law enforcement officers from various agencies combed the home room by room with the aid of a bomb-sniffing dog.

An exhausted Leslie Valentino stood in the kitchen watching and monitoring the progress. Although the FBI was responsible for coordinating and executing this operation, as the representative from the National Security Agency, she was in charge of the overall operation. Leslie had flown in from Bar Harbor on the red-eye because she felt that her presence would be critical in evaluating the big picture and keeping her finger on the pulse. She felt certain that a massive assault on the United States was imminent. Her intuition told her that Rex and Trissy could very well provide the information needed to unravel the plot. Somehow, they had been swept up into this lethal game—or had they become willing participants vowing heart and soul to treasonous acts against this great nation? She had to dig deeper to find the truth, but now time was of the essence.

"Ms. Valentino, we found a rather angry and uncooperative Mrs. Bent asleep in the master bedroom. She will be out shortly and, hopefully, in better spirits," Captain Richter reported over the loud barking of a crazed golden lab named Schnapps.

"Thank you, Captain," Leslie replied, watching in amazement as the deputy dog stood on his hind legs, paws extended, clawing at the upper reaches of the kitchen wall.

"Well, I've heard of people climbing the wall, but not dogs," Captain Richter remarked, observing the loyal four-legged officer making several attempts to scale the nine-foot wall.

"Either he didn't like the wallpaper, or something has tickled his olfactory system," Sergeant Jones, the dog's handler, observed. Moments later, Schnapps was enveloped by a cloud of plaster and the ear-shattering, nerve-wracking barking gave way to a loud whimpering sound and an occasional sneeze.

"I must say that these retrievers can uncover just about anything. The trouble is you never know if they've found old toys, empty whiskey bottles, or clandestine contraband," Captain Richter complained as the dog began to get on his nerves.

"Good boy, Schnapps" the sergeant praised, giving his best friend a crunchy, mouth-watering treat.

"Well, I think we might very well find something of interest in the attic," Captain Richter concluded.

"I do believe it's a lead worth pursuing," Leslie added.

"Jones, the entrance to the attic is in the hallway leading to the master bedroom. Would you and Sergeant Schnapps please follow that trail?" Captain Richter requested in an unusually polite manner.

"Absolutely, Captain," Jones replied without hesitation, before wondering why his unreasonably demanding and always unappreciative boss was behaving so out of character.

"Captain, we have found the mother lode," Agent Abercrombie reported with zeal.

Captain Richter and Ms. Valentino followed Abercrombie to Dr. Bent's office, where a large wooden box lay in the middle of the room.

"'Medical Supplies,'" Captain Richter read from the label on the side of the box.

"Talk about mislabeling!" the agent remarked, grabbing a plank and prying it open, exposing thousands of unmarked glass ampoules.

My God, what form of death and destruction is contained within these evil glass vials? Leslie wondered.

"A/E," Agent Spike "Sharkie" Holt blurted, staring at the computer screen while attempting to decipher the code.

"What have you found, Sharkie?" Captain Richter asked.

"Captain, I was able to break into Dr. Bent's personal files. The most recent correspondence is this letter he drafted today at o-seven-forty-five," Sharkie replied.

Captain Richter, Leslie, and Agent Westin leaned over Sharkie's shoulder to read from the flickering screen. The letter was addressed to Yassar Yacsole, President of the World of Islam. The letter simply read:

> *The A/E gifts arrived intact. They shall be distributed throughout the land. Soon the population will be decimated. Allah is great, and our mission unstoppable.*
>
> *Your humble servant,*
>
> *R*

The concentration was intense as each government agent attempted to comprehend the meaning of *A/E.*

Suddenly, the tension in the room was broken by a loud pounding from up above. Each step elicited a hideous creaking sound as the rafters strained to support a great weight. The ceiling began to bow, and most felt certain it would snap. The muffled bark left no doubt as to who had found their way into the attic.

"For Christ's sake, Schnapps and Jones sound like a herd of migrating elephants," the captain complained, staring at the ceiling, anticipating a structural collapse.

"Captain, look at these icons," Sharkie requested. "I've opened these programs and have come to the conclusion that Dr. Bent has software capable of not only converting English to Arabic, but also encrypting text," Sharkie surmised.

"I'd say this case is pretty well a slam dunk, and it's time to execute the guilty party," Captain Richter announced gleefully.

"Not so fast, Captain. There will be no cowboy justice as long as I'm in charge," Leslie reminded the volatile FBI agent.

"That's odd, Captain. This letter was never sent," Sharkie discovered, much to his amazement.

"That's not so unusual. I would assume that Dr. Bent ran out of time and intended to complete the letter later today," the captain rationalized.

"Perhaps," Leslie said. "But all he had to do was hit send, and his message would have been translated, encoded, and delivered instantaneously," Leslie added.

"Indeed," Sharkie confirmed.

"As I recall, you said that the letter was drafted at o-seven-forty-five. Is that correct?" Leslie asked.

"Yes, ma'am,"

"Is this the original message, or have there been revisions?" Leslie inquired.

"The original."

"Captain, here again we have a discrepancy. I know for sure that Dr. Bent has been at work since o-seven-hundred. I'd say we have a glaring problem with the timeline," Leslie concluded, much to the executioner's dismay.

"Ms. Valentino, you're starting to sound like a sea lawyer," the captain criticized sarcastically.

"No, Captain, I'm sounding like a trained attorney who cut her teeth as a federal prosecutor in the DA's office in Houston. Thus, I use brains instead of brawn, and indisputable evidence rather than testo-twisted, ball-busting, wild-ass guesses to arrive at my conclusions," Leslie snapped back, after deciding to take a more aggressive position in dealing with this bowed-up bozo.

"Haven't you overlooked the fact that Mrs. Bent could have drafted the letter for her husband?" Captain Richter suggested, after choosing to ignore Leslie's estrogen-ridden rage.

"Possibly, but it was never sent. Why?" Leslie asked as the captain began to appear more and more agitated.

"Ms. Valentino, surely you aren't implying that these upstanding citizens were set up?" Captain Richter huffed in disgust.

"Anything is possible. Frankly, I am troubled by how quickly and easily this entire investigation has proceeded," Leslie replied.

"Damn, it's hot up there," a sweaty Sergeant Jones announced, entering the office with the rambunctious, dusty, tail-wagging Schnapps at his side. "Captain, there must be at least five hundred pounds of plastic explosives in the attic, a box full of detonators, and half a dozen drones, complete with remote controls," Sergeant Jones disclosed as he handed Captain Richter a lump of what appeared to be white clay.

Schnapps barked affirmatively in an attempt to confirm his partner's story.

"Drones were used in the attack on the *Stennis* Carrier Strike Group," Leslie reminded all who were present, as the horror of that fateful day was relived momentarily.

"It appears that we have vials of A/E, and a means to deliver the deadly liquid. I would suppose that the plastic explosive would be detonated once the planes are over their intended targets, thus maximizing the distribution of the deadly contents," Captain Richter surmised.

"I can't seem to find any reference to the abbreviation A/E on the computer," Sharkie said, continuing to work the keyboard in an attempt to dig deeper.

"It probably stands for 'Assholes with Estrogen,'" Captain Richter mumbled.

"Captain, my hearing is excellent. I suggest that you become part of the solution, and not part of the problem, before you find my foot in your 'A' and my 'E' crushing your atrophied 'Ts'. Have I made myself perfectly clear?" Leslie growled, glaring at Captain Richter as the room suddenly fell silent.

"Somewhat," the captain responded defiantly.

"No, sir. I need a yes or no," Leslie insisted, but no response was forthcoming. "Well, seeing that the cat's got your tongue, perhaps we should get back to work," Leslie suggested, after deciding that the timing wasn't right to crush the captain's fragile ego.

"The only viable possibility, in my estimation, is that A/E reflects the contents of the vials," Agent Abercrombie suggested.

"Absolutely, but that would lead us to the conclusion that the vials contain a mixture of anthrax bacillus and Ebola. My God, a weapon of mass destruction, combining a deadly bacteria with a flesh-eating hemorrhagic virus," Leslie suggested, to the shock and horror of those in the room.

"And we must assume that both agents have been genetically engineered to act synergistically in order to kill millions," Sharkie surmised.

"That would unleash an evil genie, which no one could put back into the bottle," Agent Abercrombie added, opening the solid French doors to the office closet and revealing dozens of wooden boxes stacked to the ceiling.

"Oh no!" Leslie whispered, surveying the solid wall of boxes marked *Medical Supplies*.

"I want this house taken apart to see if there are any other hidden surprises," Captain Richter announced to the crowd, which had squeezed into the small office to visualize what had been uncovered.

"Seize everything in Dr. Bent's chamber of horrors. Sharkie, have the computer geeks analyze the hard drive byte-by-byte," Captain Richter ordered.

"Yes, sir," Sharkie replied as he began to detach the wiring leading to various peripherals.

"Agent Abercrombie, call the regional office in New Orleans and have them dispatch a hazardous waste vehicle immediately, and do not disclose what is being transported," Captain Richter insisted.

"Will do," the agent responded promptly, walking into the living room with his cell phone in hand.

"Corporals Garrison and Sams, front and center," Captain Richter barked, looking around the room for his photographer and evidence-gathering expert. He was irritated that he couldn't find the men right away because they always stood out in a crowd. Garrison, a crime scene photographer, looked like an African Dudley Do-Right, while Sams, a bungling micro-evidence-gathering expert, was the spitting image of Mr. Magoo.

"Yes, sir," Garrison replied from outside the crowded office.

"Garrison, photograph everything in this house and, most importantly, everything in this office, before it is moved," the captain ordered. "Sams?" Captain Richter yelled, but there was no response. "Sams, where in the hell are you?" he screamed at the top of his lungs.

"Here I am, Captain," Sams replied, jumping up and down and waiving his arms wildly before charging through the sea of humanity that had gathered in the living room.

"Sams, I need every vial in this office and the boxes they came in dusted for fingerprints. Next, there are drones and explosive containers stored in the attic. I expect everything to be examined thoroughly, and I mean down to every last damn molecule," Captain Richter ordered as Sams began to perspire.

"Yes, sir," Sams responded immediately as he attempted to snap to attention. However, the warm room and Sam's excessive body heat combined to generate a fog-like mist on his glasses, the sight of which was not reassuring to Captain Richter in the least.

"And Sams, do be especially careful," the captain insisted as his visually impaired evidence expert wiped the condensation from his glasses.

"As always, Captain," Sams acknowledged as he began to squint, mistakenly staring at Sharkie instead of the captain, the identity error escaping him completely.

"Blind as a bat and dumb as an ox," the captain mumbled about Sams while leaving the office for the kitchen. Leslie was close on his heels.

"What kind of Green Acres Agency are you running around here, Captain? I'm starting to think that the FBI stands for Frickin' Barnyard Idiots," Leslie critiqued with brutal honesty, wondering how Sams had made it into law enforcement.

"Grrrrr," Captain Richter roared, choosing to ignore the comment from the woman who had now become a thorn in his side. "Why would those bastards at the NSA send me an irrational, estrogen-driven female?" Captain Richter mumbled as he approached Corporal Carpenter, who was standing in the kitchen with Trissy. "It's about time," Captain Richter growled at what he perceived to be an inordinate amount of time taken to flush the criminal out of her bedroom.

"Is this Mrs. Bent?" Leslie asked, looking at Trissy, who appeared dazed and confused. "What's wrong with her?" she asked Corporal Carpenter.

"She tried to choke me," Trissy blurted before the corporal had a chance to reply.

"That's not true," the agent insisted.

"Well, then, how do you explain this bruising around her neck?" Leslie asked, brushing Trissy's hair to the side.

"Damned if I know," Corporal Carpenter replied, shrugging her shoulders.

"Captain Richter, is your agency now supporting a policy where torture is condoned and one's legal rights ignored?" Leslie asked, knowing full well that an inquiry would have to be held on this matter.

"Mrs. Bent obviously fell while resisting arrest," the captain replied, in an effort to protect his agent.

"I see. Mrs. Bent, I'm Leslie Valentino," the National Security Agency operations director said.

"Mrs. Bent, I've taken the liberty of making you a cup of coffee. Would you like anything in it?" Sergeant Jones asked, handing her a piping hot mug.

"Thank you, no," Trissy replied appreciatively, accepting the black brew. With her mind clouded by illness and the sedative, Trissy did not want her journey toward full consciousness to be interrupted or even delayed by sugar or cream.

"You're welcome," Jones replied as Sergeant Schnapps looked at Trissy, smiled, and wagged his tail.

What warranted this invasion? Trissy thought as she struggled to make sense of the chaos around her. She was aware of the tremendous noise coming from the crowd, but whenever she focused on any one individual their lips appeared to move out of sync with their voice.

How bizarre, she thought.

"Mrs. Bent," Captain Richter said loudly, in an attempt to gain her attention. However, there was no response. Trissy continued to survey and analyze the invaders. She didn't hear her name or see the agent who, by this time, was standing beside her.

"Mrs. Bent!" Captain Richter shouted as he grabbed her by the elbow.

Trissy was aware of her arm moving and coffee being splashed over the rim of the mug and onto the floor. Yet it took her a moment to realize that someone was tugging on her elbow. She looked to her left and was briefly startled. There he was, the ornery beady-eyed man in black, half Johnny Cash and half G.I. Joe.

"Take your hands off of me!" Trissy insisted, attempting in vain to free herself from his vice-like grip. "Let me go and get the hell out of my home!" However, the more she struggled, the greater Captain Richter increased his unyielding grip on the petite nurse.

"Captain, let her go," Leslie ordered in a firm, authoritative voice

"In due time, Ms. Valentino, of course you realize that this is an FBI matter," Captain Richter winked, snickering. In his mind the FBI was on the front lines of national security, and not this pitiful, passive representative sent from the herd of sheep running the NSA.

"How dare you! You either let her go now or I'll have your badge, Captain," Leslie demanded. The captain's cavalier attitude and his gesture were more than Leslie could stand. She was in charge of this operation, and the FBI was functioning under her authority. Such insubordination would not be tolerated.

Captain Richter chose to ignore the command, disregarding the threat. He had dedicated his life to protecting the United States of America and her citizens from harm. The raid he had planned and executed had been enormously successful. Not only had he prevented weapons of mass destruction from being unleashed, but he now held a terrorist in his hands. He detested the thought of releasing his prisoner to the dysfunctional, liberal judicial system. Mrs. Bent's death should be swift and by his hands. She and her husband were undoubtedly guilty. Oh, how he wished he could be judge, jury, and executioner.

"Captain, did you hear me?" Leslie queried, raising her voice.

"You're hurting me!" Trissy screamed, struggling to free herself.

The United States was under attack and all indications pointed toward a forthcoming final massive assault. Time was of the essence. Leslie needed answers, and she needed them quickly in order to effectively defend this great nation. The emails Rex had sent to the CDC and the NSA over the last week were of strong interest. She was unsure how the information he provided related to recent terrorist attacks, but Carencrow now appeared to be the epicenter for terrorist operations. Her intuition told her that, directly or indirectly, Trissy and Rex could provide information invaluable to national defense. She had some very important questions to ask Trissy, and now was the perfect opportunity with Rex at work. Leslie needed Trissy calm and cooperative, not agitated or possibly injured. Realizing that the situation was escalating, she positioned herself in front of Captain Richter.

"Damn it, Captain, let her go, NOW!" Leslie growled, waving her finger at the FBI agent.

Suddenly, there was the shattering of glass. Trissy had lost her grip on the coffee mug, and it fell to the floor. Exhausted, she stood in Captain Richter's grasp gasping for air, her oxygen-starved muscles twitching, and her pulse racing. Trissy had ceased struggling.

The captain, realizing that his anger and rage were now far too evident, released his grip and shoved Trissy toward Leslie. Leslie embraced the frightened emergency room nurse and led her toward a large glass table adjacent to the kitchen, where she helped her onto a seat.

"Jones, cuff Mrs. Bent and read this traitor her rights," the captain ordered. "Corporal Carpenter, pick up the glass and mop up that crap before someone slips and falls. We surely don't need another bogus worker's compensation case," Captain Richter ordered, before storming down the kitchen hall toward the garage.

"Jones, let me make myself perfectly clear. Mrs. Bent is not to be cuffed or your head will roll along with the captain's. Trust me, I have the power and the authority to draw and quarter you both, and will do so without hesitation. Now, if you would, please bring us two cups of coffee, both with cream and sugar," Leslie insisted, her voice resonating in a hard, unyielding tone.

Captain Richter stopped dead in his tracks, looking back toward the kitchen. His eyes reflected anger and frustration. Sergeant Jones looked at the captain for clarification of the conflicting orders. Captain Richter said nothing, but stood glaring at his nemesis, grinding his teeth in defiance.

"What an adolescent display of machismo," Leslie whispered, continuing to comfort Trissy, while Jones and Schnapps went into the kitchen to search for two coffee mugs.

The now dejected captain continued his march toward the outdoors and freedom, where the coronary-clinching nicotine gods offered some relief from the cruel and unforgiving world.

"Why me, and why does that crazy bitch have to remind me of my ex-wife?!" Captain Richter screamed into the night as a flock of buzzards circled above.

CHAPTER 25

WITH EVERY MINUTE THAT ticked by, the madness and mayhem in the emergency room intensified. Today, the patient volume and acuity had been extremely high. There had been dozens of admissions, many of which had to be held in the emergency room, because the floors were at capacity—or so it would seem. In actuality, there were not enough ICU, telemetry, or floor nurses. Most had been driven off by the low pay and lack of esteem, while others abhorred the dangerous working conditions and the long, grueling hours. Yet, whatever the reason, there was a common denominator: all disdained management. Needless to say, the ER was a mess. The hallways were congested, with sick patients everywhere—some were standing and some were squatting, while others were confined to wheelchairs. Most were complaining, and several were waiting for a bed on the hospital floor to clear. Additionally, four ambulance crews hugged the walls attempting, to stay out of the way while the patients they had transported lay immobilized on portable stretchers for hours

"Welcome to gridlock, ER style," Rex shouted over the crying, moaning and groaning, coughing, and vomiting. All sounds were intermingled with angry conversations from the multitude of dissatisfied pateints. "Sheila, as coordinator you have to do something about this mess," Rex insisted, glancing at his watch.

Sheila was clearly overwhelmed by the chaos. The demands and the expectations had suddenly become too great. Rex could see the hair on the back of her head begin to rise as her glowing emerald green eyes darted rhythmically back and forth. The normally relatively calm and stable charge nurse was undoubtedly frustrated. For a moment she looked like a lemming ready to jump from a cliff and swim to its death. Clearly, Sheila was ready to cross that fine line dividing sanity from insanity. Down, but not out, she reached deep into her cerebral cortex to rekindle the anger she had so mercilessly bludgeoned her fourth husband with.

"Well, Rex, what would you like me to do, pull a bed out of my butt?" the frazzled buxom bombshell fired back.

The exchange was interrupted by another ringing phone. "Rex, it's for you," Sheila said, placing her hand over the receiver. "It's Doctor Gonzales, and he sounds like he's in a pissy mood."

"Great, that's all I need, a mad, manic Mexican," Rex moaned, placing the phone to his ear and listening for a moment. "Yes, sir, I'll be right there," Rex replied apprehensively, before handing the phone back to Sheila.

Over the years, Rex had committed thousands of intentional (and quite a few unintentional) corporate infractions in this fairytale hospital setting. Yet, he had never been called back to the woodshed. It was highly unusual for the non-confrontational, fast-talking emergency department director to demand that anyone come to his office.

"All is not right in the Land of Oz," Sheila concluded. She now sensed that Rex had been a key topic in the a.m. meeting with Teresa Talon and the muckity-mucks.

"Perhaps it's happy hour, and Speedy just wants to have a *cerveza*," Rex rationalized.

"Possibly, but today is the Day of the Dead in Mexico. There's no doubt in my mind that somewhere along the way you have insulted Dr. Gonzales, and possibly his ancestors. May I suggest you bring a peace offering of some kind?" Sheila suggested reassuringly.

"Rex, stay focused and don't take it personally!" Boom Boom shouted in support.

As Rex walked past Teresa's office, the two briefly locked eyes before her blinds came crashing down, eliminating any opportunity to gaze into the nursing director's glass tower, from which all could be seen but nothing appreciated. Teresa's actions were so abrupt and purposeful that Rex chuckled.

All this managerial disaster/hospital executioner needs is a stockade outside her office, from which daily hangings and floggings could be observed by the peasants, Rex thought to himself as he marched by.

In short order, Rex arrived at his destination.

Emergency Room Director

Dr. Gonzo T. Gonzales

"Well, I guess this is the place," Rex whispered after reading the brass plaque. "*Ay, caramba!* If the damn flip-flopping politicians had ever built that border fence, this meeting would have never been," Rex rationalized while fighting the urge to knock. "In fact, what a fitting end to a miserable day: called into an office to talk to a man who has all the warmth and charisma of a rabid, tequila-tipping hyena," Rex justified while rapping his knuckles against the highly polished oak door.

"Come in and sit down!" Dr. Gonzales growled. The tone in his voice had an ominous quality that registered immediately. Rex entered but remained standing in order to survey the field of battle. Dr. Gonzales was also standing, but with his back toward

Rex. The fearless leader kept sniffling and repetitively tweaking his nose. It was apparent that Speedy had just put on a finely pressed, brilliantly white lab coat, which he only wore when attempting to appear authoritative.

"I told you to take a seat," Dr. Gonzales lashed out in an uncharacteristically aggressive manner as he turned to face Rex.

"Here?" Rex asked, pointing to the only chair in the small, cramped office.

"Don't be a wise ass. I am certainly not going to allow you to sit in my chair," Dr. Gonzales shot back, before they both slowly and cautiously took their respective seats.

"My apologies, Gonzo, I had no intention of insulting you," Rex responded humbly as he fought to restrain his anger generated from the pompous, portly prick.

"Rex, I need to be perfectly blunt. The nurses don't like you, the staff physicians can't stand you, and management despises you," Dr. Gonzales disclosed with a sense of joy while waiting impatiently for Rex to squirm.

"Gonzo, I don't want to ignite your sombrero, but you're dead wrong," Rex replied calmly as the corners of his lips turned upwards.

"There you go again, exhibiting flagrant disregard for authority. Wipe that damn smile off your face," Dr. Gonzales ordered, pounding his desk.

"Gonzo, I don't understand. For over ten years I have remained relatively loyal to this thankless hospital, as well as our Medicaid/Medicare-embezzling employer. Furthermore, I have always made myself available to fill empty shifts that no one else wanted," Rex replied in his own defense.

"That was in the past. You've done nothing for us today."

"I see."

"Most importantly, you've become public enemy number one. There's no one in this hospital that gives a damn about you," Dr. Gonzales relayed, raising his voice.

"What's not to like? I'm courteous, professional, and lovable. Surely, you have the wrong man," Rex replied.

"Rex, you have jeopardized the profitable contract that the Rock Hard Group has nurtured for years with this superb hospital, and I refuse to stick my neck out for you any longer. We have come to the conclusion that we are over staffed, and you must go," Dr. Gonzales shared with great satisfaction as he handed Rex an un-stamped envelope.

"Surely this is some kind of a joke. You've been here for three months, I have only spoken with you twice, and now you can no longer lend me your support?" Rex asked, staring at Speedy in disbelief before opening the letter.

Suddenly, Dr. Gonzales became agitated. He began to squirm in his seat, madly picking at his face while making a violent snorting sound in an attempt to inhale through congested nasal passages.

It didn't take Rex long to get the gist of the message. Below the formal letterhead he read:

Dr. Bent,

Effective immediately, your services are terminated.

Regards,

Gonzo T. Gonzales, M.D.

"Well, Gonzo, I would say that you and your cronies put some time and effort into this letter. I guess those creative writing courses have really paid off after all. However, I am rather disappointed. I thought these notices always arrive on a pink slip," Rex concluded, watching Dr. Gonzales madly tweak his nose.

Rex had fully expected a response, but Gonzales appeared preoccupied. It was obvious that the conversation had come to an abrupt end. Rex stood and opened the door, but hesitated after hearing yet another strange sound. At first he was certain that it did not originate from Speedy because hyenas are supposed to laugh, not moan, groan, or gasp.

"Gonzo, I think you should really do something about that cold," Rex suggested, turning around.

However, once again, there was no response, probably because Dr. Gonzales was pale, diaphoretic, and struggling for air while grabbing his chest. Rex recognized the symptoms immediately. There was no doubt that the sorry, self-serving bastard was having a myocardial infarction.

"Oh, by the way, I appear to have lost my privileges at this fine institution, so I can't stick my neck out for you. But, given the fact that we're close personal friends with a common bond, I can tell you that your cigarettes are in your top pocket, the defibrillator is located just down the hall, and I believe you dial nine-one-one for emergency medical services," Rex shared with his former employer, before gently closing Gonzo's office door. "That's extraordinary. Usually you can't kill the maggots," Rex quipped after hearing a thud.

Rex gazed at the soon-to-be obsolete brass plaque and thought of his termination and the cold, calculating manner in which it had been delivered. He felt the anger within him surge as he slapped the termination letter against the palm of his hand.

"Thank God! This is the best thing that could have ever happened. My sentence at this rock quarry has been served, and the ball and chain severed. It's time to chase a few rainbows, especially given the fact that socialized medicine is just around the corner," Rex announced joyfully, strutting down the hall. As he passed Teresa's office he noticed that all the lights were off, and the *Gone Fishing* sign was proudly displayed.

"That figures. The executioner has already left for her usual four-day weekend while the slaves toil away," Rex chuckled, ambling back into the emergency room, convinced that no one could ruin his evening.

"Well, you don't appear to be bleeding anywhere. How did your meeting go with General Santa Ana?" Boom Boom asked with great curiosity.

Rex said nothing. He simply handed the termination letter to his trusted friend and coworker.

"Those bastards!" Boom Boom shouted.

"What?! What is it?!" Sheila asked, seeing the anger on Dr. Witherspoon's face.

"Sheila, Rex has been fired," Boom Boom announced.

"No, it's not possible," Sheila responded.

"Rex, forget everything I have ever said. Take this very PERSONALLY!" Boom Boom insisted without hesitation.

"Rex, sometimes the line between being laid and being screwed becomes blurry. In your case, there is little doubt. You've been screwed!" Sheila added as the phone rang yet again.

"C'est si bon," Wan blurted loudly in agreement, without knowing what the conversation was about, as he scurried by on some obscure mission.

Sheila shook her head at Wan's remarks, while briefly observing his bizarre behavior.

"This phone is becoming a pain in the ass," Sheila complained.

"ER, Mofuz," Sheila growled.

"No!" Sheila shouted as she listened intently.

"Oh my God, Rex, it's Trissy. The CIA, the FBI, the NSA, the state police, and the city police have raided your home. Trissy has been placed under arrest, and they're looking for you!" Sheila relayed.

CHAPTER 26

REX MADE IT HOME in record time. As he turned onto Mallard Drive he could see dozens of cars lining both sides of the street. As he eased the Mustang into the drive he could see that all the lights in the house were on. *Surely this has to be a mistake*, Rex thought to himself.

A moving truck blocked his access to the carport, so he pulled his sports car onto the front lawn and shut down the engine. As Rex stared through the front windshield, preoccupied with all the activity going on inside and outside the house, he didn't notice the two FBI agents, Coco and Tango, approaching.

The two burly men dressed in black, each with their revolver drawn and pointed at his head, stood adjacent to his pride and joy. No sooner had Rex cracked the car door than Coco grabbed it, jerking it wide open.

"Whoa," Rex blurted as Tango grabbed his scrub top, pulling with such force that he was ejected from Ford's masterpiece. Within seconds, Rex felt himself being burrowed into the hard, cold ground—his head and face constrained, his hands bound, and the middle of his back put under intense pressure.

"Cuff him," Coco shouted while Tango patted Rex down.

"No weapons," Tango announced, as the dazed physician was yanked to his feet.

"You have the right to remain silent…" Coco began, as Rex was escorted toward his home.

"What in the hell is going on, and who are you people?" Rex demanded to know, while spitting grass and dirt from his mouth. However, he never received a reply, and his Miranda rights continued to be read.

"…and if you do not have an attorney, one will be appointed for you. Do you understand your rights?"

"Of course I do," Rex replied angrily, watching his office furniture being loaded onto a stark, white truck without any identifiable markings.

The two men shoved Rex through the carport, past the rectangular heap of molten metal. With his hands cuffed behind his back, the men turned Rex sideways, rushing through what remained of the kitchen hallway door, which the battering ram had demolished during the raid.

Trissy and Leslie had remained sitting at the kitchen table since their earlier encounter with Captain Richter. Leslie had learned a great deal from Trissy in a short period of time. However, their conversation was abruptly terminated by what sounded like a herd of stampeding buffalo.

"Take it easy," Rex shouted, stumbling forward. "Damn it," he growled as he lost his footing and fell.

"You clumsy son of a bitch," Coco blurted, as each agent grabbed Rex by the arm, dragging him through the hallway and into the kitchen where the two gorillas righted their prisoner and began dusting off the dirt, grass and leaves, which Rex had accumulated during his capture.

"He looks better already, Coco," Tango announced with great satisfaction, as he and his partner continued to make Rex look presentable, thus downplaying their strong-arm tactics.

"Rex!" Trissy shouted, standing up quickly and rushing toward him with outstretched arms. Her efforts, however, were cut short by the ever-hostile Captain Richter, who had returned to the kitchen after a thirty-minute hiatus.

"Not so fast," Captain Richter ordered, grabbing Trissy by the shirt and jerking her away from her husband and back into her seat, where, in one fluid motion, he cuffed her wrist to a leg of the heavy kitchen table.

"Captain, this is inexcusable," Leslie protested as Rex lunged forward to attack the sorry bastard who had treated Trissy so roughly. But he had only advanced one step when his efforts came to an abrupt halt. Coco and Tango did not budge, even though Rex struggled with all his might.

"How dare you treat me and my wife in this manner!" Rex shouted at Captain Richter.

"Captain, we have successfully apprehended Dr. Bent," Coco announced with pride.

"Strong work, Corporal. Has he been informed of his rights?" Captain Richter asked.

"Absolutely, Captain," Coco replied.

"Tango, make sure you search his car," the captain insisted.

"Yes, sir," the agent answered, before swaggering down the kitchen hall toward the carport.

"Coco, please continue to maintain a firm grip on the good doctor. We must make every effort to ensure that he's not injured," the captain requested with arrogant gestures in a sarcastic, condescending tone.

"That may be difficult, Captain, because this sorry excuse for a human being looks quite fragile," Coco snickered as he briefly considered breaking every bone in Rex's body.

"Dr. Bent, I am Captain Richter of the Federal Bureau of Investigation. Thank you for saving us the time and effort of hunting you down. We recently received some rather shocking information about you, your wife, and your recent activities," Captain Richter began, while examining the disheveled physician.

"I'm sure," Rex said as he stared into the eyes of this power-hungry little man who stood before him.

"Thus, we found it necessary to obtain a court order to search your home," Captain Richter added, moving closer. "And, from what we've uncovered, it appears that the allegations are true. You and your wife have indeed committed treasonous acts against our great nation." Rex shook his head, and Trissy looked on in disbelief.

"I have no idea what you're talking about. We are law-abiding citizens, and I demand that you release us immediately!" Rex insisted.

"In good time, Doctor; however, if you would, please tell me about the thousands of vials you so conveniently stored in your office."

"Vials, what vials?" Trissy shouted as tears started to stream down her face.

"Captain, this is neither the time nor the place to interrogate Dr. and Mrs. Bent," Leslie said, in an attempt to console Trissy.

"Ms. Valentino, I would be most appreciative if you would leave the police work to the professionals. I, personally, will decide not only the time and the place, but also the means and the forcefulness exercised in extracting intelligence. Do I make myself perfectly clear?" Captain Richter said in an unyielding tone.

"Captain, the Nazi storm troopers were crushed. You, as well, shall have your day," Leslie assured the tyrannical captain, who had blown an important and timely opportunity for her to gather invaluable information.

"You're mad! I have no vials stored in my office," Rex replied, raising his voice defiantly.

"Well, now, I believe we have obtained your fingerprints from several of those mysterious nonexistent vials. Tell me, Doctor, what biological agents are contained in those glass ampoules?"

"I want to talk with my lawyer—NOW!" Rex insisted.

"Also, I need to know what your plans were and who your accomplices are. Now, that's not too much to ask from someone bound for the gallows, is it?" Captain Richter growled, as his face came within inches of Rex's.

"How in the world does a maggot like you become so delusional that he thinks he is judge, jury, and executioner?" Rex fired back, not intimidated by the captain's arrogant demeanor or his bad breath.

"If you're asking how I have become so successful, obviously it is the result of hard work and my unique God-given ability to catch bad guys," the captain responded curtly. "Now, Doctor, if you don't know anything about the vials, perhaps you can enlighten me with regard to your goods stored in the attic?" Captain Richter asked as his frustration and anger quickly became more evident.

"Go to hell!" Rex growled.

"No, sir, you're going first!" Captain Richter instinctively fired back, before taking a moment to collect his thoughts. "Now, so much for pleasantries, I'd also like to know about the drones and the hundreds of pounds of napalm," Captain Richter demanded while grabbing Rex by the front of his scrub top and twisting the fabric.

"Piss off!" Rex replied calmly, unfazed by the intimidation.

"You had enough explosives to destroy the entire neighborhood. And we ain't talking fireworks, boy. Surely you aren't going to deny knowledge of these weapons?" the captain sneered, while pulling Rex closer.

"Captain, if you must know, I was developing napalm enemas to use on assholes like you," Rex replied with a smile so broad that it sent Richter into a rage.

The captain immediately released his grip and stepped back, reaching for his side arm with his other hand. Within seconds, the Colt .45 was out of its holster and leveled at Rex's chest.

"Captain, put that weapon away—NOW!" Leslie yelled at the top of her voice as the enraged FBI captain moved closer, placing the barrel under Rex's chin as Coco continued to restrain the prisoner.

"No!!!" Trissy screamed, fighting to free herself and help Rex.

Captain Richter ignored both pleas as his finger wrapped even more tightly around the trigger.

"I must admit, Captain, at first I thought you were just another loose cannon. Now, I realize that you are just a stocky pansy with a pistol," Rex concluded with his signature Cheshire grin.

"AH!" the captain screamed with bloodcurdling intensity as he buried the barrel of the pistol deep into the space between Rex's mandible and neck. Still, Rex did not flinch. He remained cool and collected.

"Even a maggot like you couldn't kill a man in cold blood," Rex said, taunting the captain, while thinking that perhaps he had taken the pansy analogy in this macho standoff a bit too far.

"Captain, stand down!" Leslie ordered, as Trissy began to shake with fear. She was nearly hysterical knowing that Captain Richter was about to discharge his weapon.

"Oh, was I tempted," Captain Richter said, rationalizing that any grand jury, if convened, would find him not guilty in Dr. Bent's accidental death. However, to avoid a potentially career-ending misunderstanding, he holstered his weapon. "You'll live to see another day in hell from a cell on death row while I bask in the glory of capturing your sorry, treasonous ass," the captain announced proudly, realizing how highly successful his flawless mission had been. He had won a skirmish in the war on terrorism.

Everyone breathed a sigh of relief as the tension in the room eased considerably.

"Tubbs, take Dr. and Mrs. Bent down to the station and book them. The felony charge: treasonous acts against the United States of America," Captain Richter ordered as Coco finally released his vice-like grip.

"Yes, sir, it would be my pleasure," Tubbs replied smartly as Captain Richter released Trissy from the shackle, which had kept her bound to the kitchen table.

"I trust you will both enjoy your stay on death row. By the way, rest assured that we still execute traitors in this country," Captain Richter said with a chuckle, leaving the kitchen to survey the home one last time.

"Well, that's comforting," Rex whispered as Trissy's hands were cuffed behind her back.

"Rex, what are we going to do?" Trissy pleaded.

"No worries, my love," Rex assured his beautiful wife, desiring to wipe the tears from her eyes.

"Now, then, let's go for a ride in Corporal Tubb's nice patrol car," the burly, knuckle-dragging officer insisted, shoving his prisoners through the kitchen hallway and out into the carport.

THE PATROL CAR WAS parked on Mallard drive with the engine running while Corporal Tubbs and the various law enforcement agencies took time to congratulate one another for a job well done.

Rex and Trissy sat quietly in the back, each with their hands cuffed behind them. With the exception of the frequent reports coming across a police radio, the silence was deafening. Rex looked at Trissy. She sat quietly staring ahead at the impenetrable metal mesh separating the front from the backseat.

Rex thought about how the ambient light cast a captivating silhouette, accentuating Trissy's striking beauty. The vision was in stark contrast to the dusky, malodorous stench permeating the vehicle.

"Man, it stinks in here," Rex said, trying to break the tension in the air, for he knew that Trissy was mad as hell. But there was no response. After several moments Rex felt he had to reach deeper into his conscience to retrieve what few interpersonal skills he had remaining. "Personally, I found the captain to be a rather pleasant chap. Wouldn't you say, Trissy?" he joked, in an attempt to break the eerie silence.

"Damn you, Rex! You almost got yourself killed!" Trissy screamed.

"All right, all right, but it wasn't my fault," Rex said in his own lame defense.

"What do you mean it wasn't your fault? You provoked and then purposely taunted that lunatic to the point that he nearly turned into a raging homicidal maniac," Trissy lectured.

"It was rather gratifying, I must say," Rex replied calmly.

"Rex, that nut had the crazy eyes that we only see with patients who are either psychotic or have fried their brains on some illegal high potency street drugs. And you nearly pushed him over the edge," Trissy complained.

"Well, I didn't care for the way the bastard was treating you. Frankly, he pissed me off!" Rex argued.

"Well, pissed off and dead are two different issues. How in the world would I go on living without you, you old varmint? " Trissy growled, moving closer and placing her head on his shoulder.

"What do you mean, 'old varmint'? As I recall, our birthdays are only a day apart," Rex replied in a huff.

"Yes, Rex, nine years and one day, to be precise. Boy, you have really developed quite a selective memory," Trissy replied.

"I have found it to be rather helpful over the years. Now, tell me, how are you feeling?" Rex asked with concern, after realizing now was the perfect time to change the subject.

"Physically or emotionally?" Trissy inquired suspiciously, although she had not finished giving Rex a piece of her mind.

"Physically, my love," Rex qualified.

"Physically, much better than this morning, but for a while it was nip and tuck. I think that shot you gave me did the trick. In fact, I slept beautifully until the FBI came a-knocking. Now, emotionally, I'll just have to let your imagination run wild," Trissy added in an attempt to reopen the discussion on the altercation that could have proven fatal.

"Thank, God. I was so worried about you," Rex said sincerely, kissing Trissy on the forehead, again, wisely choosing to ignore Trissy's emotional well-being.

"I love you," Trissy said, looking into Rex's eyes.

"I love you, too," Rex replied as he kissed Trissy on the lips.

Suddenly, the drivers' side door opened, and Officer Tubbs squeezed in behind the wheel.

"Okay you two lovebirds, it's time to go to Sing Sing," the officer chuckled as he lowered the rear driver's side window. Rex and Trissy took one last look at their home.

"Smile for the camera," Corporal Coco requested as a bright flash appeared from out of nowhere. Clearly, Rex and Trissy had been caught by surprise. They were blinded by the light.

"Nice shooting, Coco," Officer Tubbs snickered as Coco lowered his camera.

"Thank you. Captain Richter thought this would be the perfect career-enhancing photo op," Coco replied as Tubbs rolled up the window, placing the police cruiser into gear. Slowly, the vehicle started rolling forward.

"That's comforting. Does the captain have any other surprises in store for us when we reach the jail?" Rex asked as his vision slowly started to return. There was no reply. Rex and Trissy watched quietly as their once-peaceful neighborhood rolled by. "Trissy, what in the world was that madman talking about when he referred to vials with biological agents, drones, and napalm? And, who in the Sam Hell is he to insinuate that we're terrorists?" Rex questioned.

"Rex, I have no idea what captain crazy eyes was referring to, but from what little I gathered, the Gestapo found something in your office, as well as the attic," Trissy said, trying to remember bits and pieces of information she had overheard.

"Well, the only thing he'd find in either location is dust bunnies. By the by, who was that lady you were sitting with?" Rex asked as he, too, tried to put the pieces together.

"Her name is Leslie Valentino. She said she was from the National Security Agency. In fact, now that I recall, Leslie is the one who received your correspondence with regard to the blue Asian sailors and their mysterious deaths," Trissy remembered, just as Rex's memory was simultaneously triggered by the name.

"Ah, of course, she's the one who replied that the information we had provided was 'of interest and would be explored in due time,'" Rex suddenly realized, gritting his teeth. "Frankly, I'm surprised the bureaucratic bimbo is here. Did she happen to mention what brought her to our quiet little town of Carencrow, or why due time just happens to be tonight?" Rex asked with a hint of sarcasm.

"Yes, as a matter of fact she did. It was your email," Trissy replied, wondering why Rex was getting so suspicious.

"Well, then, why do you suppose she invited all of her playmates—the FBI, the CIA, the state police, and a gaggle of unidentified bozos?" Rex asked, coming to the conclusion that Leslie was the ringmaster of this circus.

"She didn't say, but my impression is that she's in charge," Trissy replied as she struggled to find a more comfortable position, an impossible task with her hands cuffed behind her back.

"I knew it. Well, then, what did she talk about?" Rex inquired with great interest as he tried to unravel the mystery.

"She asked mainly about us," Trissy replied.

"It sounds like Leslie was gaining your confidence before picking your brain. Now that I think about it, there seems to be quite a few brain-picking buzzards in this town. I wonder why the government would fly in another vulture?" Rex asked, also struggling to get comfortable.

"Who knows, but she was kind enough to defend me from Captain Richter's talons," Trissy replied with a sigh of relief.

"For that I owe her a debt of gratitude, my love," Rex admitted, while thinking of ways to ensure the evil captain's early demise.

"Well, if we ever get out of this mess, I believe an apology is in order," Trissy suggested.

"Yes, dear," Rex responded submissively, and out of habit, for these were the two words which the male species had adopted to survive the trials and tribulations of marriage. "By the way, did Leslie ever share with you what position she holds with the NSA?"

"No, no she did not. Why? Would it matter?" Trissy asked.

"I was just curious. Trissy, are you sure Leslie didn't ask about vials or explosives?" Rex prodded.

"No, she didn't," Trissy answered as she suddenly recalled overhearing a conversation among all the chaos.

"Did she ever mention the dead Asian sailors, the strange illness which had befallen the emergency room nurses, or our near-death experience with the Asian road warriors?" Rex inquired.

"No, not a word, but…" Trissy said, pausing.

"But what?"

"It's probably nothing, but I do remember hearing someone saying, 'all the proof we need is on the computer,'" Trissy disclosed as Tubbs listened intently to their conversation.

"What? Christ, what in the world could they have possibly found in our home?" Rex wondered out loud.

"Weapons of mass destruction, perhaps?" Tubbs said, beginning to think these were the dumbest terrorists he had ever known.

"WMDs, that's absurd!" Rex growled in response.

No, it's not, Trissy thought. "Rex, it appears that we've been set up. Someone planted weapons of mass destruction in our home and then informed the authorities," Trissy concluded, recalling the bizarre events that had occurred over the last few days.

"That's just not possible. I locked the door this morning before leaving for work and, and…" Rex suddenly paused, struggling to remember exactly what he had done so early in the morning.

"And what, Rex?" Trissy asked, patiently waiting for the other shoe to drop.

"And, I think I set the alarm, but I can't be sure. Well, one out of two isn't bad," Rex confessed, not believing he could have been so careless.

"What do you mean you can't be sure? Rex, how could you, especially after we were almost killed last night?" Trissy argued.

"Trissy, I am truly sorry. I was running late," Rex apologized.

"Rex, a stampeding herd of wild elephants couldn't have awakened me this morning. I was dead to the world. The vials of whatever, the explosives, and the computer trail must have been planted today," Trissy surmised.

"Well, then, I'd say that we're probably in big trouble," Rex concluded, looking around the confines of the police cruiser.

"Rex, that has to be the understatement of the year. My God, what else could possibly go wrong?" Trissy wondered, unaware that her husband had more unsettling news.

"Well, now that you mention it, I was fired," Rex confessed.

"What!" Trissy shouted.

"Speedy was kind enough to deliver the news late this afternoon. In fact, he was so choked up with emotion that, when I left his office, he was clutching his chest," Rex grinned with satisfaction.

"Oh, Rex, I am terribly sorry," Trissy empathized, looking at her husband. The occasional streetlight would briefly reveal Rex's eyes, from which Trissy could always judge her husband's state of mind. However, this glimpse into his soul was lost in the shadows as the police cruiser continued onward.

"I knew we needed a change in our lives, but losing my job, having our home seized, and being branded as traitors is rather drastic," Rex said, in an attempt to lighten the moment.

"Well, somehow we'll find a way out of this mess," Trissy said, trying to convince herself and her husband.

"Absolutely, that's why it's time for us to go on the offensive," Rex rationalized enthusiastically.

"Against whom, Rex?" Trissy asked, her fingernails digging into the back of the beige vinyl seat.

"Why, GeeHad, and possibly Chum, of course," Rex stated emphatically.

"And just how do you propose we achieve your objective, now that the police have placed us in irons?"

"You don't have a hairpin on you, do ya?" Rex inquired.

"Rex, that trick only works in the movies," Trissy replied as the police cruiser turned onto the blacktop nestled high on the levee restraining the raging Cajun river.

Seconds later, there was a sudden brilliant bank of lights bouncing up and down and closing very rapidly. Rex and Officer Tubbs were both startled as they looked to their left.

"However, I do happen to have a nail file," Trissy joked, moments before realizing the impending danger.

"Look out!" Rex screamed as the police cruiser was suddenly T-boned by a rather large truck traveling at a high rate of speed. Rex was thrown violently into Trissy on impact, and the police cruiser rolled over onto its hood. The crippled cruiser rapidly began to pick up speed as it slid down the steep embankment.

The splash was unmistakable. Rex, Trissy, and Officer Tubbs were now trapped upside down in a dark tin coffin, submerged in a very unforgiving body of water.

CHAPTER 27

I T HAD BEEN SNOWING heavily for two days, and a thick blanket of sparkling white powder now covered the grounds. Darkness had fallen several hours prior and, as usual, the weather outside was merciless. A violent nor'easter was whipping frigid arctic air through the small seaport town of Bar Harbor, Maine. The sustained winds were blowing at forty knots, with gusts in excess of sixty knots. The wind chill factor was a bone-chilling minus twenty degrees Fahrenheit.

Earl Vassar, the National Security Agency's chief-of-staff, had been at work at the Bayview since 5:00 a.m. analyzing, digesting, and then reanalyzing the volume of intelligence which had been collected over the past twenty-four hours. With yesterday's destruction of Grand Central Station and today's loss of the Coast Guard Cutter, *Freedom*, there was a sense of urgency such as he had never felt before. At his insistence, briefings were now held every three hours throughout the day. There had been no time for breakfast or lunch, yet he was neither hungry nor fatigued, until he glanced at his watch.

"My God, it's been a hectic day," Earl whispered as his eyes finally focused on the dial, 1930. His mind and his body had been fueled by an intense surge of adrenaline, augmented by frequent shots of espresso, both of which were starting to wane. He had just finished reviewing the latest intelligence. Earl placed his reading glasses on the desk, shut his eyes for a moment, and then gently massaged his temples. When he opened his eyes, he felt that all of his senses had suddenly been magnified. The smell and the sounds of the crackling fire intensified. The entire room was now bathed with a warm glow as light reflected off the stained mahogany paneling surrounding the study. Even the pictures adorning the walls, depicting hunting scenes from long ago, came to life. Suddenly, Earl felt empowered and confident, as if touched by the hand of the Medal-of-Honor winner who had built this spectacular estate.

"Time for a break," Earl said aloud, pushing himself away from his desk, rocking backwards in his chair. His thoughts drifted back to his days at Notre Dame and his glory years as an all-star fullback. Oh, how he had enjoyed playing offense. There was something very satisfying about taking the pigskin and diving through the hole with reckless abandon. He chuckled as he remembered flattening several of his opponents who had the audacity to attempt to keep him out of the end zone. But his position at the National Security Agency called for a change in tactics. He felt that he was constantly on the defensive, and only with accurate, timely intelligence could he go on the offensive and take the battle to the terrorists.

The faint sound of knuckles rapping against his door awakened Earl from thoughts of long, long ago.

"Come in," Earl announced. As the door slowly opened, Director Anderson appeared. "Mr. Director," Earl said, standing to greet the director. "I wasn't sure if someone was at the door or if I was hearing tree limbs rattling against the house," Earl confessed, extending his hand.

"Your must forgive me. My hands are crippled by such bad arthritis that I can no longer announce my arrival with quite the same enthusiasm," the director responded with a smile, briefly ignoring his painfully swollen and contorted fingers to shake Earl's hand.

"Not to be presumptuous, but it sounds as if you need some new knockers, Mr. Director," Earl responded in jest, although he knew how incapacitating Director Anderson's autoimmune disease had become.

"Well, I wouldn't go that far, Earl," Director Anderson laughed. His voice and mannerisms left no doubt that he was extremely tired. However, he had certainly not lost his sense of humor.

"Please, Mr. Director," Earl said, pointing toward the plush wingback chair situated in front of his desk. The exhausted director accepted the invitation without hesitation. As he took the seat, he could hear his knees grind as they were flexed, and then cracked as he attempted to slow his descent into the down-filled cushion.

"Damned arthritis!" Director Anderson complained, after surviving the rough landing.

"Well, this weather is so foul that my joints are starting to ache as well, Mr. Director. May I suggest a lubricant appropriate for both of us?" Earl inquired, walking to the magnificent teak bar, which housed a rather extensive collection of libations.

"I thought you'd never ask. What do you suggest?"

"Sambucca, straight up," Earl responded, taking the initiative and pouring two rather healthy doses of the clear sedative into crystal snifters.

"Earl, I thought you were going to suggest a lubricant, not lighter fluid," Director Anderson quipped.

"Mr. Director, as your personal bartender, I wholeheartedly recommend this fine elixir without reservation. Trust me, this is the fountain of youth, guaranteed to eliminate whatever ails you," Earl proclaimed, handing over the high-octane nightcap.

"Earl, you would have made a fine barkeep, and an even better snake oil salesman," Director Anderson responded, swirling the potent liquid, fully expecting it to eat through the glass at any moment.

"I'll take that as a compliment, Mr. Director. To the eradication of your arthritis and our joint effort to rid the world of terrorism," Earl proposed as the two men brought their glasses together.

"To the war on terrorism," Director Anderson confirmed, before taking a sip.

Earl was savoring the intense joy derived from the licorice-flavored liquor as it gently eroded his esophagus and attacked his stomach lining. He looked at Director Anderson, only to find a different reaction. The director's face was so distorted that he was almost unrecognizable.

"Whoooa!" Director Anderson gasped. "How in the world do you drink this stuff, Earl?" the director asked, struggling to catch his breath.

"It's an elixir from the gods, guaranteed to warm your cockles," Earl proclaimed with pride as he held his glass to the light.

"Earl, Drano would be less caustic to your system, and probably wouldn't kick like some ornery old mule. However, I must say that now that the pain is starting to subside, I'm feeling somewhat euphoric and am experiencing an intense yet pleasurable bodily warmth. I just hope that my cockles haven't been singed!" Director Anderson joked, placing his glass on Earl's desk before pushing the dangerous liquid as far away from him as he could.

"Well, it is definitely an acquired taste, Mr. Director," Earl chuckled.

"I should say," Director Anderson agreed, watching in amazement as Earl took another sip. However, it was now time to get down to business. Terrorism had once again arrived on American shores and claimed thousands of innocent lives.

"Earl, I understand that the death toll at Grand Central Station stands at six thousand five hundred and is rising rapidly. The president and the public, as well as the press, are demanding answers." Director Anderson shared the gut-wrenching facts openly with his longtime friend.

"Mr. Director, everyone has worked tirelessly to avoid such a disaster, and I can assure you that each man and woman will continue to give one hundred percent," Earl replied, knowing how disappointed the director was, and feeling that he had let down the entire nation.

"Earl, you retain my utmost confidence, but the fire-breathing dragons hunkered down in Washington have instantaneously developed their own politically motivated conclusions. The flames from the attack have yet to be extinguished, no one has been laid to rest, and already Congress is insisting upon an inquiry and demanding that heads roll. Unfortunately, it would appear that you and I are destined for the guillotine, unless we can find some plausible answers as to how this happened and provide viable solutions to ensure that it never happens again," Director Anderson stressed.

"Yesterday we were quietly praised for successfully preventing the *Mecca* from sailing into the Chesapeake Bay, where the explosive-laden vessel would've wiped Washington, DC off the map," Earl replied, shaking his head.

"As you very well know, a politician is a different animal," the director politely confessed.

"I should say! Yes, unfortunately the donk-enas are thriving. Who would have ever thought that a politician could successfully breed a donkey with a hyena. In public, they cackle like publicity starved hyenas, glad-handing and posing for the cameras, while behind the scene they rip your throat out and show their ass," Earl growled sarcastically.

"Unfortunately, Earl, that's the no-loyalty game that is played in Washington. No one gives a damn if you saved their skin yesterday. All that matters is what you can do for them today," Director Anderson admitted as Earl began to cool down.

"Mr. Director, I feel the heat and without question will remain loyal to you and dedicated to our mission, even if dragged through the political gates of hell. However, despite today's disaster and our pending political demise, I do have some good news," Earl announced with confidence, choosing to focus on the positive and move forward with their conversation.

"Earl, your timing has always been impeccable. I could certainly use some good news," Director Anderson replied as he leaned forward in his chair.

"Mr. Director, our big break came late this afternoon. I'd like to say it was the result of hard work but, honestly, it was also a matter of luck," Earl conceded.

"Earl, for God's sake, don't keep me in suspense! What have you uncovered?" Director Anderson asked impatiently.

"As you recall, last week several grossly disfigured and discolored bodies washed ashore in Galveston, Texas. The very next day an emergency room physician, Dr. Rex Bent, sparked our interest when he mentioned taking care of blue-tinged Asian sailors who had died quickly and violently from unknown causes. Dr. Bent is employed at Carencrow Regional Hospital in Carencrow, Louisiana, a small, obscure town two hundred miles to the east of Galveston, but only thirty miles inland. We thought it wise to scrutinize the traffic originating from and destined to Carencrow over the last two weeks. Interestingly enough, today it became apparent that the content within the correspondence pinpointed the sleepy little town and the surrounding area as terrorism central," Earl disclosed. There was no doubt that Earl had a high degree of confidence in the agency's most recent intelligence that had been compiled.

"So Leslie's hunch was right," Director Anderson remarked.

"It would appear so."

"Earl, what exactly led you to this conclusion?" Director Anderson inquired, deciding to probe deeper into the analysis.

"Specific details regarding each mission were disclosed prior to and after the execution of these heinous crimes. For example, there was outgoing traffic that praised the success of the attack on the carrier group *Stennis*, while other messages reflected disappointment regarding the *Mecca* and her mission against the capitalistic infidels. Additionally, we have recently concluded that orders directing the attack on Grand Central Station appear to have originated from Carencrow," Earl stated emphatically.

"Good God!" Director Anderson replied with a great deal of fervor before instinctively reaching for his snifter of Sambucca, which he had abandoned so abruptly several minutes earlier. "Bottoms up," Director Anderson said as he raised his glass. He had anticipated a rather stout kick, but the potent libation went down rather smoothly. He looked at his empty crystal snifter and thought to himself that perhaps all the liquor needed was time to breathe. "I really shouldn't, but I believe I'll have one more snort," he requested, digesting the most recent intelligence which Earl and his team had compiled.

"A wise choice, Mr. Director, no one can fly on just one wing," Earl responded, refilling both snifters.

"Well, it certainly seems plausible that some obscure town in the middle of nowhere is ground zero for coordinating and executing terrorism within our borders," Director Anderson replied.

"I was initially convinced that the terrorists operating in this country had multiple autonomous cells, each acting independently, with orders to destroy America. However, it now appears that they have established a base, and there is in fact a chain-of-command," Earl concluded.

"That's interesting. However, it doesn't explain the radiation poisoning that claimed the sailors' lives. Have you uncovered any intelligence on the topic?" Director Anderson asked, knowing how imperative this issue was with regard to national security.

"No, sir," Earl replied candidly. "Unfortunately, Mr. Director, we have not come across any messages referencing nuclear materials or an attack with nuclear weapons. However, we did intercept one electronic message addressed to Wonsan thanking the North Koreans for their support and contribution to the war against the United States.

"Good God, Earl."

"And, interestingly enough, just today we uncovered traffic originating from North Korea to Carencrow, but addressed to a different email address. The message was encrypted with a code the North Koreans have never used. Thus, we have had difficulty breaking it, but our best men are working on this challenge as we speak. Most importantly, I feel confident that we will have it cracked within the next twenty-four hours," Earl assured the director.

"Time is of the essence. We need to know the significance of that message ASAP! Furthermore, we must assume that the terrorists have smuggled a nuclear weapon into the United States and intend to detonate it within days," the director stressed.

"I agree, but if a nuclear weapon did reach our shores, why did the sailors succumb to radiation poisoning? I suppose it's possible that the weapon was leaking weapons-grade plutonium. However, it's more plausible that the WMD is a dirty bomb. In any case, it appears that North Korea is the only link we have to the nuclear threat," Earl shared.

"Do we have any other leads?"

"Yes, the mystery of the cargo ship, *Il-sung*," Earl replied.

"Ah yes, the elusive *Il-sung*. Is there any possibility that the cargo ship's task was to transport the WMD?" Director Anderson asked, feeling quite certain that he already knew the answer.

"That's not only possible, Mr. Director, but highly probable. We have come to the conclusion that the dead Asian sailors were crewmembers. Here again, we are working aggressively with the Coast Guard and the Navy to locate that vessel. In fact, we have narrowed our search to Louisiana and the state's multitude of tributaries, many of which could easily provide access and shelter for a vessel of that size. If she's not on the bottom of the ocean, we'll find her," Earl assured Director Anderson.

"Earl, there is a very fine line between being labeled a hero or a bum. The terrorists were successful in their attack on Grand Central Station. They will NOT unleash a nuclear weapon on our watch!" Director Anderson stated emphatically.

"If the potbellied pig poker from North Korea has left a calling card, we will locate it, disarm the weapon, and neutralize the terrorists," Earl stated with confidence and conviction.

"As you know, this morning I dispatched FBI agents and CIA operatives to Carencrow. Would the president consider activating the National Guard to assist in our efforts?" Earl requested.

"Unfortunately, it's out of the question. In light of the Grand Central Station devastation, activation of the National Guard in any location other than New York City will cause a state of panic that would sweep the nation."

"Understood. We will run deep and silent. I'll call in several overdue favors," Earl responded, knowing that whatever it took, he would get the job done.

CHAPTER 28

ARL CHECKED HIS WATCH. It was a quarter past eight in the evening. Director Anderson had just left his office when his phone rang. He immediately looked at the caller ID.

"Leslie, where have you been? I've been worried about you."

"It's been a long day, and we still have a great deal to do," Leslie replied while standing just outside on the Bents' front porch.

"I'd say, especially after catching the red-eye. Can you bring me up to date?" Earl asked, getting right down to business.

"Briefly, the Bents were apprehended earlier this evening and are now in custody. In their home we found thousands of vials of a hazy brown liquid, hundreds of pounds of napalm, several large drones, and incriminating emails and data on Dr. Bent's computer."

"WOW!" Earl blurted out. He hesitated for a moment before continuing, "Leslie, that plan sounds rather ambitious, even for a highly motivated renegade physician. As you know we did a rather exhaustive background check on the doctor. In no way does he fit the mold of a traitor."

"Earl, I am in total agreement. In fact, my suspicion is that everything had been planted. No effort was made to conceal the WMDs or the other items, and the story of being attacked while driving home is true. In fact, what remains of Mrs. Bent's vehicle is smoldering under the carport. Hell, the metal is so charred and twisted that there is no way you could even make out either the manufacturer or the model."

"That's interesting."

"Most importantly, I had a lengthy discussion with Mrs. Bent. She said that she cared for the Asian sailors when they arrived in the emergency room several days ago and has been ill ever since. When the FBI swept the house there was a trace amount of radiation found in the master bedroom and bathroom, and when they passed the Geiger counter over Mrs. Bent, the machine went berserk. Yet no source was found," Leslie emphasized.

"It would appear that Dr. Bent and his wife have become a threat to the terrorists and the execution of their plans. They must be protected at all costs until we can find that nuclear weapon," Earl added, resolute.

"What nuclear weapon?" Leslie blurted loudly, leaving no doubt that she had been caught off guard.

"Forgive me, Leslie, I had intended to brief you earlier," Earl said apologetically. "The latest intelligence reports have led us to the conclusion that the North Korean cargo vessel *Il-sung* smuggled a nuclear device, most likely a dirty bomb, into Louisiana," he disclosed.

"That would explain the dead and dying Asian sailors," Leslie quickly surmised.

"Precisely," Earl replied. "Leslie, we have also been busy rereviewing and analyzing all the communications from within that sleepy little town and the surrounding area. Your hunch was right on target; Carencrow is terrorism central."

"I knew it!"

"The Coast Guard and the Navy are searching by sea and air for the *Il-sung*, while local authorities are looking for terrorist encampments. They're all focused on a two-hundred-mile radius surrounding Carencrow," Earl disclosed.

"Well, then, all roads lead to and from the Bents. It's imperative that we find out exactly what they know. I'm convinced that, either directly or indirectly, they can lead us to the bomb."

"Leslie, where are Dr. and Mrs. Bent now?" Earl asked as static suddenly rumbled from the speaker in Earl's office.

Instantaneously, both nature and man pierced the quiet of the night. Leslie had not heard the question. The wind began to howl and leaves rustled as FBI agents walked across the frozen lawn, trampling through the fallen foliage. Simultaneously, cold car engines were fired up and gunned. As Leslie adjusted the volume on her earpiece and stepped away from the house, she was startled when powerful camera lights unexpectedly illuminated the front yard.

"Damn it!" Leslie shouted, scurrying for a quiet area within the shadows.

"Leslie, are you all right?" Earl asked, raising his voice in concern. Moments later, the static coming across the line was reduced to a distracting roar.

"I will be, as soon as I kill one sorry son-of-a-bitch!" Leslie responded instinctively while she watched Captain Richter gallantly basking in the light, as the camera from a local TV station began to roll.

Leslie growled, knowing full well that the captain had notified the media.

CHAPTER 29

GEEHAD SAT AT HIS desk, intently focused on the flickering light radiating from his computer screen. The room was dark, with the exception of one desk lamp, which cast an eerie shadow in his dreary office. Earlier in the evening, he had accessed the Islamic World Organization website located in Riyadh, Saudi Arabia. From that address, utilizing a special code, he was able to bring up the daily prayer video from which he could extract the orders he was expected to carry out.

"Yes!" GeeHad shouted in joy, pounding his desk uncontrollably.

"What is it, GeeHad? What brings you such great pleasure?" Hobnob asked.

"All is well, Hobnob, our reign of terror is scheduled to begin in the morning!" GeeHad announced joyfully.

"Excellent!" Hobnob replied loudly.

"Our great people have endured much over the centuries. It's time for us to rise and strike down our enemies, wherever they may be. The decadent West has found great pleasure in ridiculing our religion, our beliefs, and our way of life. Now it's time that we free ourselves from the humiliation and oppression that the United

States of America has brought to our shores," GeeHad announced with pride.

"Allah is great!" Hobnob shouted.

"Mark my words, the infidels will be defeated in a battle that's the mother of all battles. Our god is greater than the nonbelievers could ever imagine. We are about to unleash the Islamic version of shock and awe. Monuments shall crumble, fires will rage, and the smell of death will be in the air. Panic and chaos will ensue. Government and financial institutions will experience a meltdown. The east and west coasts will be uninhabitable. Commerce will grind to a halt,and the infidels driven inland and into obscurity. America will cease to exist!" GeeHad proclaimed.

"It will be my honor to follow you into battle!" Hobnob shouted with pride.

"Open a bottle of Chardonnay, Hobnob. It is time we celebrate," GeeHad commanded. But his thoughts of joy suddenly turned to sadness, as he thought about Abdul. The Bents had killed his lover and confidante, a loss which he personally vowed to repay. However, watching Hobnob sashay over to the bar, he felt aroused, and pleasant thoughts returned as his servant started dancing around the room.

"As you wish, GeeHad," his humble servant replied.

"Now, let us see what death and destruction has occurred in this evil land, with and without our helping hand. It's time for the news," GeeHad announced with an air of excitement. As the flat screen came to life, the death and destruction of today's early morning attack on Grand Central Station came into view. The horror was surreal. GeeHad and Hobnob were most impressed. They sipped on their wine while watching buildings crumble and thousands scramble for their lives.

"Oh, no," GeeHad sighed as Mohammad's brilliantly executed New York City disaster disappeared from view and an anchorwoman appeared, while at the bottom of the screen the words *Breaking Story* kept flashing.

"What in the hell is this?!" GeeHad shouted, increasing the volume.

"We have just received word that a terrorist plot has been uncovered in a small town in Louisiana," Laura Flaaten announced. "We will now take you live to that location, where our reporter, Ryan Murray, has the latest details," Laura added, before the screen briefly went black.

"Ah, Hobnob, I do believe we are about to be entertained by a heartwarming local story," GeeHad chuckled.

"This is Ryan Murray reporting live from Carencrow, Louisiana, where state, federal, and local authorities just completed raiding the house behind me. I have with me tonight Captain Richter, a senior FBI agent, and the man responsible for conducting this highly successful operation," the reporter announced gleefully, knowing that he had captured a career-enhancing story. "Captain Richter, what was the nature of your mission, and why was it necessary?" the reporter inquired, probing for answers to questions which had been discussed before the camera started rolling.

Captain Richter looked very much like a figurehead on the bow of the ship with his chin raised high, his jaw clenched, and his chest thrust forward. There was a moment of silence as the media-savvy FBI agent pretended to collect his thoughts, which had actually been rehearsed for days.

"Our mission is to protect the United States of America and all Americans from terrorism at home. We have taken an oath to defend our great nation. In this instance, our actions were necessary to save lives and to protect property," the captain replied in a deep, booming voice.

"Can you share any of the specifics with regard to tonight's raid?" the reporter asked, pretending to inject some element of sincerity while pushing the microphone toward the captain.

"Yes, indeed," Captain Richter responded as he wrenched the microphone from the reporter's grasp. The publicity-driven captain then began to deliver a sermon with confidence and authority while pacing back and forth across the lawn. "Now, as you and your viewers may assume, there are very sensitive issues of national security involved. Thus, I am not at liberty to disclose all of the details. However, it is of the utmost importance that we, as Americans, learn to be vigilant. Several days ago, the FBI received an anonymous tip that Dr. Rex Bent and his wife, Trissy, were engaged in alleged terrorist activities. We were astounded to find that the Bents had not only frequented radical Islamic web sites but had also contributed to several of these organizations," Captain Richter began as the reporter reached for the microphone. However, the muscular captain quickly brushed his hand away.

"Furthermore, coworkers and neighbors were very forthcoming. Two emergency room nurses, who like to be referred to as Mean and Evil, have worked with Dr. Bent and his wife for many years. Each was convinced that the Bents had organized and were running a major sleeper cell. Mr. Richard Haney, a next-door neighbor, told us of shady characters entering and leaving the Bents' home at all hours of the evening. All of these credible sources were in agreement that the Bents had been behaving quite suspiciously," Captain Richter announced as the reporter made another unsuccessful attempt to retrieve his microphone. "Our investigation was quick and comprehensive. It soon became readily apparent that these traitors posed a clear and present danger to our national security and had to be neutralized," Captain Richter concluded.

"Are you implying that the Bents were killed during the raid?" the reporter inquired, feeling very fortunate to have gotten a word in edgewise.

"I'll get to that question in just a minute. As you are well aware, the FBI has assumed the lead role within the National Security Agency. Thus, my superiors requested that I not only plan, but also execute a raid on the Mallard Drive property. I can assure you that our actions were swift and decisive. Tonight, only moments ago, this sleeper cell was crushed, weapons of mass destruction seized, and the Bents captured," Captain Richter added, before striking his best Rambo-like pose.

"Yes, but were the Bents taken alive?" the reporter grunted as he fought for and successfully retrieved his microphone.

"That captain is a pompous ass. He is cold, bold, and brainless, as are most Americans," Hobnob chuckled.

"Agreed, but he is rather comical," GeeHad replied, before taking a sip of wine.

"You were absolutely right. The infidels have taken the few morsels we have provided and fabricated them into their own worst fears. They are starting to attack their own people and the resultant feeding frenzy is really quite entertaining," Hobnob observed.

"Hobnob, would you be kind enough to pour me another glass of wine?" GeeHad requested, handing his warm and affectionate servant his empty class.

"Yes. Well, that was very interesting, Captain," the reporter said. "Captain, if you would, please standby, while I talk to the Bents' neighbor, Mr. Haney."

"Certainly," Captain Richter replied, as he widened his stance and clasped his hands behind his back.

"By the way, I am sorry about the microphone," the captain whispered, leaning forward. "Occasionally, my hand will involuntarily wrap around an object and hold onto it with tremendous force. It's the damnedest thing," Captain Richter whispered.

"No need to apologize," the reporter growled, struggling to control his anger, while motioning for Mr. Haney to come closer. "Please, Mr. Haney," the reporter said, encouraging the paranoid old country boy to pick up the pace.

Mr. Haney made it his business to know exactly what was going on in the neighborhood. Now in his mid-seventies, he walked stooped over and exhibited a slow, shuffling gait. As he finally approached the microphone, he looked toward Captain Richter with an air of distrust.

"Mr. Haney, thank you for joining us at this late hour. I understand that you have lived next to the Bents for many years. What kind of people are they?" the reporter asked, placing his arm around the frail gentleman.

"I don't rightly know. I never see 'em," Mr. Haney replied, rubbing the mucus from his nose with the back of his hand.

"Well, what kind of characters do you see hanging around their home?"

"None, because they're never home."

The young reporter shook his head. His immediate concern was that the old goat was going to diminish the value of his story, and that the viewers watching his live broadcast were going to switch channels. "Now, Mr. Haney, have you noticed anything suspicious next door, sir?"

"Yes, now that you mention it. Like clockwork, every Wednesday morning at five a.m. all I ever hear is the sound of clinking bottles as the Bents' take their garbage to the curb. If you ask me, they're a bunch of damn winos!" Mr. Haney added, before wiping his nose and rubbing his hand on his overalls.

The reporter lowered his head in frustration and spoke softly into the microphone.

"Well, your stories have been quite interesting, Mr. Haney. Let me personally thank you for your time." Ryan reluctantly motioned the captain to come closer.

"Captain Richter, exactly what did you and your men find in the Bents' home?"

"Well, I really shouldn't say, but there were a multitude of weapons of mass destruction," Captain Richter replied, with strong emotion.

"Surely you must be joking?" the reporter blurted out spontaneously as he studied the captain's face, fully expecting a smile, which would reveal the hoax.

"The war on terrorism is no laughing matter, son. The Bents had amassed a lethal array of WMDs. Millions of Americans could have lost their lives," the captain replied in a stern but scolding manner.

"My God!" the reporter gasped. "What types of weapons? Chemical, biological?" he asked with great concern.

"That is a matter of national security. The public will be advised as soon as it is deemed appropriate," the arrogant captain replied.

"What do you mean a matter of national security? The public has a right to know, and they have a right to know—NOW!" the newly invigorated reporter shot back. In an instant, Ryan Murray's natural journalistic instincts surfaced and his quiet reserved demeanor had been replaced by an aggressive style more conducive to his surroundings. There had been something very strange about his TV station being lured to this scene on such short notice, especially given the circumstances surrounding the raid. Something was missing from the story, but he just couldn't put his finger on it. "Well, then, Captain, let's get back to a question I had asked earlier. Where are the Bents now?"

"Cuffed and on their way to jail. The FBI, in conjunction with the National Security Agency, the CIA, and local authorities, has crushed this cell. Furthermore, the computer, which was seized in this raid, has already proven to be of great value. This information, in addition the to the emails to and from this evil little town, will allow us to quickly locate and capture all additional accomplices operating in Carencrow. Make no mistake, we will turn Carencrow upside down until we've captured every one of these radical Islamic terrorists," Captain Richter replied bluntly.

"Oh, shit!" GeeHad screamed, after realizing that his plan had backfired. He could ill afford closer scrutiny at a time when final preparations meant the difference between success and failure in their Holy War.

CHAPTER 30

THE EXPLOSION WAS UNFORGETTABLE. Suddenly, metal was contorted and twisted, and glass shattered. In an instant, the entire cab had been violated, hurling Rex away from the point of impact and into Trissy, before she was slammed against a very unforgiving car door. However, the stout, knuckle-dragging Corporal Tubbs took the brunt of the trauma. His seatbelt had held fast, so he had no chance to avoid the intrusion. His door was displaced so far into the cabin that the metal crushed all the ribs on the left side of his chest. A heavy, black chrome-laden truck had struck the police cruiser squarely on the driver's side. The force of the impact had not only flipped the cruiser onto its hood, but had also knocked it off the levee.

"Oooh, oooh," Trissy and Rex moaned collectively as the crippled vehicle rapidly gained speed, sliding down the steep embankment. Each time the vehicle came in contact with a mound in the uneven terrain, it was lifted momentarily, only to come crashing down on the roof, which collapsed more and more with each jolt. All the while, the four wheels of the police cruiser continued spinning, hopelessly clawing at the cold night air. Corporal Tubb's arms and head flailed about aimlessly within the rapidly constricting space, while Rex and Trissy were tossed about unmercifully. The bone-jarring ride abruptly came to an end when the vehicle struck the muddy water. However, on impact the sound of the splash had been absorbed by the turbulent Cajun River, where a pulsating roar and angry, howling whitecaps were ever-present.

"Oh," Rex moaned as he struggled to clear his mind and right himself from an unnatural position. "Trissy, are you all right?" Rex screamed, attempting to rouse his beautiful wife. There was no response. In the dim light radiating from the dashboard, Rex could see that Trissy lay motionless, partially submerged and contorted on the ceiling of the condemned metal coffin. With his hands cuffed behind his back, Rex reached down and grabbed the back of Trissy's shirt collar, lifting her head and neck free from certain death. Suddenly, time had become the enemy, and unlike any other adversary, time remained unbiased and unyielding. There was no way for him to assess her airway, breathing, or circulation. And spinal immobilization, so critically important in avoiding paralysis in any trauma patient, also had to be ignored. These were mentally painful but instantaneous decisions predicated on survival, and survival alone.

As frigid water continued to surge into the compartment, the sheriff started to rouse.

"What—what in the hell is going on?" Corporal Tubbs cried, attempting to free himself. Upside down and lodged in the driver's seat, he started to panic as he struggled to keep his head from submerging in the rising waters while frantically attempting to open what remained of the driver's side door.

"Tubbs, unlock the rear doors!" Rex yelled, holding Trissy upright while placing his face against a metal grid separating the front from the back seats. There was no response. The sergeant was disoriented, seriously injured, and now fighting for his life, as well.

"Help!! God hel…" Tubbs screamed as the water level quickly rose. However, his plea for divine intervention was soon squelched by the rising tide. He had been unable to extricate himself from the grip of his unyielding seatbelt.

"Oh, Christ, now we're really in trouble. Trissy, Trissy please, honey, wake up!" Rex yelled, shaking her as best as he could given the constraint of the shackles.

Suddenly, the swift current snagged the vehicle, and it rolled. Rex and Trissy were tossed back onto the car seat, and the sheriff saved from a watery grave. The police cruiser was now upright with the front angled downward thirty degrees and rapidly gaining speed as it was whisked downstream. The surging water was quickly approaching the level of the dashboard. Tubbs coughed incessantly as he fought for a breath. "Tubbs, unlock the damn door!!" Rex shouted, kicking at the front seat in an attempt to gain the lethargic officer's attention.

"I can't swim! I can't swim!" the officer yelled as he thrashed about while struggling to unfasten his seatbelt.

"Corporal, Trissy and I can help you! We're excellent swimmers. Please, unlock our door and give me the keys to these cuffs," Rex pleaded as Trissy started to come around.

"I can't swim! I can't swim!" Tubbs screamed in terror as the water level continued to rise.

"Rex, what happened?" Trissy moaned, struggling to regain full consciousness.

"Trissy, try to open your door!" Rex shouted, ignoring her question.

Suddenly, the officer turned around and opened a small compartment within the protective mesh. Rex heard the rattling of keys and felt something strike his right shoulder. By the time Rex looked up, the sheriff was gone.

The large man must have slid out the passenger side door, Rex thought to himself as he frantically searched the submerged seat with his bound hands for what he believed to be the keys. As he twisted his upper torso, his hands struck a sharp metal object on his right thigh.

"Thank God!" Rex shouted in delight, wrapping his hand around the wide metal ring.

"What—what key is it?" Rex shouted in a loud, panic-stricken voice as he fumbled through all the keys on the large key chain.

"Trissy, turn your back toward me, quickly!" Rex insisted while continuing to fumble for the right key in the dark murky water.

"Rex, what in the hell is going on? I don't remember going for a swim," Trissy replied as the cold water continued to awaken her from the effects of a mild concussion.

"Got it!" Rex screamed with great satisfaction. "Oh, Christ!" Rex shouted in anguish as he frantically searched for the keys he had just dropped.

"Rex, what is it?" Trissy yelled, looking over her shoulder to see what her husband was doing. Rex appeared to be hopping up and down on the backseat.

"Rex, stop splashing!" Trissy added as the small waves Rex was generating with his movement slapped against her cheek.

"I dropped the damn keys! Don't move!" Rex insisted, continuing his unorthodox search. "Got 'em!" he shouted enthusiastically, after successfully snagging the key ring. "The police association is just going to have to consider coating their keys with non-skid, or accidents like this will be inescapable," Rex quipped, once again searching for the right key. However, his fingers were rapidly becoming quite numb, and he was keenly aware that he was losing dexterity. Rex had little doubt that the frigid waters would soon render his desperate efforts useless.

"Thank God! Trissy, don't move a muscle. I've got it!" Rex said, grabbing her handcuffs and fumbling for the keyhole. "There it is!" he shouted. The bond, which had only moments ago assured a certain death, was broken as one cuff, and then the next snapped open.

The police cruiser continued to gain momentum as the raging waters hurled the damaged vehicle downstream. The cruiser was now totally submerged and sinking very rapidly. With their necks flexed, Rex and Trissy hugged the ceiling, struggling for life as they consumed oxygen from the only remaining, and quickly shrinking, pocket of air.

"Trissy, my door was crushed in the accident. Try to either get your door open or break the window!" he shouted, attempting to unlock the shackles preventing his escape.

Trissy took a deep breath and submerged herself. She quickly found the handle on the passenger side door. It pulled back easily, but the door did not budge.

"No luck, Rex!" Trissy yelled as she came up for air. "But I have an idea," she said, taking another deep breath and quickly disappearing.

"Trissy, we're running out of TIME!" Rex emphasized as his body began to shake and his teeth began to chatter, before realizing that Trissy had gone.

Trissy put her shoulder into the door and pulled back on the handle. She gained leverage by planting her feet against the vertical metal bar dividing the back seat. Extending her legs and pushing with all her might she could feel the door open ever so slightly. In an instant, the swift current grabbed the door and flung it open violently, sucking her out of the vehicle and propelling her into the dark, unforgiving Cajun River.

"Thank God!" Rex shouted as his steel cuffs sprung open. He inhaled the last vestige of air before submerging to help Trissy. But she was gone, and the door was wide open. He frantically felt for her arms or legs while struggling to fight the ferocious and unyielding current. Rex was not about to leave his gorgeous wife behind in this wicked watery grave. Suddenly, he was thrown toward the surface, and then violently pulled back down while heavy objects struck his twisting and turning body from every direction. It was as if the river was toying with him before deciding whether to take his life. After what seemed like an eternity, Rex broke the surface and filled his lungs with the thick musty air that blanketed the river.

"Rex!" Trissy shouted, as he took in several deep breaths and struggled to gather his wits.

"Trissy, are you all right?" Rex shouted as they joined hands and kissed.

"Absolutely!" she said with a smile.

"Trissy, have you seen Tubbs?" Rex asked as the current continued to whisk them downstream.

"No, and quite frankly I haven't been looking for him."

"Well, for Christ's sake, don't you think something that large would float?" Rex said.

Corporal Tubbs was only ten yards away and struggling to stay afloat. His large arms kept slapping helplessly at the water, briefly raising his head and torso above the murky depths. Each time the moonlight reflected off the sheriff's silver badge, a beacon of hope flashed. However, the intensity with which the corporal fought for his life was rapidly diminishing. He was exhausted. There was no way he could make it to shore.

"There he is!" Trissy yelled after a brilliant flash of light caught her eyes. As Rex and Trissy swam to the corporal's aid, they were extremely fortunate to avoid being impaled by heavy, jagged floating projectiles. When they reached the officer, all that was visible on the surface were the back of his head and his arms. There was no purposeful movement, although the waves and the current generated a bobbing and rolling motion, which gave the illusion that he was still alive. Immediately, Rex grabbed the corporal under the chin, while rolling him onto his back and raising his face out of the water.

"Badges? He needed the stinking badge," Rex shouted, kicking furiously toward shore.

"Between Sheila's addiction to *Young Frankenstein* and yours to old westerns, I believe I'm going out of my mind," Trissy shouted, grabbing the large man by his arm. Together they fought the dangerous current.

Yards from shore, Trissy, in an utter state of exhaustion, attempted to touch bottom. "The water is still too deep!" she shouted as she kept swimming.

Finally, all reached the muddy banks of the Cajun River. With one last burst of energy, they moaned and groaned and tugged the large man's torso up onto the slippery shore.

Trissy collapsed, gasping for air as her knees and elbows kept sinking deeper into the wretched, malodorous mud. Rex as well struggled to meet the demands of his oxygen-starved body. His breaths were so rapid and deep that he quickly became dizzy. With his thought process gravely impaired and his eyes unable to focus, he felt that he was about to pass out. He fought to remain conscious and crawled closer to Corporal Tubbs. Instinctively, he tilted the corporal's head back and pinched his nose, but before Rex could deliver his first life-sustaining breath, Tubbs began coughing up water. Rex quickly rolled him onto his side to prevent aspiration, while checking his vital signs.

"Thank God, no need for CPR," Rex announced with pleasure.

Huffing and puffing, Rex rolled onto his back. Moments later he was struck by the thought that his dizziness was the result of his hyperventilation, and that his hyperventilation was not only the result of the tremendous expenditure of energy but also of his body attempting to replenish the heat which had been lost in the frigid waters. He made a conscious effort to slow down his breathing, and as he did so, his dizziness quickly resolved. He began thinking more clearly, and his vision improved dramatically. Almost immediately, the ever-present ominous threat from above became apparent.

"There'll be no free lunch tonight, you vulturous, beady-eyed bastards," Rex said defiantly as his eyes focused on a herd of Carencrow buzzards circling overhead.

"Trissy, are you all right?" Rex asked, staggering to his feet. But he did not listen for a reply, because he suddenly became aware of a great deal of activity on top of the levee. One hundred and fifty yards upstream he could see a stationary big, black truck. With the headlights on, Rex noticed steam rising from beneath the hood. The engine was obviously running. He was also able to focus on the large chrome bumper and immediately remembered seeing a massive, towering array of chrome seconds before the police cruiser was struck.

"First it was a Hummer, and now a truck. What is it with large vehicles, chrome bumpers, and the desire to kill us?" Rex wondered as he scrambled up the levee to confront his assassin. Just before reaching the top, Rex heard an engine being gunned and wheels spinning on the loose gravel road. Suddenly, the black truck roared past him, and a number of police vehicles raced toward the levee. Rex hesitated for moment but then turned and started running down the large man-made embankment.

"Trissy, it's time to go!" he shouted. Trissy slowly rose to her feet. She was covered from head to toe with thick mud. She bent over, placing her hands on her knees in an attempt to stabilize her weary body as she looked up toward Rex, who was frantically scampering down the hill.

"What do you mean, it's time to go? Rex, I'm half frozen and totally exhausted!" Trissy complained as sirens wailed and flashing blue lights flooded the night sky.

"Trissy, we have been set up, and I do believe that Captain Richter and his storm troopers have every intention of locking us up and throwing away the key. Our escape is the only chance we have of clearing our good names," Rex said, taking off his pants and tying each leg into a knot.

"I'm not sure about this, Rex," Trissy confessed, staring in amazement at her half-naked husband. "Rex, now is not the time to revert to the nineteen-seventies and take up streaking. Please, put your pants back on!" a shivering Trissy pleaded as Rex waded waist-deep into the muddy water.

"Come on in, the water's fine," Rex said, holding his hand out toward her as she began to walk back into the rolling, thunderous river of death.

"Well, I must say it certainly feels a lot warmer the second time around," Trissy admitted.

Corporal Tubbs had rolled onto his belly and was attempting to stand. Bright white lights from multiple flashlights were now scanning the river, searching for signs of life. Rex lifted his pants into the air, and then brought them down quickly into the water. He wrapped his hands tightly around the drawstring in order to trap a pocket of air.

"Now, that's a fancy trick," Trissy freely admitted.

"It's standard operating procedure for survival at sea, compliments of the United States Naval Academy. My only regret is that to pass the test I had to wear a speedo and tread water in an icy cold pool for forty-five minutes," Rex recalled as Trissy held on to the base of Rex's improvised flotation device.

"Feet up, booty down," Rex instructed as they left the security of the muddy bank.

The treacherous current whisked them downriver, just as a beam of light illuminated a very fortunate Corporal Tubbs.

The action continues in *Crisis: Black*.

ABOUT THE AUTHOR

J OHN IS THE COFOUNDER of 5VS (5 Vital Signs), a start-
up committed to saving the lives of wounded American
soldiers by allowing the medic, or any soldier within one
hundred yards, to triage on the battlefield. He is a board
certified Emergency Room physician.

He graduated from the United States Naval Academy (BS),
in Annapolis, Maryland, and the University of Texas (MBA) in
Austin, Texas. Later, he completed his Doctorate of Medicine
(MD) at the University of Texas Medical Branch in Galveston,
Texas, and finished the Louisiana State University Emergency
Medicine Program in Baton Rouge, Louisiana.

ACKNOWLEDGMENTS

Commander Rex Bent, USN (ret)
Cathy Maroney
Pat Walsh
Sir Richard Thornton
Tyson Cornell
Alice Marsh-Elmer
Hailie Johnson
Heidi D. Barnes
Michael Evenbly
Agnes "Sissy" Barr Davis